Praise for *Who You've Got to Kill*

"Ó Fiaich unapologetically exposes the shrapnel of war-torn Iraq, as he weaves the intricate, shocking display of political puppetry on both sides of the war, revealing its ugly effects on the lives of the innocent.... The cinematic, twisting plot superbly navigates a series of explosive events that lead this battle-ready political thriller to its gripping conclusion."

—*Kirkus Reviews*

WHO
YOU'VE
GOT TO
KILL

RUSSELL Ó FIAICH

BOREAS PRESS

Published by Boreas Press, Oak Park, Illinois
ISBN: 978-0-9985119-2-4 (paperback)
ISBN: 978-0-615-69421-4 (e-book)

Cover design by Juan Pedro Alvarez
Book design by Maureen Cutajar

For Joan
First and Forever

You've got to kill who you've got to kill to save who you've got to save.

—Mantra of combat Marines in Fallujah, Iraq

Prologue

Fallujah, Iraq

To Sam Belmonte the squad of Marines moved with the ease and grace of a snake, slowly elongating and quickly contracting, gliding from side to side, undulating over obstacles in its path. Like a serpent using all its senses to divine and react to even the most minute changes in its environment, the squad used the combined senses of all its members to wend its way through the streets of Fallujah. In Belmonte's mind, the squad functioned as a single living organism, an organic whole: predatory, deadly, and intent on survival.

Insurgent snipers had targeted local police units with great effect, and intelligence had narrowed the area from where the firing was coming to one block near the center of the city. It was the squad's mission to clear the houses and businesses in this sector of these insurgents.

The squad leader signaled a halt, and Belmonte, along with the other Marines, knelt on one knee and waited. The squad leader hustled over to Belmonte and crouched down.

"It's that one there," he said, nodding across the street to a two-story, cement-block house at the end of a courtyard.

Belmonte sighted through the scope of his M16A4 rifle toward the door of the house. Thirty yards he guessed, ninety feet. He scanned the windows in the second story of the house. No movement. There was no blare of a radio or TV or the squeals of children playing. Still, Belmonte felt there was something odd about the solid stillness of the rough brick building amid the clatter of the vehicles on the streets and the baleful bleating from the slaughterhouse on the corner. The heat was intense, rising in shimmering waves off the brick and cinderblock buildings. Belmonte took off his helmet and wiped the sweat from his face with his sleeve. His uniform was soaked and gritty from the heat and dust.

"So what's it going to be, Sergeant?" asked Belmonte, putting his helmet back on.

"We're going to clear from the bottom up," said the squad leader. "You'll head the assault team. We have the courtyard secured. The windows are covered. Go!"

Belmonte was first through the gate of the courtyard and was quickly followed, one after the other, by the three remaining members of the assault team. They ran in a line toward the door of the house, each marking off a sector of the courtyard with their rifles so that every square inch of the low walls to the sides and front was covered. When Belmonte reached the door, he fired into the lock, which disintegrated in a shower of brass and wood. The team leader kicked the door open and rushed into the main room of the house at a crouch, the barrel of his rifle sweeping from left to right. Belmonte entered right behind him, head up and rotating three-hundred-and-sixty degrees to survey the entire ceiling. The other two Marines took positions at the door and at the bottom of the stairwell leading up to the second floor. The room was empty, and except for the faint scent of saffron and mint that pervaded most Iraqi homes, there were no signs that it had been recently occupied.

"Signal the stack to join up," said the team leader to the Marine at the door.

"Wait, not yet," said Belmonte, his eyes still probing the ceiling.

"What the hell are you talking about? We got a foothold here, and we got to keep moving up. Give them the signal," repeated the team leader.

"No wait," Belmonte insisted, "Something's not right."

"Bullshi…"

Before the team leader could finish, Belmonte spotted flakes of plaster begin to dislodge from around a tiny crack in the ceiling and yelled, "Mouse hole," as he squeezed and held the trigger of his rifle, sending nearly a full clip of rounds screaming into the widening crack.

Down from the barrel of an AK47, six-hundred rounds per minute at over twice the speed of sound ripped through the team leader's Kevlar helmet and vaporized his skull, flooding the room with a pink mist. The body of the team leader toppled forward, but Belmonte grabbed the collar of his tactical vest and yanked him up. Backpedaling toward the door, Belmonte tried to shout, "Break contact" but choked on the blood-soaked air. Then the chaos of hell descended on the Marines. The impact of hundreds of rounds exploding into walls, ceilings, flesh and bone filled the house with a blinding miasma of brick dust and blood. The Marine by the stairs kept trying to raise his rifle as his body jerked in spasms from repeated hits by an automatic weapon. The Marine at the door fell to his knees, blood gushing from his nose as his sinuses blew apart from the concussive force of the rounds trapped within the four walls of the room. Huge chunks of concrete and plaster rained down on Belmonte as he sprayed the ceiling and, with one hand, half dragged, half heaved the corpse of the team leader toward the doorway. Over screams and the roar of automatic weapons' fire, Belmonte yelled to break contact and plunged into the courtyard. As he stumbled away from the door, he saw the squad leader racing toward him while a phosphorus grenade arched overhead toward the second floor window. And then blackness. And silence. A soundlessness so deep and complete that Belmonte was sure he must be dead.

*   *   *

"Today you serve Allah in a great cause. Get to your feet," the sniper ordered.

The old man stayed on his knees begging for the lives of his daughter and her children, his whole body shaking, his arms swaying above his head as if clearing a path for his pleas. His daughter was behind him. She too was kneeling but facing away from him, her back shielding the young boy and girl who were huddled together.

Thin ribbons of smoke hovered in the air from the gun fight with the Americans. The sniper could see down to the room below through the holes the bullets had chewed in the floor. A dead Marine lay sprawled by the door, his eyes staring, vacant and accusing. The sniper looked again at the old man.

Animals, he thought, lower than animals, mere insects. They swarm to wherever they sense safety. They buzz greedily even around those who wish to slay Islam. He'd seen too many of them accepting the handouts of the invaders, mimicking their ways in pathetic flattery, growing comfortable under their protection. The disgust he felt was so great that he could taste it, a bitter, sour bite at the back of his throat that made him want to retch. Such betrayers of the faith deserved to die the death of cowards, he told himself.

"Get up," he demanded.

The old man leaned forward, pressed his face to the floor at the sniper's feet, and began to pray. The sniper raised the butt of his rifle over the old man's head. "I said get up."

"Leave him alone. Can't you see he's old and sick? His hands shake too much to hold a gun," screamed the woman.

"Koos," he bellowed and kicked her in the stomach. Her body coiled and twisted like a hooked worm, and then she vomited. He was surprised at how soft she felt, her gut like a great pillow. The stench of her bile blended with the sweet smell of cordite in the small room.

"He will serve well enough, as will you and your filthy children," he said more to himself than to the woman.

"When, brother, when? More Marines are through the courtyard entrance. They are almost here." A second sniper held a cell phone in front of him with his back against the wall, his head twisted so that he could see into the courtyard from the second story window. He was a good soldier, but young and inexperienced. The first sniper heard his fear.

"Wait. Wait till the first man reaches the door, then do it," he said in a slow, steady voice to calm him.

The first sniper turned his attention back to the woman. "You and your children come with us now, or I will kill you here," he said, and lowered his rifle to the old man's head. When she didn't move, he fired. Blood splattered her face and arms. She leaped to her feet screeching and clawed at the sniper's face. Her sudden fury startled him, and he fell back. When he stumbled, her hands pulled the rifle from his grip. For an instant he stood facing her, transfixed by the wildness in her stare. Then he grabbed his rifle with one hand and slapped the woman across the face with the other, knocking her to the floor.

The young boy rose and looked to his mother and then up at the sniper, his eyes darting between them, wide with terror. His older sister lay curled behind him in the corner with a blanket over her head, shaking violently, of no help to anyone. The boy's knees trembled beneath the hem of his blue shorts as he took one uncertain step toward him.

"Don't," said the first sniper, and stabbed his rifle into the boy's chest.

"They are at the door," screamed the second sniper.

"Now. Do it now," the first sniper ordered.

The second sniper pressed twice on the cell phone pad. A red flash and a ball of searing heat filled the window an instant before the sound of the explosion roared through the room. In the moment of silence and stillness that followed, the first sniper grabbed the boy and threw him down into the stairwell. He watched as the second sniper hauled the girl to the top step and kicked her off it. She rolled slowly, flopping over each stair, the blanket still covering her.

"I will take care of the woman. Go," the first sniper demanded.

He snatched the woman's hijab from her head and wound her hair through his fingers. He looped the thick strands around his wrist; and in one movement, yanked her to her feet and slung her over his back like a sack hung from a braided rope. She squirmed and writhed as he hauled her behind him, her fingers prying at his hand. At the bottom of the stairs, he stepped over the body of a dead Marine, slipping on broken brick; and the woman wrenched free of his grip. She staggered to her son who was lying face down in the debris and clutched him to her. She began to sing to him.

"The house is burning, we must go now," shouted the second sniper.

Through the doorway, the first sniper could see black smoke and sparks spilling off the roof from the fire set by a phosphorus grenade. They would soon be engulfed in flames.

"Shut up," the first sniper yelled to the woman. He pulled her and her son up and tried to separate them, but the mother only held her son tighter. Her father's blood on her arms made them slick and difficult for him to grasp.

"It will be sahel for your family. They will be hacked to pieces and dragged through the streets," she hissed as he tried to pry mother and son apart.

"You pig," he said, and swung his rifle at her ankles, sweeping it back and forth. She tried to dodge the blows, backing away, high-stepping like a wooden puppet, her son still wrapped in her arms. When the woman was near the door, he pushed her to his brother who slammed a fist into the side of her head, stunning her. The boy had become wide-eyed and catatonic. The first sniper then turned to the daughter. She lay in a heap, the blanket covering her. When he tried to force her to stand, she kept collapsing; so he lifted her and, balancing her dead weight between his forearm and chest, propped her in front of him.

"Today we will see each other in Heaven," he said to the second sniper. He tore the blanket from the girl and twisted her face so that she had to look at her mother. Then he nodded once to the second sniper, who shoved the mother and her son out the door ahead of him.

*   *   *

Belmonte clambered to consciousness hearing a high whine. It was like the oncoming rush of a distant train, a drone that dropped in pitch and became more distinct as the engine sped closer. It was a train, he was certain. He could feel the vibration of the tracks; sense the rumble of the steel wheels bouncing the ties. The rails were shaking now; and the noise filled his head, punching his skull from the inside. He must be on the tracks. He had to get up before the train rolled over him.

"Fuck, man. Look what they did to us, man. Fuck."

Belmonte opened his eyes and saw the face of another Marine. He was crying and lying on his stomach next to Belmonte, shaking Belmonte's shoulder.

"He's gone man. He just disappeared. Ain't nothing of him left," cried the Marine.

"Who?" asked Belmonte, still groggy.

"Sarge, man."

Over the Marine's voice, Belmonte heard the voices of other injured Marines. They were crying for help. Bodies littered the courtyard.

"I can't feel my legs," said the Marine beside him.

Belmonte looked down and saw that the Marine's right leg was severed just below the knee, the calf and foot lying at a ninety-degree angle to his body. His boots were missing, and the dust around him was wet and dark with blood.

"Shit, we got to get you some help," said Belmonte.

"You're the one who needs help, amigo. Your face looks like you been in a razor fight. Anyway, there ain't no fucking help. Everyone's down," said the Marine, who rolled over onto his back, leaving the piece of his leg where it lay on the ground.

The heat from the burning house roiled black smoke into the courtyard. Belmonte's eyes started to burn. He sat up and reached for the first aid kit attached at his waist on his left side. He undid the flap and pulled out a rubber tourniquet. Kneeling over the Marine, he wrapped it around his right thigh. As he tightened the tourniquet and tied it, Belmonte thought how small and insignificant the limb seemed inside the leg of the uniform.

"There, you'll be fine until help comes," he said; but the Marine ignored him, as if unaware that part of him had been torn off.

Belmonte lifted the Marine's head and pushed his pack under it. The Marine opened his mouth and started to speak when his face split into a crimson blossom of muscle and bone. An instant later, Belmonte heard the rattle of gun fire as dust kicked up around him.

He reeled toward the sound and saw a woman holding a boy stumble from the house in front of a man with a rifle. The man fired into the courtyard. A Marine on the ground near the door shuddered under the impact of the rounds. Another man came out of the house carrying a young girl, and he too fired into the wounded Marines. The group began edging along the front of the house toward the wall of the courtyard, the men firing continuously through the smoke.

Belmonte reached for his rifle and aimed, but the armed men were shielded by the others. As Belmonte tried to get a clear shot at the gunmen, the young boy broke from the woman's arms and began running toward Belmonte, his legs pumping furiously. As the woman lunged after the boy, the armed man pulled her back. She screamed and flailed. The boy ran until he was almost to Belmonte, and then he stopped and raised his hand as if waving. As Belmonte stared at him, his rifle raised, the boy's arm spun away from his body; and he crumbled to his knees, turning his head to follow his arm. Then he fell on his face into the dust. The woman keened and thrashed against the sniper's hold before she buckled. Belmonte

fired; blood splashed on the wall behind the man. The man staggered and dropped the woman, who crumpled to the ground. The
other man caught him as he fell and dragged him and the girl
toward the wall of the courtyard. When they reached the wall, the
man released the girl and heaved the wounded man over the top.

Free from the sniper, the girl began to crawl, slowly at first and
then faster until she scuttled over the sand like a crab toward a
receding tide. The sniper picked up his rifle and sprinted after her.
He was almost upon her when he dived, slid in the dirt, and
grabbed her foot. The girl flipped on her back and kicked the sniper
in the face. He let go of her; and she scrambled backwards, churning
the dust with her heels, her abayah billowing as her knees rose and
fell. The sniper, still on this stomach, steadied his rifle and fired in
Belmonte's direction.

"Dammit. Return fire," screamed a voice behind Belmonte.

"I can't, man, he's covered by the girl," Belmonte shouted back.

"Fuck it, he's killing Marines."

Belmonte ignored the stinging in his eyes and took a deep
breath. He held it and sighted through his scope. He let air escape
from his lungs for an instant before he pulled the trigger. Belmonte
saw the girl's body rock and become still. The sniper jumped up and
raced back into the swirling dust and soot. Belmonte fired once
more before the gunman leapt the wall and disappeared.

"Looks like the motherfuckers got away," said a Marine, stepping
to Belmonte's side.

Another Marine appeared, lifted his rifle, and pointed with it to
where the woman, girl, and young boy were lying in the courtyard.
"What the hell we gonna do about them three?" he said.

Belmonte struggled to his feet. "That can wait," he said.

Chapter 1

SLIDELL ROLLED OVER in the narrow bed and reached across the twisted sheets to touch his wife before he silenced the syncopated scolding of the alarm. He wasn't ready yet to open his eyes so he had to imagine her face as his hand traced the edges of the frame holding her picture on the nightstand. When he was certain that his fingers had found her lips beneath the glass, he mouthed a kiss and then slammed a fist down on the clock-radio.

Slidell left the house by 6:30 a.m. and headed north on I-5 toward Camp Pendleton, weaving in and out of the tangled strands of traffic on the outskirts of San Diego before he hit the open stretch of ocean highway leading to the base. It was going to be a hot summer. June, and already he had to turn on the car's air conditioner to survive the morning drive to the camp. The chilled air tightened the skin on his face, which somehow tricked his mind into thinking that his body was taut and ready for the push and shove of the day— which it wasn't; which it hadn't been in a long time.

He hated the commute. He had tried everything to keep his mind occupied on the long drive: listening to books on CD, dictating briefs and letters for his legal cases, learning Spanish. But as the road opened and the car eased into a steady cruise, the hum of the tires and the drone of the engine were a white noise that blanketed the car's interior, and memories of Mary would rush to fill the silence. His thoughts always returned to her, to the two of them, and what they might have had together. Then he would battle with a guilt that overwhelmed him. The recrimination was a barbed hook imbedded in the meaty flesh of his palm. It hurt like hell and was impossible to get rid of without intensifying the pain. He had even considered selling the house and moving on base to avoid the commute, but he couldn't bring himself to do it.

Slidell was still thinking of his wife when he arrived at Pendleton.

"Good morning, Captain," said Corporal Fallon. She stayed seated behind her metal desk outside his office instead of standing at attention and gave him a mock salute, the back of her hand flat against her forehead, pressing against her blond bangs, her pale blue eyes crossed, and her pink, curled tongue peeking out of the corner of her mouth.

"At ease, Marine," he replied, returning the same mock salute with a quick crispness that hers lacked. No matter how bad his mood, he couldn't help laughing at the manically comic mask she put on for him every morning. This was a game they played together when no other officers or enlisted personnel were around to witness it. Slidell knew no disrespect was intended, and no disrespect was taken.

"The Colonel wants to see you ASAP, Captain, about a new case," she added, and winced.

"Please. Not first thing. I'm not even awake yet. Where's my coffee?"

"It's on your desk along with the file he wants to discuss with you. The file is labeled 'Belmonte'," she called after him as Slidell disappeared into his office.

She was right about the coffee. It was there on his desk perched on the far corner in the one bare spot left by toppled piles of papers. As he stretched to reach the Styrofoam cup, his stomach pushed against a file jammed with documents, which bumped another file, which knocked over the cup, sending brown sludge cascading everywhere.

"Damn it," he shouted as he looked around the room for something to wipe up the coffee. Except for the dozens of files strewn across the floor and the papers covering the top of the bookcase, there was nothing else in the room, no diplomas or pictures on the walls, no framed awards or commendations, no photographs. There was nothing to mark the room as his, not even a nameplate on the desk announcing his rank and station to the occasional visitor. This was how he preferred it.

"Is this what you're looking for?" asked Corporal Fallon, standing in the doorway to his office and holding out some paper towels.

"Where's that damn file I'm supposed to look at for the meeting with the Colonel?" he growled, grabbing the towels from her.

"On your desk sir; it's the one with all the coffee on it," she answered.

*   *   *

"Good morning, Chuck," said Colonel Stubblefield, who sat leaning over his desk with his large hands clasped as if he were a bishop awaiting the confession of a penitent. Colonel Stubblefield was not the kind of officer to laud his rank over his subordinates by feigning an indifference to them. Instead he shoved it in their faces with an attention so focused and unwavering that it invariably unnerved them.

"Good morning, sir," said Slidell. Every time he entered the Colonel's office he got the impression that it was unusually small. In

fact, the office was large, as befitted the Marine Regional Defense
Counsel, Western Region, commanding the Marine Corps' defense
counsel in the western half of the United States and also those in
Iraq. The smallness of the office was an optical illusion caused by
the massive size of Colonel Stubblefield. He was a bear of a man,
over six feet seven inches tall, and weighing almost three-hundred
pounds. He dwarfed everything within his orbit. The illusion was
also caused by his color. Colonel Stubblefield was onyx, a black so
black that it fooled the eye into seeing shades of the darkest blue and
deepest purple.

"Have a seat," Stubblefield said, motioning to the chair at the
front of his desk.

Slidell moved into the chair, sitting on the edge, back erect, head
up, Marine style. He was not yet comfortable enough with the
Colonel to lean back and sit easy.

"You look like shit," the Colonel added.

"Thank you sir," said Slidell.

"You're welcome. How do I look?" asked Stubblefield, turning his
broad face in profile and lifting his chin.

"Beautiful sir, you look beautiful," answered Slidell.

"You're goddamn right I do," Stubblefield said, running his bear-
paw of a hand over the dome of his shaved head. "And this is how
you should look. Not like the sack of crap I see sitting there." The
Colonel slowly pushed aside the granite and cut glass trophy in
front of him and leaned in closer to Slidell. "It takes effort. I work
out two hours a day. I get my hair cut once a week, whether I need it
or not; and I make sure I screw my wife the same day I go to the
barber. When's the last time you had any sex, Chuck?"

"Sir, the Corps may own me; but my sex life is still private,"
Slidell said in exasperation.

"I thought so. Not getting any, nada, zip. It shows." Colonel Stubblefield rose out of his chair and walked over to the credenza across the room. He picked up the single piece of paper lying on its polished mahogany surface and then turned to Slidell.

"A soldier, especially an officer, isn't supposed to be a monk. Gotta keep the mind sharp," he said. He returned to his desk and sat down, carefully placing the paper in front of him and smoothing it down with both his hands as if it were a finely-embroidered linen cloth.

"This is a missive all the way from the Pentagon. Know what it says?" asked Stubblefield, looking up from the letter.

"No sir, I don't," answered Slidell.

"Well, I'll tell you. It says, right here, that your life is about to become a holy, living hell."

"I don't understand, sir," said Slidell.

"You are to represent one of the three Marines accused of murdering civilians in Fallujah. The incident is already being reported in the news media. High-profile cases for the military are hell, pure and simple."

"Thank you, sir," said Slidell, not really knowing what to say.

"Don't thank me. I didn't pick you. Your new client, Corporal Belmonte, did as is his right under the Uniform Code of Military Justice," said Stubblefield.

Slidell was silent, momentarily taken aback, and then he asked the obvious question.

"Why me, Colonel?"

"Because Belmonte wants a military lawyer with combat experience in Iraq. And guess what? It turns out that you are the only defense counsel in the Western Region with combat experience in Iraq. Ain't that a bitch?"

* * *

Fallon was waiting for Slidell when he got back to his office after his meeting with Colonel Stubblefield. She had a fist full of pink telephone message slips that she handed to him as he passed her going through the doorway.

"What are these?" he asked, flipping through them on the way to his desk.

"The beginning of hell," she answered.

"Were you listening to what the Colonel and I were saying to each other?" Slidell eyed her with a mixture of surprise and accusation.

"Of course. It's impossible not to. Colonel Stubblefield's voice is like thunder in an echo chamber. You were a bit harder to hear. But I managed," she answered smiling.

"So what are these?" Slidell asked again, returning his attention the phone slips.

"They are all calls from reporters: the *Union-Tribune*, the *Globe*, the *LA Times*, the *LA Daily News*, even *Time* magazine, you name it. They want to know about the massacre, as they're calling it, and about us representing Corporal Belmonte," Fallon answered.

"When did these calls come in?"

"They started even before you got here this morning. My phone has been ringing since I opened the office."

"Does Colonel Stubblefield know about these calls?"

"He's the one who told me to give them all to you," said Fallon, smiling and backing out the door.

"That son-of-a-bitch," said Slidell.

Slidell sat down and spread the slips out in front of him. He counted over a dozen. His first instinct was to sweep them all into the circular file beside his desk, but he stopped himself. This was a new age, the age of openness and transparency, especially in government. It would not do to ignore them. But he hated reporters. He knew they all had an established agenda before they even started to investigate. They'd interview you and then cherry-pick your words, taking them out of context to fit their agenda and cobble together the story they wanted told. It had happened to him often enough that he now approached reporters as he would a hooked barracuda on the floor of an open fishing boat. You kept a safe distance from it, and only when it was absolutely necessary did you handle it and then only with utmost caution. Right now he had nothing to say about the Belmonte case. He hadn't even reviewed the file or interviewed his client. It was the perfect time to talk to reporters.

Slidell picked out one of the slips at random. It was from *Time*. Might as well start at the top, he said to himself.

Chapter 2

SHANAHAN'S WAS A bar discovered by mistake. It did not advertise itself, not even with the blue flicker of a dying neon sign or a ripped and sagging canvas awning. Its entrance was a pocked wooden door with a rusted knob set flat against the wall of a dirty brick building down an isolated side street. Its patrons did not frequent it to socialize, party, or flirt. Shanahan's was not a bar for amateurs. It was a bar for professionals, professional drinkers.

"If this is Shanahan's, it must be Thursday," Slidell said to himself as he pushed an empty tumbler to the bartender's side of the bar for a refill of straight whiskey. The rotund, red-faced man in a filthy white shirt and a filthier white apron tied around his ample middle shambled over and poured amber liquid into the glass from a bottle without a label. The bartender counted out three dollars from the stack of bills Slidell had placed on the bar when he first sat down. He then shoved them into the pouch of his apron and walked away without uttering a word. When the stack of bills disappeared, so would Slidell.

Slidell had given up drinking at the officer's club. He had been seen there too often, by too many, unable to find his car keys, unable to extricate his wallet from the back pocket of his uniform trousers, and unable to grab the handle to the door of the club without several fumbling attempts. Instead, he had taken his drinking to remote dives off base. Every Thursday it was Shanahan's.

The only nod Shanahan's gave to atmosphere was a juke box that played nothing but country songs. As Willie Nelson began his sonorous wail, Slidell took the letter Colonel Stubblefield had given him out of his shirt pocket. He unfolded the envelope and removed the letter, placing it in front of him on the faded veneer of the bar. Drops of spilled whiskey instantly spread stains, blurring the ink of some of the words. Slidell snatched up the letter and fluttered it in the stale air to dry before any more of the text was lost.

"Is that some kind of fairy-assed signal for another drink?"

Slidell looked away from the stained page to see the unsmiling face of the bartender.

When Slidell just stared at him looking confused, the bartender pointed to the letter dangling between Slidell's thumb and forefinger and said, "Waving that fucking piece of paper like some sort of fucking semaphore. What do you think I am, some fucking Boy Scout?"

"Yes, I will have another drink," said Slidell, noticing that his glass was empty again. "And could you please wipe down this bar once in a while?"

The bartender slowly poured Slidell a whiskey, being very careful not to fill his glass as high as the last time. Taking three more dollars, he walked away without cleaning the bar.

"Belmonte," thought Slidell. He would meet him for the first time tomorrow when he arrived at Pendleton's brig from the Navy hospital in Germany on his way from Iraq. Slidell already knew what he would be like. "Just a kid," he thought, "a kid accused with other Marines in his squad of disobeying orders, of breaking the rules of engagement, of murder in time of war." The press was trumpeting it as a massacre. The public was dividing itself into opposing camps of screaming slogans: "Marines are Murderers" versus "Killing the Enemy is not Murder." The written charges against Belmonte and the other two Marines were precise. Purged of the legalese used by civilian lawyers and devoid of adjectives and adverbs, they were as sharp as the blade of a finely honed KA-BAR. The charges included multiple murder, kidnapping, assault, and making false statements. The prosecution was asking for a sentence of death.

"Shit," Slidell whispered as Willie Nelson moaned the closing words of his song.

"I'm done with you, do you understand? Finished. I can't take this anymore. I don't care what happens to you now." A woman was yelling somewhere behind him. The pain of her words mimicked the lyrics of Nelson's song, and Slidell would have laughed if he hadn't turned and seen her face. She was standing over a man sitting in a chair rocked back against the wall at one of the round wooden tables opposite the bar. He was smiling, his fist raised to her, the middle digit rigidly extended. Her high cheek bones, wide set eyes, and fine features should have made her attractive; but the shape of her face had shifted to an angry mass that pinched her eyes and twisted her lips.

"Fuck you, too," she screamed and kicked the leg of his chair, causing him to jolt upright and shoot his arms out to recover his balance and keep from falling. She straightened to her full height, lifted her head, and pushed her mop of red hair back before turning and walking out of the bar. As she passed Slidell, something fell from her purse.

"Hey miss, you dropped something," he called as she stepped out the door. She did not stop and did not return.

"Oh hell," he said and slid off the stool.

Outside, he saw her standing by the door of her car, rifling through her purse.

"Miss," he called again.

"Get the hell away from me," she screamed.

"No, no. You don't understand," he tried to explain. "You dropped something back there in the bar." He held out his hand to show her and realized that it was a set of keys on a heart-shaped ring.

"I said leave me alone. Get away or I'll call the police." She was screaming even louder now, almost hysterical.

"Okay. Look. I'll just put them down right here on the sidewalk and go back inside. See?" said Slidell, crouching down and placing the keys in front of him. As he stood up, he raised his arms over his head, opened his hands, and stepped back. The woman looked down at the sidewalk and then back up at Slidell.

"Have a good evening," he said and returned to the bar.

His drink was still there, the glass half empty. He hoisted himself up on the stool, drained the tumbler in one gulp, and signaled for another drink. The woman's hysterics had somehow unnerved him. He spun around on the stool and looked at the man she had first screamed at. He was sitting at the table, his head lolled back. His eyes were closed and the shit-eating grin was still on his face. Slidell could not tell if he was resting or passed out. To hell with both of them, he thought.

He turned back to the bar and continued to think about the Belmonte case. The reporter from *Time* had intrigued him. He had an East Indian name, Amarphal Singh, if he remembered correctly.

He had spoken in a lilting rush of words that at first made it difficult for Slidell to understand him. When he finally adapted to the cadence of his accent, Slidell managed to comprehend what he was saying. He told Slidell that he wanted to write a story from the perspective of the accused Marines. It would be well researched and factually accurate. He was not looking for headlines. It would be published, if it were published at all, well after the press's current feeding frenzy was over. He gave Slidell his editor's name and telephone number at *Time* so that he could check on his legitimacy as a reporter for the magazine. He sounded young but straightforward and professional. Slidell wondered if he could believe him.

The sharp clink of the bottle against the rim of the glass as the bartender poured him another drink brought Slidell out of his reverie.

Chapter 3

THE DISTANT GREY mound, low against the burnt-brown hills of the Santa Ana Mountains, became more and more distinct as Slidell drove along the narrow road toward it. Soon he could distinguish the squat, flat-roofed, concrete buildings of the brig, and, as he got closer, the high chain-link fence topped by razor wire that stretched along the entire perimeter of the compound. It was so desolate and devoid of color that it seemed to Slidell that it could be a station on the moon, anchored in the dust of an ancient crater.

As the steel mesh door to the small cell swung open, the young Marine inside jumped to attention. "Sir," he shouted.

The Marine standing erect in front of Slidell was thin, much too thin. His blue prison uniform shirt hung over his shoulders like a sheet on a veiled statue; and his beltless, bloused trousers billowed up to his waist from his boots. Like a statue, he seemed rigid and brittle underneath.

"At ease," said Slidell, and then he turned to the Marine guard just outside the door of the cell and nodded.

The guard stepped quickly around Slidell into the cell and gave the Marine a stiff punch on the shoulder, instantly spinning him around. He jerked his arms behind his back and ratcheted metal cuffs around his wrists. Then the he bent down and attached rugged plastic shackles to his ankles."

"You can forgo the shackles," said Slidell.

"Sorry, sir," said the guard looking up at Slidell. "I have my orders. This detainee is to be shackled whenever he leaves the cell."

Slidell knew that the three Marines accused of the premeditated murder of civilians in Fallujah had been classified as maximum-security inmates by court order. This meant that they were each confined in isolation to individual eight by nine foot cells containing only a bed, toilet, sink, and desk. They ate alone, exercised once a day alone, and were shackled when leaving the cell. Still, he hoped that the guard might relax the requirement for shackles when the detainee was in the presence of his attorney. Apparently it wasn't going to happen.

"We're going to a room where we can talk in private," explained Slidell to the Marine.

Slidell almost gagged on the fumes of cheap beer and regurgitated chow as they walked along the grey corridor of the brig past several bays housing up to thirty inmates. The stench was overwhelming. Several of the bays held Marines arrested the night before for drunkenness. Slidell had represented a legion of soldiers accused of intoxication and substance abuse and knew that very early this morning—reveille at the brig was 5 a.m.—the inmates had been ripped from their alcohol-induced comas and made to mop up the puke drying and congealing on the floors. They had been provided mops and buckets for this purpose but nothing for the hangovers that threatened to behead them. As Slidell passed, they swayed and moaned over the handles of their mops.

"Here we are, sir," said the guard, stopping at a metal door with a square, thick pane of glass imbedded at eye level. The guard selected a key from the ring attached by chain to his pistol belt and unlocked and opened the door. The room was empty except for a wooden table and two chairs. Illumination came from two small windows high up near the ceiling on opposite walls and a single, shaded bulb hanging above the table.

Slidell pointed toward the Marine; and the guard, understanding the signal, removed the handcuffs.

"I'll be outside the door if you need me, sir," said the guard.

"Just a moment," said Slidell, stopping the guard as he was leaving the room. Slidell turned to the Marine.

"It's Belmonte, is that right?" Slidell asked, pronouncing the ending 'e' like the long 'a' in say.

"Yes, sir," said the Marine.

"Do you drink coffee, Belmonte?"

"Yes, sir."

"How do you like it?"

"Two creams and two sugars, sir."

"Would you get us two coffees, one black and one with two creams and two sugars?" Slidell asked the guard.

"Yes, sir, right away." As the guard was shutting the door to the room, Slidell saw him give Belmonte a look that said the Marine would pay dearly for his coffee with two creams and two sugars.

"Sit down," said Slidell, pulling out for himself the chair facing the door.

Belmonte remained standing until Slidell was seated, and then he sat down.

Slidell decided to dispense with the preliminaries and get right to the point. "I'm Captain Slidell, and I'm the lawyer you asked for."

When Belmonte looked confused, Slidell added, "You requested a lawyer with combat experience in Iraq."

"Oh, yes sir."

Slidell noticed Belmonte smile quickly and relax a little.

Do you know why you're here?" he asked.

"I know why they say I'm here," answered Belmonte after a slight hesitation.

"Good answer, very good," thought Slidell. Belmonte had listened to the question and thought before he answered it. A good sign, just what Slidell wanted in a client.

"And why do they say you are here?" continued Slidell.

"Killing civilians, sir," said Belmonte. Slidell saw that he didn't hang his head when he said this. He had looked straight at Slidell when he spoke.

"And did you?"

Belmonte did not hesitate this time before he answered. "It was not murder, sir."

Slidell took a deep breath and looked around the room. He sensed the muscles in the back of his shoulders involuntarily tense and wondered why. Perhaps it was just the feel of the room, its smallness, its sparseness, the way it felt confining. His gaze returned to the table and Belmont's shadow cast upon it from the light above. The shadow appeared so still that it could have been painted there. Slidell raised his head and looked into Belmonte's face.

"Listen to me carefully. Your opinion doesn't matter. Nobody gives a damn about your opinion. Nobody will listen to it if you speak it. It is irrelevant, worthless to your case, of no help to you at all, a hindrance, an obstacle, a peril. Do you understand me?" pressed Slidell.

The confidence Belmonte had exhibited a moment before disappeared, and his eyes slid down and away from Slidell's. He gave no answer, so Slidell tried again.

"I am interested in facts, not opinion, conjecture, speculation, guess, or bullshit. When I ask you a question, you answer with facts, nothing else. Anything else will get you hung."

Belmonte looked up, and Slidell leaned forward until he was almost nose to nose with him.

"I am not exaggerating to make a point, so I will repeat it. Anything other than facts will get you hung. Are you beginning to understand?"

"I think so, sir," answered Belmonte.

"We'll see." Slidell said these two words quickly and without emphasizing either to erase any skepticism they might imply. "I'm going to ask you my first question again. Did you kill civilians?"

Belmonte raised his hands from his lap and placed them flat on the table. His eyes slowly focused on Slidell. "Yes, sir," he said, his voice clear and steady.

Slidell leaned back into his chair and nodded his head in approval of the answer. Yes, he said to himself. Now he could defend this boy.

*   *   *

Belmonte sat on the metal bed and rubbed his back just above his right kidney where the guard had punched him before shoving him into the cell. "Ask for coffee again, and this comes with it," the guard had whispered in his ear just before he buried his fist next to his spine. The sharp knot of pain melted and spread into a dull ache; and as he massaged the bruised muscle, he felt himself begin to slide into despair. But he subdued the impulse. He would not show weakness of any kind, not now and not ever. Slidell had shaken his confidence. He had made him feel weak and helpless, temporarily robbing him of something essential that he had struggled hard to get and keep.

Belmonte thought back on that struggle in an attempt to retrieve what he felt was slipping away from him. He had begun to see his life as a crucible that could have destroyed him but instead had made him strong. The memories he had once avoided and suppressed he now willingly brought forth, reviewing them again and again to sustain that strength.

Ever since he was old enough and strong enough, his father had made him work the farm. It was just the two of them together, no hired help. And nothing he ever did on the farm was right. His father saw to that. He was called a dumb-fuck and fuck-up no matter what he did, no matter how hard he tried to please. And his ignorance and transgressions were punished by beatings. He could not count the number of times he had to miss school until the bruises faded and the swelling subsided. It wasn't until he was almost finished with high school that he realized that his father only belittled and humiliated, never taught or corrected. It was as if he did not want him to succeed at anything. The sense of failure his father planted and nourished in him turned to anger and then to violence.

He got into fights and took delight in destroying what others cherished until he beat up a kid so badly that the boy was in a coma for three days. That did it. He was eighteen and charged as an adult with assault and battery. The judge gave him a choice—jail or the Marines. Either way he would be out of town for a long time. He chose the Marines. And it was in the Marines, he now understood, that he found himself. There was the abuse, physical and verbal; but he was familiar with it, comfortable with it even. He witnessed the unformed and frail personalities of young recruits like himself obliterated through isolation, intimidation, and exhaustion. But he also saw that they and he were not left to flounder because, in the place of their former selves, they were given the mindset of a Marine and the rigorous training to be successful soldiers. Within that mindset were confidence, loyalty, and mission.

And in Iraq, he surprised himself with his ability to use his training and intelligence to accomplish a mission and to keep himself and others alive. Combat had taught him that you relied on the men on the ground next to you. That's what kept you alive and drinking beer. That's why he had chosen to be represented by a Marine lawyer instead of the civilian lawyer the other accused Marines had decided on. But now he wasn't so sure he had made the right choice. Slidell had made him feel like he was back on the farm, back in high school—a no-account who was sure to fuck-up. Slidell made him feel small and stupid.

Belmonte's heart began to race. He leaned back against the wall of the cell and tried to steady his heartbeat by slow rhythmic breathing. He closed his eyes to concentrate; but when he did, he was instantly overcome by a sense of dread. He felt as if he were standing on a cliff leaning farther and farther over the edge as he fought against the urge to jump. He opened his eyes and focused on the pale green wall opposite him. The feeling began to fade, and his heartbeat slowed. This had happened to him once before in Landstuhl, Germany, after his arrest. He and the other two arrested Marines in his squad were undergoing a medical exam before being sent back to the U.S. for trial. Belmonte shook his head to rid himself of the memory. He had to hold himself together. His life and the lives of his two squad members depended on it. Belmonte stood up. He would never falter, he swore to himself.

"Semper Fi," he whispered.

Chapter 4

CONGRESSMAN JAKE BLAKELY lay down next to the young girl sprawled on his bed. Such a beautiful child, he thought, and touched her face to feel the softness of her skin. Her eyes were shut tight, so tight that her lashes had disappeared between the slits of her lids. She began to moan. "Soon, my darling, soon," he whispered in her ear. The drug was taking effect, and it would not be long before he could have his way with her.

She was a Dominican, dark the way he liked them, and the perfect age for what he wanted. Thank god for Santo Domingo, he thought, the Bangkok of the West, providing an endless supply of pubescent females to men like him. It was so easy, women, pretending to be their mothers, bringing them from the Dominican Republic in their brightly colored dresses, bringing them to him. Pretty flowers to be plucked.

He sat up and leaned over her. Grabbing her wrists, he was raising her arms to the top of the headboard where the nylon rope hung when the Colorado State Anthem blared from the cell phone beside the bed.

"Shit," he bellowed. "Not now, goddamn it, not now." But, 'Where the Columbines Grow' played only seconds more before he answered it.

"Hello," he said.

"Jake, Jake is that you?" said a voice all too familiar to him.

"Yes, Mr. President," he replied.

"Jake, I hear we have a problem. There's talk that funding for the war may be cut off."

"It's more than talk, sir. Right now we barely have the votes to continue funding, and some of our stalwarts are beginning to balk. Momentum on the Hill is against us. By the time the bill hits the floor for a vote, we may be outnumbered."

"Then crack that whip of yours. You've got a reputation for making it sing. Get the bastards in line." Blakely heard a clink, faint but unmistakable, ice in a glass. The old man was drinking again.

"It's not that easy. Everyone is tired of seeing our casualties mount with nothing to show for them. Our people need to convince their folks back home that we're starting to win this war. I need your help, Mr. President."

A pause, then another clink, "Well, what can I do for you?"

"We need kills, sir. We need to show that the insurgents are dying in greater numbers than we are. Get me kills sir, and I can get you votes." The girl opened her eyes, rolled them around, and then tried to lift her head. Blakely clamped his hand over her mouth. Her fingers climbed his arm like nervous spiders and then clutched at his wrist.

There was a long pause and then the President spoke. "You know the situation we are in there. It's complicated. We're trying our damnedest to prop up a government that's on our side. Hell, everybody's shooting at us, Sunnis, Shiites, insurgents-from-god-knows-where, you name them. The new prime minister is trying to come up with a coalition that can get something done for once, and the son-of-a-bitch doesn't want to piss off the Sunni or Shiite leaders in his parliament. That means containing us so that we can't pursue their armies and then kick the shit out of them in a real old fashioned war."

The President's words were tired, like the crumple of old newsprint; and he sounded as if he were reciting a CIA or State Department position paper by rote. Blakely had heard it all before, in one form or another, and just wanted to tell the President to pour himself another drink, and shut up. Instead, he forced himself to listen; something new might be gleaned from the drivel.

"Our troops are hunkered down in locales they are struggling to subdue street by street. The prime minister won't agree to let us out of them, and we've got to go along to get along. We need him and the semblance of a government in that shit hole of a country. We just can't have another government collapse and face the onset of total anarchy. It's bad enough as it is. For now, we're stuck where we are."

It's not that complicated, thought Blakely. Not if you had a set of balls. "I'll do what I can," he said, "but I can't guarantee anything."

"I understand," said the President, and then there was silence.

Blakely snapped the cell phone shut, stood up, and placed it back on the table beside the bed. He wondered if the old man had understood him, wondered if he really understood anything these days. The old man had his lucid moments; but, whether it was from the drink or something more insidious, they were becoming few and far between. Would he even remember their conversation in the morning?

The girl stirred and emitted a soft, low moan, almost a purr. She was ready. Now it was his turn. Blakely picked up the small pink pill on the table and examined it in his palm. Magic, pure magic. In less than a minute after taking it, he would be able to go all night with the girl. He placed it on his tongue, and then swallowed.

Chapter 5

GABIR AL-ASADI HAD always been a surprise to others. His mother, happily settled into her fallow years, had nearly died of surprise when she felt his life inside her. And his father too was surprised after seeing seven daughters born before the son he had silently prayed for. A frail boy, plagued by illness as a child, he grew to be a robust man. Since he was a slow student, few thought he would become a scholar. But he never gave up on a subject until he mastered it. In his teens, he showed evidence of a hungry mind that eventually took him all the way to Stanford University in America. Considered a minor player in the politics of Iraq, to the surprise of all, he became the prime minister. That was his strength and his gift, the ability to surprise. He had come to rely on it.

Al-Asadi looked out over the rooftop veranda at the city spread below him. Here he could behold the city's former beauty. From the perspective of the roof, the strife of its people was muted; and the rubble of its neighborhoods seemed bound again with mortar. The scene invigorated him and renewed his hope. Baghdad was a city for the ages and would someday return to its former glory, he mused.

Al-Asadi forced himself to leave the veranda and return to his office. As he stepped through the doorway, he immediately felt the difference in temperature. The breeze from the north that glided over the veranda and cooled his skin did not enter the room. The air inside sat stale and heavy. He would meet with the American soon. He had arranged the meeting for the hottest time of day, the time of day when the electricity was shut off, the time of day that the air conditioners and fans would be useless. He wanted the American to be uncomfortable away from his 'Green Zone' and its perpetually raging generators. He wanted him to swelter in the heat and to sweat.

He went to his desk and sat. He thought again of his gift and how he must use it. He surprised others because he studied them, studied them until he understood them. It was this understanding, more than anything else, that unbalanced others and gave him an advantage over them. Take the American for example. He understood his kind. They were mad men whose minds whirled in upon themselves. They believed they were best in all things and remained ignorant of the value of others. They mistrusted ways different than their own. The fingers of his right hand involuntarily contracted into a tight fist as he thought of their arrogance. The Americans believed it was their destiny to impose their mode of life throughout the world. They got their way either by seduction, through the use of their vast wealth, or by brute force. That would not happen here, he vowed, but for now he would use them to grow his power; he would be the seducer. Al-Asadi tried to calm himself and poured tea from the urn at his desk. He took a sip and winced. The dark liquid had lost its warmth and was bitter.

There was a knock at the door; and it was immediately opened by a tall, white-haired man in his late sixties. For a moment, al-

Asadi was a boy again, quaking before his teacher, his schoolwork not completed, his studies neglected. Hakim was his secretary now but had been his tutor when he was young. A close cousin of his father, Hakim was discrete, not ambitious for himself, and devoted. Al-Asadi had known him all his life.

"The American is here, ya sayyid," Hakim said, and bowed slightly.

"Show him in; and have some fresh tea brought to us, please," said al-Asadi.

"Do you wish it brought to the veranda?" asked Hakim.

"No, here is fine," he said, as Hakim backed out of the room and shut the door.

Odd, thought al-Asadi, looking at the gold watch on his right wrist; the American was exactly on time. Usually, he and his cabinet members were kept waiting by the Americans for such meetings, especially by the generals. It was strange, too, that he had been requested to meet privately with this American. No matter, Hakim would be listening as always.

As a final preparation for the meeting, al-Asadi prayed to Allah for resolve. He must remain strong in his faith. His was a land of ties among families and tribes going back more than a thousand years, ties so tight and strong they could not be loosened or broken by the violent squabbles that families sometimes suffered. He would make those ties a source of strength, a sword held to the throat of the West. Such a weapon would cause the West to fail again in its effort to dominate the East. Of this he was certain. There was another knock at the door and Hakim ushered in the American.

"Good afternoon, Mr. Prime Minister. My name is James Arndt from the State Department. It is so good of you to meet with me on such short notice," said the American.

The American stood with his hand out to him. Al-Asadi did not offer his hand to the American in return. Instead, he said, "If this meeting is to have any worth to either of us, then we should begin without pretence, Mr. Arndt."

"What do you mean?" asked Arndt, lowering his hand.

"You are not from the State Department. Your office is with the White House. Before your president entered politics, you were in his law firm. You are off the radar, as they say. Even the American press doesn't know who you are. But that does not mean that I am unaware of you," said al-Asadi, watching Arndt's face for a hint of surprise. He found none.

"All I can say right now is that I have access to the ear of the President, Mr. Prime Minister," said Arndt.

Al-Asadi turned his back on the American, walked over to the entrance to the veranda, and stood looking out on the city. It would not be long before the muezzins would call the faithful to prayer from the minarets of the city's mosques. When he faced the American again, al-Asadi was smiling.

"Indeed, and what is it your president wishes to hear?" he asked, motioning for Arndt to sit down in the cane chair opposite his.

Chapter 6

THE SUN WAS setting over Baghdad. The air was beginning to cool; and, in the west, the honed edge of a horizon the color of raw sapphire sliced into a cerulean sky. Hakim considered this the best time for reflection. The wild occurrences of the day, which besieged him and which he struggled to tame, were replaced by comfortable routine and satisfied expectations. He leaned his head back, exhaled the cigarette smoke floating in his lungs, and watched as the white, lucent cloud spread above him. He settled more deeply into his chair.

"You did well today with the American, Gabir," he said. Al-Asadi was reclining on the couch in his private office reading some papers, his shoeless feet resting on a satin pillow.

"Thank you, Hakim; but you must not flatter me. I am still your student in these matters," said al-Asadi.

Hakim was always honest with al-Asadi. He did not flatter or pander. In fact, al-Asadi had performed brilliantly with Arndt. He had combined the crudity and cunning of a camel trader with the wit and intellect of a poet, which he was, to wheedle out of the American his true mission. The American had been out-classed.

"The Americans want to be unleashed, Hakim. They want to be able to pursue the armies that harass them. In return, they promise us the world; but it cannot be done."

Hakim studied the relaxed figure of al-Asadi and thought how his friend used his mind like his body. Al-Asadi was sometimes too relaxed in his thinking, too casual about his conclusions.

"Perhaps it could be done," he said.

"Don't talk such madness," said al-Asadi. Then, setting the papers on the floor beside the couch, he turned to Hakim. "Or is it not madness you speak?"

Hakim wondered if perhaps he were mad. Yesterday, the situation had been dire for their new government. Internal feuding among the Shia councils had broken into armed conflict and threatened to unbalance the fragile truce between the Sunni and Shiite factions in the city. The leaders of the Sunnis were starting to take advantage of these internecine battles and had authorized several attacks against Shiite conclaves. Hakim drew a tight breath through his cigarette and listened as the dry paper and sour tobacco crinkled to ash. He knew civil war threatened if the feuding could not be stopped. A solution had eluded him and Gabir, but now Arndt and his president may have unwittingly placed into their hands the means to avert a civil war and hasten the Americans' defeat. Before he could be sure, he needed the litmus of Gabir's mind to test his sanity.

"Strange is it not, Gabir, that in a place where killing is everywhere, the death of a mother and her children could become so big a matter," he began.

"You speak of the death of al-Ogedi's niece and her children in Fallujah," said al-Asadi. Hakim nodded.

Al-Asadi raised his feet off the pillow and swung his legs to the floor, sitting upright on the couch. "Naseri's sons were fools for using her house to hide from the American soldiers, and now Ogedi blames Naseri for the death of his niece and her children. He has many scores to settle with Naseri. This one gives him a legitimate claim for the mayhem he has brought against him. He is strong enough to defeat him and will try."

"The incident has caused blood to spill throughout Baghdad as the factions choose sides between Naseri and Ogedi," added Hakim.

"It gets worse by the day," said al-Asadi. He stood and walked behind Hakim, placing his hands on the curved rim of the chair's back.

Hakim turned and looked up at him. "Ogedi has always been trouble for us, Gabir; Naseri an ally. If Ogedi's army is weakened, Naseri becomes stronger and gains greater influence among the councils. And as he does, so do we," he said. "He could convince them to end their fighting. The bloodletting among the Shiites will stop, and the Sunnis will then have no advantage over them."

"And how do you propose to weaken the army of Ogedi?" asked al-Asadi.

"We unchain the Americans and set them loose on him," answered Hakim.

Al-Asadi closed his eyes and was silent for a moment. Then he shook his head. "Parliament would never give permission for the Americans to attack Ogedi's army," said al-Asadi.

"No, but you as prime minister could authorize a military operation against Ogedi, using our army with the Americans in support," said Hakim.

Al-Asadi walked to the window behind his desk and stood with his back to Hakim. The sky was still bright enough to absorb the light of the stars and made his form appear as a shadow. "And what excuse do we use for mobilizing our army?" he asked.

"Our excuse will be the truth, to put an end to the fighting and prevent a civil war," answered Hakim.

"But Ogedi's supporters in Parliament will surely see through this. They will accuse us of supporting Naseri over Ogedi. They will call for an election to oust us and may well get it," said al-Asadi. "In any case, such a scheme might increase the fighting. Ogedi's supporters would surely rally to his aid," he added.

Hakim rose from the chair and faced al-Asadi. "Neither will happen, Gabir. Ogedi is not liked by many who support him out of fear. Without his army, Ogedi has no influence over them. They will be free to follow Naseri," he pressed. "Already the people are shouting that the blood of Ogedi's family was spilled by the Marines as an act of revenge. If this were proven, Naseri's sons could not be held accountable for their killings. Ogedi will then have no excuse to continue his fighting against Naseri. Our attack against him will be seen as an attempt to quell a groundless vendetta and bring peace. The objections of Ogedi's supporters will ring hollow, Gabir; and they will achieve nothing."

Al-Asadi stepped back from the window and did a slow about-face like a soldier on parade. "No, no, it will not work. Our army is not yet ready to fight," he said.

"Perhaps not, and that is why it would be, in reality, an American operation. The Americans would get what they want, victories they could tout as their own," said Hakim.

"And we would get what we want, the gratitude of Naseri, a balance of power among the factions, and an end to the conflict," said al-Asadi.

"Precisely," said Hakim. "And our coalition in Parliament would remain intact and become stronger."

"But there are too many missing pieces to this puzzle," said al-Asadi.

"There is only one missing piece, Gabir, and that piece is the American Marines. You must make it clear to Arndt what is needed," said Hakim.

"And what is needed, Hakim?"

"For Naseri's sons to be absolved of the killings of Ogedi's niece and her children, there must be no doubt that the American soldiers are the ones responsible. For this to happen, it must be the Americans themselves who hold their soldiers accountable. Arndt is a lawyer. He will know what is required and how to accomplish it. Do you understand me, Gabir?"

Al-Asadi thought for a moment and then said, "To hear you speak, we have been delivered a great gift in the deaths of the woman and her children."

"Yes," said Hakim and smiled as he remembered the words of the Quran, repeating them to himself, "This Quran guides to the best path, and brings good news to the believers who lead a righteous life, that they have deserved a great recompense."

Chapter 7

A RNDT GRIPPED THE arms of his seat as the airplane ascended through the clouds. He hated this part of flying most, not being able to look outside the small window and see the ground or focus on the horizon to get his bearings. Blind, he would begin to hallucinate, imagining the plane slowly banking, its nose arcing into the roll that would plunge him toward the earth. He began to breathe heavily; and the passenger next to him, a large woman in army fatigues, looked over at him with concern.

He closed his eyes and tried to control his anxiety. He bent his thoughts toward his meeting with al-Asadi, forcing himself to forget that he was in a cramped seat, bolted to a thin metal tube hurtling through the sky, nearly six miles high. He had been warned that al-Asadi was a shrewd man, his shrewdness sharpened by a cunning advisor and confidante. His experience of al-Asadi verified that warning, and he had watched him closely. While Arndt spoke, Al-Asadi never took his eyes off of him or lost his pleasant smile, even when Arndt purposefully but subtly challenged him.

Arndt knew well the game al-Asadi was playing. It was one he had mastered long ago or come as close as anyone could to mastery. In the game to grasp and hold power, allegiances shifted as quickly as the sands of a fast flowing river; groups, parties, or factions constantly formed and reformed alone or together to possess the greatest share. You did what you had to do to keep the power you had or to get the power you needed. Al-Asadi was struggling to keep his power, and to do that he was willing to set his army upon his own people. He just needed the appearance of a legitimate excuse. The Marines' guilt for the killing of the family of Ogedi would give al-Asadi the excuse he needed to put down with force Ogedi's vendetta against Naseri and eliminate the threat of Ogedi to his leadership of Iraq. Arndt had promised him that excuse in return for al-Asadi's granting American forces the freedom to expand military operations far outside of Baghdad.

Arndt felt a weight pushing against his left shoulder and opened his eyes. The female soldier next to him was asleep and snoring softly, her body leaning heavily against his. Arndt pushed her away with both hands; and she woke up with a snort, startled. She looked at him and then shut her eyes and was instantly asleep. He wished he too could sleep; but the stale, recycled air that hissed down at him in a tepid stream made him hot and uncomfortable. Right after takeoff, he had reached up to shut the nozzle off; but it was stuck open. He again looked out the window and saw that the plane was through the clouds. Far below him, the clouds resembled the undulating dunes of a white sand desert. His tension eased.

When al-Asadi made his startling proposal, he acted as if subverting the American military justice system was a reasonable request. He convinced Arndt in the steady thrust of his argument that it was. As he reviewed his conversations with al-Asadi, Arndt realized that his proposal was not only reasonable but plausible. Apparently al-Asadi knew what most American lawyers knew but did not want to admit—that the autonomous courts in the countless counties, towns, and cities scattered across America were not much different from those of the pseudo-democratic third world. Nearly all could sometimes be corrupted.

Arndt had learned early in his legal career that the American legal system was corruptible and that justice could be bartered and sold, often at enormous gains—monetary and personal. As a young US Attorney in Chicago, he had been involved with Greylord, the code name for a federal investigation that swept the Cook County criminal and civil courts clean of over ninety corrupt judges, lawyers, and other court personnel. The corruption not only involved fixing the outcome of traffic and misdemeanor cases but also of high-profile murders and big-money corporate disputes. The fix was in from the very bottom to the top of the Cook County court system and involved some of the most respected judges and attorneys in Chicago.

The plane lurched, and Arndt noticed that the clouds had risen into billowing towers, surrounding the plane. The seat belt sign flashed above him; and the pilot's calm, steady drawl oozed from the speakers along the plane's fuselage.

"We will be experiencing a little turbulence for the next few minutes, folks, so please buckle up. We're going to fly around this weather, so don't worry if you feel the plane change direction a couple of times. Everything's fine. Just sit back and enjoy the ride."

The woman next to Arndt woke up, pulled a magazine from the pouch in front of her, and began leafing through the pages. Somehow this simple act of nonchalance angered Arndt. He tightened his seat belt and pressed back hard into the cushion of his seat, more to control his emotions than to brace himself.

Arndt marveled at al-Asadi's audacity in making the proposal. Al-Asadi must have known about his reputation, but he couldn't imagine how. As a senior partner in one of the nation's most powerful law firms, Arndt had skillfully used the power and wealth of his firm to guide cases to the ends most beneficial to its clients and partners. Such guidance often involved discreet but lucrative offers to judges and opposing council. In many cases, these offers were accepted, sometimes to his surprise.

He preferred a positive approach, one that benefited all parties; but, when necessary, he applied a different form of persuasion to achieve the result he wanted. This method also was successful but made enemies, and enemies were a liability. His skill had earned him the moniker —a moniker that no one called him to his face—of "The Fixer." Because of this skill and their long personal and professional history together, the President turned to him when faced with difficult and delicate matters.

Finally, al-Asadi assumed that he would be willing to sacrifice the lives of a few soldiers for the greater cause of an American victory in Iraq. Al-Asadi was correct. Arndt had no illusions about the guilt of the soldiers. The secret reports he had read confirmed that the killing of civilians by the US military was widespread. Due to the tactics of the insurgents, collateral damage was an unavoidable, even necessary, part of operations in Iraq. The rules of engagement had been relaxed to the point where there was almost no difference between a civilian and a combatant once the shooting started. Whether the Marines killed the mother and her children to save themselves or in retaliation for the snipers hiding in her home made no difference to him. If the Marines had to serve as sacrifices to their country then so be it. They would just be another casualty of the war.

But was the military justice system just as susceptible to subversion and corruption as the civilian justice system? Arndt wondered; and as he did, a plan began to form that would guarantee the guilt of the Marines. He would fix this problem for the President but without his knowledge. The President must never know the means he took to achieve the end. All he needed to know was that al-Asadi was persuaded to permit American forces to expand their operations in Iraq. Arndt would protect the President by shielding him from what had to be done to attain that persuasion, even if he had to sacrifice himself to do it.

As the plan settled in his mind, the rocking of the plane began to soothe rather than worry him. His body relaxed. Just before Arndt fell asleep, the name of the man who would carry out his plan came to him.

Chapter 8

A RNDT WAITED, STANDING at the window of his fifth-floor office in the Old Executive Office Building across from the White House. Although the room was small and sparsely furnished, the view from his window offered a broad sweep of the District of Columbia, from the White House south, over the green expanse of the Ellipse, to the Washington Monument. He enjoyed this vista as he composed himself for the meeting about to take place.

Arndt had selected an office in a remote part of the nineteenth-century edifice. He wanted it unobtrusive and isolated from the other rooms in the building that housed the majority of the White House staff. The view was a bonus. His title on the White House roster was "National Park Service Liaison." Arndt had chosen this title. It was a joke for his own amusement, and he smiled thinking of it.

He was a member of the board of the National Park Foundation. The NPF was a not-for-profit organization that functioned as a charity for the National Parks. If anyone inquired about him, his cover would appear legitimate. But, he was not troubled by any official duties; and no one had inquired. As the rest of the staff, both high and low, engaged in no-holds-barred infighting, Arndt anonymously carried out his duties. He knew that he had but to dial a certain number on his cell phone, and the President would answer it, any time and any place. But he would not call the President about this meeting. The President would never know it had taken place.

The person Arndt awaited would arrive soon. He was always punctual. Arndt congratulated himself. He had chosen well, picking a foot soldier of the party, a Washington veteran intimately familiar with the hidden threads of real power, someone who could get things done discretely, without leaving a traceable path. Arndt was certain that he could rely upon this person to do what was necessary. But the man was no fool, nor a blind patriot. What Arndt was asking him to do would be risky, personally and politically. He would need persuading, and Arndt was prepared.

Footsteps sounded in the hallway. Arndt turned from the window toward the open office door. He was coming. Arndt recognized the stride. The sharp, rapid report of heel against marble signaled impatience and entitlement. Arndt was ready to deal with both.

The clacking ended when Blakely stepped through the door and onto the carpeted floor.

"What's this all about, Arndt?" Blakely asked Arndt this question with unadorned animosity. He made no secret of his dislike of Arndt, either to him personally or to the President. Arndt knew that Blakely had been attempting to undermine his influence. Blakely blamed Arndt for the President's failure to appoint him to a cabinet position. In fact, it was true. In covertly vetting Blakely for the position of Secretary of Defense, Arndt had inadvertently discovered Blakely's dirty little secret, a secret that could make Blakely a political liability. Blakely never knew the reason that the President passed over him for the appointment. Now that secret was about to become Arndt's asset.

"It's good to see you, Congressman. It's been a while. Please sit down. By the way, how's your beautiful wife Cindy? Is she still with that organization helping orphans in war-torn countries?" said Arndt, walking past Blakely and shutting the door.

"Cut the crap. First, I don't like being summoned—by anyone, but especially by you—and second, I don't appreciate being kept in the dark about why I'm being summoned."

Blakely remained standing.

"You take the couch. It's much more comfortable," said Arndt, maneuvering the winged-back chair to the front of his desk to face the couch and sitting down. "I promise I won't take much of your time and that when our meeting is over you will be glad you came."

Blakely reluctantly sat down. He feigned an air of bored impatience that Arndt found childishly petulant rather than insulting. Blakely was hiding his curiosity.

"The war funding bill must pass," Arndt began. "The President is counting on you." Arndt immediately sensed that he had chosen the wrong tone and that Blakely would pick up on it. He did.

"Start lecturing me you arrogant prick, and I'm out of here. I don't need you to tell me what the President requires in Congress. Just get to the point."

"I'm sorry," said Arndt. "I didn't mean that the way it sounded. Please, let me start again." He had to keep Blakely in check, at least for a while longer. "This war is the President's legacy. History will judge him by its outcome, and the outcome of this war is in a delicate and precarious balance. It could go either way for the President, success or failure. Now more than ever, he needs his most trusted allies, those he knows he can depend on." Arndt paused, waiting.

"The President can count on me; he always could; he always can," responded Blakely as if on cue. Arndt could see the curiosity in

Blakely's eyes and knew what he was thinking. What would be asked of him, and what would be granted to him? The President would be grateful to those who sacrificed to help him in this crisis; and the gratitude of the President, the most powerful man on earth, must be curried. Arndt had dangled the carrot in front of Blakely's nose, but he might have to brandish the stick above his head. He would see.

"The President heard the advice you gave him a couple of weeks ago and agrees with you," said Arndt. Blakely's self-satisfied grin lasted a moment too long, and Arndt almost lost his composure with the bastard.

"The President has put in place the mechanism to secure the battlefield victories needed to renew public support for the war. That support will translate into the pro-funding votes in the House you need to get the bill passed." Blakely nodded. "But for this to happen, you must do two things," said Arndt.

"Anything," said Blakely. He was now a full-fledged member of the team. But would he remain one after what was said next? Arndt wondered.

"First, you must delay the vote on the funding bill." Blakely nodded and shrugged his shoulders as if to say, no problem.

"The second thing you must do is crucial. It is beyond your official duties. It is off the record, totally. But it is of the utmost necessity to the President as commander-in-chief that it be done, and that it is you who do it." Blakely moved to the edge of the couch, listening.

"You've heard the news of the Marines accused of murder in Fallujah?" asked Arndt. "It's all over the media."

"Yes, of course. But what does that have to do with me or the funding bill?"

"Everything," said Arndt. "The Marines must be found guilty at their court-martial, and you are to make certain that they are."

Blakely gaped at Arndt in disbelief, then abruptly stood up and started to leave the office. Arndt blocked his way.

"You're insane," said Blakely. "You're asking me to commit a crime. Those soldiers may be innocent for god's sake. Get out of my way. I want nothing to do with this."

"The President needs that bill passed to continue the war—to win the war. It can't happen unless those Marines are found guilty, trust me," said Arndt.

"I don't give a shit. I'm not going to do it." Blakely pushed past Arndt. "And I don't trust you. The President doesn't want this. This isn't him. This is your psychotic scheme," he said, and reached for the handle of the door.

Arndt had known this moment would come and was ready. "Wait," he said, and then he recited the number and street name of an address in DC.

Blakely froze.

"Your name is on a list," Arndt continued, "a list of persons of interest that the FBI compiled for an investigation of child sex trafficking from the Dominican Republic. You have been recorded frequenting that address, an address where children are taken for sexual encounters with adults."

Blakely straightened and turned toward Arndt. He looked ready to kill him. "You bastard, are you threatening me?"

"I'm giving you an opportunity, Blakely, an opportunity to save your career and your freedom. Your name will disappear from that list—forever. All I'm asking is that you help the President."

Chapter 9

F ALLON COVERED HER face with her hands and groaned silently as soon as Robert Anderson disappeared through the doorway. She felt the heat radiating from her cheeks. Shit, she said to herself. He'd only been waiting to see Captain Slidell for how long? Five minutes? She'd lost track of time in his presence. However long it was, she wished she had those minutes to live over again. She would be prepared the second time. She couldn't look at him when he spoke to her. He'd asked her questions. She remembered that, except she couldn't recall what she said to him. She knew though that she had made a fool of herself. Her whole body told her so, from her flushed face to the sick feeling in her stomach.

It was the fault of her damn fantasies. When he had called for an appointment with Captain Slidell, his voice had been dreamy, almost hypnotic. He had announced his name and the reason for his call, and it had all sounded like he was telling her a beautiful story. "This is Robert Anderson," he had said. "I am an attorney with Boswell, Noonan, and Clark and have been assigned by my firm to the team representing the other two Marines on trial with Corporal

Belmonte. I would like to meet Captain Slidell." Silly, but she had imagined him a handsome prince, tall and dark, just from the sound of his voice. Every other time in her life when she had met someone with a sexy phone-voice, he turned out to be a frog. But when Anderson walked into her small office that also served as the waiting room for the Western Region Defense Counsel Offices, she had immediately become unnerved. At 6'2" with hair that covered his head in black waves and the face of a model for GQ, he was a prince. And now she wished she could turn herself into a tiny mouse and skitter under her file cabinet and hide so she wouldn't have to face Robert Anderson when his appointment with Slidell was over. But it wasn't to be so. She heard Slidell saying goodbye and then Anderson's footsteps in the hall coming her way. "Oh, shit," she said again.

She pretended to be busy, staring at her computer screen as she typed nonsense on the keyboard, nmvoeojhiontgm, ngaoshjgonjthnt he's beautiful lnjvoasdnrolhjogfhsdnlgosehj. She did sneak a peek at his ass as he walked past her desk—god it was gorgeous—and was still ogling at it when he stopped and turned around.

"I enjoyed our talk while waiting," he said.

Fallon bobbed her head once, but didn't look up from her computer.

"If you would give me your number, I'd like to call you," Anderson added.

Fallon almost blurted out, "You got to be shitting me," but caught herself. She grabbed a piece of paper, wrote down the number of her cell phone, and thrust her arm toward him.

"You can let go of it," he said, trying to pull the paper from her fingers.

"Sorry," said Fallon, and released it.

"Thanks, I'll call you," he said, folding the paper and putting it into his shirt pocket. Then he was gone.

Fallon started to breathe again. She picked up the phone on her desk and buzzed Slidell.

When he answered the intercom, she said, "Sir, there is something I need to tell you."

"Yes?" asked Slidell.

"Mr. Anderson asked for my telephone number."

There was silence and then Slidell said, "Corporal, is this a matter I need to know about?"

"What I mean, sir, is that I think he might ask me out. Is there a problem with that if he does; some regulation or something that forbids it, considering we're on opposite sides of a case?" Fallon stammered.

"Actually, we're supposed to be on the same side, unless something changes. I don't think there are any regulations prohibiting that kind of relationship with a civilian; but if you do go out with him, you know you're not to talk about our case. That is forbidden."

"Of course, sir," said Fallon.

"Fine; this is your business; but, if he asks you about Belmonte or anything about his case, I want to know about it. OK?" cautioned Slidell.

"Certainly, sir."

"And Fallon…"

"Yes, sir?"

"Congratulations."

Chapter 10

THE TWO ADJOINING glass doors that faced the elevators on the thirtieth floor of the Parker Building in the center of downtown San Diego were massive. At a height of twenty feet and a width of twelve each, they were the largest single pieces of crystal glass in the world. Shipped from Amsterdam at a cost of 1.2 million dollars, they were also the most expensive. They were the last wish of Kenneth Boswell, the most senior partner of the law firm of Boswell, Noonan, and Clark, before his death at the age of ninety-seven. The other named partners had not refused him.

Anderson scanned down the list of eighty-seven lawyers whose names were written in gold on the glass and found his name, twenty-fourth from the bottom. His progress up the list had been steady, some might say meteoric, ever since he started at the firm as a summer intern from Duke Law School four years ago. Now he had been chosen as part of the litigation team defending a high-profile case involving the murder of civilians by Marines. Things could not be better. He touched the handle of one of the glass panels, and the door automatically opened with a majestic sweep.

"Good morning, Mr. Anderson," said the receptionist. She was beautiful and exotic, as were all the female functionaries at Boswell, Noonan, and Clark, another wish of the senior partner that had not been refused.

"Good morning, Maisie, has Jim come in yet?" he asked, as he turned toward the hall that led to his office.

"No, Mr. Anderson, shall I tell Mr. Patterson you want to see him when he does?" she called after him.

"Yes, if you would, please," he shouted back over his shoulder.

Anderson walked down the hall lined with oils and watercolors painted by known artists, some of them famous, without looking at a single one. When he came to his office, he hesitated before opening the door. He reminded himself that he was an associate in one of the most prestigious law firms in the country, and not a cipher in a legal aid office in a washed-out part of the city. He felt a tap on his shoulder and turned around. In front of him stood a young man in an Armani suit and a two-hundred dollar tie grinning his head off.

"Jim," he said. "What the hell are you smiling about?"

"Mr. Patterson to you, buddy boy. I'm one name above you on the golden list, and don't you forget it," said Jim Patterson still grinning.

"Not for long," said Anderson.

"Well?" asked Patterson, his smile fixed to his face like that of the proverbial Cheshire cat.

"Well what?" Anderson asked back, starting to smile in spite of himself.

"Did you get any last night?" asked Patterson, forming a circle with the thumb and forefinger of his left hand and thrusting the middle finger of his right hand back and forth through it.

"That's disgusting," he said, and opened the door and stepped into his office.

"You didn't answer my question, pal," said Patterson, following him in.

"It was just a first date for god's sake," said Anderson.

"Never stops me," said Patterson.

"Get the hell out of here," said Anderson, sitting down at his desk and turning on his computer. "I've got work to do."

"See you later. In ten minutes it will be all over the firm that you screwed your eyeballs out last night," Patterson said, laughing as he backed out the door.

"Screw you," said Anderson and pelted a wad of paper at him.

As Patterson left, the intercom on Anderson's desk buzzed. "Yes?" he said into the machine.

"A heads up," said the voice of a mature female. "Sutton's coming to see you now, and he doesn't look happy." Stella was another perk collected in his rise in the firm, his own secretary. Well not really his own. He and Patterson shared her with Jeffery Sutton, a senior litigation partner with the firm, which meant that they got last dibs on her services, way last. She was almost old enough to be his mother; but unlike his mother, she did not have any maternal instincts towards him. In fact, he thought she took a perverse delight in watching him fall on his ass.

"Thanks. What's Sutton upset about?" he asked.

"No idea. By the way, have a nice day."

Shit, he said to himself, and then Sutton walked in.

"You fucked up big time Anderson, but I'm not going to hold it against you because I'm such a nice guy," said Sutton, grabbing the chair in front of Anderson's desk and squeezing his ample backside between its arms.

"May I ask what you're talking about, Mr. Sutton?" said Anderson.

"No. Just shut up and listen," said Sutton. "The judge denied our—your—motion for release of our clients pending trial. That means they're stuck in the brig. That means they are unhappy, the ones who are paying our outrageously high fees are unhappy, and I am unhappy." Are you unhappy too, Anderson?"

"Yes sir."

"Good. Now you are going to make this right," said Sutton, tossing the judge's order on Anderson's desk. "We—you—are going to motion for a speedy trail, a very speedy trial. I want opening statements to begin in no more than eight weeks. Now get to it."

"Is that wise, sir?" asked Anderson.

"Listen. You don't think wise or unwise, you just follow instructions. Got that?" said Sutton rocking himself out of the chair.

"Yes, Mr. Sutton," said Anderson.

"I want that motion filed tomorrow morning. I'll review it this afternoon before three o'clock," said Sutton waddling out of the office.

"Yes, sir," said Anderson to an empty doorway. He pressed button number four on the intercom, and Patterson answered.

"Patterson here, who's there?" he answered.

"It's Robert. We've got a problem," said Anderson.

"I know, buddy boy. Sutton wants us to go to trial in eight weeks," said Patterson.

"How did you find out so fast? Sutton just told me." said Anderson.

"I know about everything that happens around here," said Patterson.

"How?" asked Anderson.

"I'm screwing Stella," said Patterson.

"You're kidding, right?" said Anderson.

There was only silence in response to his question, but Anderson could feel Patterson grinning right through the intercom.

Chapter 11

THE NIGHT OF her funeral, Slidell slept at the bottom of the stairs. He'd woken several times during that night feeling her body beside him. He imagined her lying there alone on the floor. Was she in pain or had she felt nothing? He had been told that she had not died instantly. He wondered if she'd been able to call out for him, if she tried. All traces of her blood had been cleaned from the wooden floor before he had arrived from Iraq. But she had not died from the blood lost from the gash in her head, the wound that had destroyed her beauty; she had died from the hemorrhaging her brain suffered after the blow of the unknown intruder. She had probably heard a noise and had gotten out of bed to investigate. He had caught her by surprise. The police said there was no evidence of a struggle. The house had been burgled, probably as she was dying.

He loved her. He would have loved her even if she had not loved him back. They had met in New Orleans at Mardi Gras; and afterwards everything for him became a colorful, noisy, bawdy, over-the-top parade. It was as if he had never lived before. He couldn't stand to be apart from her. Yet he left her, left her when she had begged him not to go on another combat tour, left her to die alone. Now there was not a day when he did not blame himself for her death. Had he been there, he knew he could have saved her.

The cab pulled up in front of Shanahan's, and Slidell got out his wallet to pay the driver.

"Nice place," said the driver, craning his neck toward the back seat and talking out of the side of his mouth. "What do they serve in there, insecticide?"

"Can you be back here in two hours?" said Slidell, tipping the driver ten bucks over the fare.

"Sure thing. The question is, can you?" said the driver.

"See you then," said Slidell, sliding across the seat and out the door of the cab.

Entering Shanahan's was like stepping from the dim light of a movie matinee into the blinding sun of outdoor San Diego, only the reverse. The interior darkness was so immediate that Slidell had to wait for his eyes to adjust before he felt safe enough to negotiate his way from the door to a vacant stool. As the outlines of the meager furnishings of Shanahan's emerged from the shadows, Slidell felt himself enveloped by a comfortable shabbiness. Benign neglect was the theme. Duct tape and dust the dominant décor. Buckled paneling and layers of cracked linoleum muted the sharp peaks of conversation to the level of easy intimacy. The saccharine smell of cologne and perfume held back the pungent odor of old, spilled booze.

"You again," said the bartender as Slidell sat down and placed his money on the bar.

"You act as if you don't like your customers," said Slidell as the bartender poured him a glass of whiskey.

"What's there to like? They're a bunch of drunks," said the bartender, setting down the bottle and wiping his nose on his apron. "I should be spending my valuable time with such losers?" The bartender started to walk away, hesitated, and then turned back to Slidell.

"Once, Frank Sinatra himself came into this bar. He was looking for someone. Found the guy over there in the corner, passed out. What he wanted with him, I don't know. Sinatra didn't even buy a drink. Didn't even say hello. Wouldn't even sign a napkin. I would've framed it. Might have turned business around, proving he came in here. What a shit. They're all shits."

"I didn't know you had napkins in here," said Slidell.

"Yeah, and screw you too," said the bartender and left Slidell for another patron.

Slidell took a sip of whiskey and let the warm, sharp liquid rest in his mouth a moment before he swallowed it.

"Excuse me. I don't know if you remember me, the other night, the keys, remember? I was the one who dropped them." The jumble of words came from the redhead who had just stepped up to the stool beside Slidell.

Slidell set his glass down and looked at her. She pushed her hair back from her forehead and held it away from her face. "Remember now?" she asked and smiled up at him.

"You didn't bring the police, did you?" said Slidell and turned back to his whiskey.

"No, I mean I just came to say I'm sorry for the way I acted. That was kind of you, bringing me the keys. I was upset. I wasn't myself. I never thanked you," she said.

"You're welcome," said Slidell, watching her reflection in the mirror behind the bar.

"Can I buy you a drink? Only I'd prefer if it were coffee and not liquor," she said.

"Is it just a coincidence you're here tonight or have you been stalking me?" Slidell asked.

The woman's smile vanished, and her face turned almost as red as her hair. Slidell could not tell whether it was embarrassment or a flash of anger.

When she didn't answer, he added, "That was meant to be amusing. I was just wondering how you knew I would be back here tonight."

"I called the bar and spoke to the bartender. He told me you were here almost every Thursday. I took a chance. I only wanted to apologize. That's all." From the tone of her voice, Slidell could tell that he had embarrassed but not angered her.

"Listen," said Slidell. "Thanks for the thanks, but I don't want to get mixed up with your wacked out boyfriend if he comes in here and sees us drinking together."

"First of all he's not my boyfriend..."

"Husband then. Even worse," said Slidell, interrupting her.

"He's not my husband either, he's my brother," she said.

It was Slidell's turn to feel embarrassed. "Oh," he said. "Look, now I really am sorry. I apologize. We're even, so let's call it a day. Nice meeting you." He turned to her and held out his hand.

She took his hand in hers. "Actually, we haven't met yet. My name's Candice, Candice McNeil." The smile was back.

"Chuck Slidell," he said.

"Would you like that coffee now?" she asked, still holding his hand.

Chapter 12

"NOT GOOD, HUH?" said Fallon scooting her chair closer to Slidell's desk. She had quietly entered his office after giving him time to read the investigation report of the civilian killings in Fallujah. It had been on her desk when she arrived at the office, and she had opened it and read it before she made the morning coffee.

"Not good at all," said Slidell, leaning back in his desk chair and pushing the open folder away from him as if it were contaminated.

Fallon picked up the folder from the desk, closed it, and put it in the brown, expanding file she balanced on her knees.

"It's pretty damn incriminating," said Slidell. "From the evidence garnered by the Naval Criminal Investigation Division, the soldiers clearly went on a rampage. The report concludes that the dead woman had been tortured. She had internal injuries, her jaw was broken, and much of her hair had been pulled out. The girl was shot in the back, perhaps trying to run away. But she took several rounds in the chest. The skeleton of an old man was found in the ashes of the house. His skull shows that he had been shot in the head, execution style. Only the boy is problematic for trial counsel.

According to the entry and exit wounds covering his body, it can be argued that he was killed in the crossfire with the snipers."

"So, will that be the case for trial counsel?" asked Fallon.

"They don't need much more for a conviction. There's the motive, revenge for the planting of the IED that killed the rest of their squad. You have the torture and executions, evidencing rage. That shows their guilt." Slidell was quiet for a moment and then said, "You think we may be on the wrong side of this one, corporal?"

"No sir, not yet," said Fallon.

"Good. Neither do I," said Slidell. "Now, let's get to work. I want to know every soldier in Belmonte's squad who left the unit within six months before that firefight, who they are, where they live, where they work, go to school, their phone numbers, and the types of discharges they received. If they're still in the Marines, what units they are with now. I also want to see their military records. Prepare the interrogatories, and get them out ASAP."

"Yes, sir," said Fallon, turning to leave.

"Oh, and get me the chain of command from squad leader on up to the commander of the Fallujah district at that time."

"Yes, sir."

*   *   *

Slidell opened the drawer of his desk and took out a new legal pad from the stack Fallon had placed there. He put it in front of him on the desk. Then he unclipped the black, government-issue ballpoint pen from the pocket of his uniform shirt. He checked to make sure that the thin piece of masking tape with his name written on it was still wrapped around its body. These pens never worked and to find one that did required that measures be taken to insure it wasn't borrowed, stolen, or sucked into the black hole that ingested seemingly tens of thousands of such instruments. He smiled as he thought how something so insignificant as a cheap pen could affect his life to the point where he would spend the mental and physical effort necessary to preserve it. As he put the pen down on the legal pad, his smile disappeared. He wondered how much more of his life might be controlled by obsession with minutia.

Slidell picked the pen up again and wrote a name on the first blue line of the yellow page of the pad. 'Belmonte.' He would go back to this page, this line, this name again and again to remind himself that the case was about one thing only, his client. From the beginning it must be about his client and never, not once, about anything else. He'd seen it happen before, the client becoming a mere pawn in the legal maneuvering and posturing of lawyers, a client lost without a guide in the maze of legal procedure and the arcane structure of the legal system, a client sacrificed in order to make a political statement or to boost the career of a lawyer. It happened most often when a case was tried because of fear, the fear of losing. Slidell knew that it was a fear more palpable for some than the fear of death, and he could point to many lawyers who had abandoned their clients' interests to save themselves from humiliation or blame.

Slidell wrote the word 'valor' beneath Belmonte's name. Belmonte was a combat veteran decorated twice for heroism. Slidell knew what that meant. He had experienced in battle what Belmonte had: each sense reaching an intensity so great that he became aware of every atom of every molecule of every particle in the matter of everything surrounding him; a focus so extreme that nothing, absolutely nothing, could deter him from his purpose. He had read about shape-shifters, Celtic warriors so ferocious in battle that their faces literally transformed into masks of horrific visages. They became unstoppable, terrifying their enemies into retreat. He knew that this was not myth but reality. Every commander he had served under had written the same thing about him in reports of his conduct under fire: he was the best field officer they had ever seen. He knew the physical courage and stamina Belmonte was capable of. But did Belmonte have mental courage and stamina? Could he bear the inevitable loss of battles in the war that was a trial for murder?

Next to 'valor,' Slidell wrote 'confinement' and then circled the word. To lock a vigorous, young man in a pen indefinitely, to restrict his movements, to limit his contact with the outside world were forms of torture, torture that often broke clients on trial in criminal cases. Slidell wondered what kind of support Belmonte would need to withstand his confinement. He wondered too if he would be able to detect the subtle signs that Belmonte was beginning to break down.

Slidell put the pen back in his pocket and looked at his watch. It was 10:25 a.m. Exactly six hours and thirty-five minutes until his first drink of the day, the Healer, as the Irish called it. He wanted a drink now. He had wanted a drink an hour ago. But he would wait until the time he permitted himself that first drink. He hadn't faltered yet. He could wait, he told himself. As he set the legal pad back in the drawer, he noticed its pages were stained with sweat from his hands.

Chapter 13

THE RECEIVER WAS barely visible in the massive hand that set it gently back into its cradle, so gently that the reuniting of the two parts of the phone made no noise at all. Stubblefield had feared that even the sound of the click disconnecting the call would erase all memory of it, and he wanted to remember this call. He needed to parse the words, hear again in his mind the inflections, feel the deliberate and accidental pauses, and study the emotional eddies left in its wake. He wanted to uncover its real meaning.

His day had been going well. He had received email confirmation of the accommodations for the fishing trip he and his wife had planned in the North Woods of Wisconsin. What more could a man wish for, he had thought, than a wife who also loved fishing? And the North Woods was their favorite getaway. The slant of the sun's rays at that latitude, especially in the mornings, gave a richness and texture to the colors of the sky and water that left a lasting imprint on his heart. And then there was his retirement. A year and a half more and he was a free man. Just thinking about it made even the worst of days bearable. But the phone call had disturbed these thoughts, had somehow diluted and thinned them to the point where they drained away like liquid through a sieve. Now he wanted them back; and, to do that, he had to get a firm grip on what General Hammond had told him.

Brigadier General Percival—Percy to only a few—Hammond got his coveted position of Chief Defense Counsel of the Marine Corps and his office at the Pentagon by kissing up and kicking down, and Stubblefield hated him. He hadn't spoken personally with Hammond for a long while. They mostly communicated by email and the weekly written summaries of the cases processed by the unit. Stubblefield preferred it this way. A phone call was unusual, particularly one where Hammond actually committed himself by giving a direct order. Hammond had stressed that he wanted the case processed quickly. "None of the pretrial procedural bullshit," he said. He didn't want that kid rotting in the brig while some nervous lawyer pranced around the legal issues trying to come up with some crap for the appeal. "Get the damn case to trial, ASAP," Hammond had demanded. No ambiguity there, thought Stubblefield; but the reasons didn't ring true from what he knew of Hammond.

Stubblefield opened the dark wooden humidor on his desk, took out a Leon Jimenez Robusto, and eyed the tube of thick rolled tobacco he held in his open palm. He preferred Cuban, but these Dominicans did him very nicely until trade with Cuba opened once again. Unbreakable directives forbade smoking in or outside any building on the base, so the taste of cured tobacco and its raw fragrance would have to do for now. He gingerly placed the cigar between his lips and spun it over his tongue. Now he could think.

Hammond had railed that the case was getting negative press and that there was a growing public clamor against the Marines. He then intimated that a quick trial would be good for the Marines and the soldiers both. Try the case before matters got out of hand and while public prejudice was not totally against the soldiers, Hammond had urged. Stubblefield knew that Hammond did not give a rat's ass for the opinions of civilians, including the press, or for the well-being of enlisted personnel unless they somehow affected his chances for promotion. Therefore, someone above Hammond was probably putting pressure on him to get the case resolved in a hurry.

In any case, it could be just as strongly argued that delay of the case was the proper tactic, Stubblefield reasoned. The ranting of the public would eventually die down, and the press would move on to other matters if you just waited long enough. Then the case could go to trial in relative obscurity. And why the phone call? Was it because there would be no record of a meeting and nothing in writing? That was not like Hammond either. Stubblefield guessed that entire old-growth forests had perished in Hammond's efforts to cover his ass in a paper trail.

Stubblefield danced the cigar from one corner of his mouth to the other as he thought. Hammond was a Naval Academy graduate. Those guys protected their own. Had one of them gotten his tit in a ringer in this mess with the Marines, and was this the beginning of a program to cover up a fuck-up? Stubblefield was disturbed by these possibilities, but what really angered him, what really pissed him off, was Hammond placing his grubby hands on a case that was under his jurisdiction and was his alone to handle as his professional judgment and experience dictated. Stubblefield put the cigar in the crystal ash tray on his desk and reached for the phone. He knew that when he was angry he made bad decisions. He needed to run this by someone he could trust, someone who could keep quiet. He picked up the receiver and dialed.

"Hey, baby doll," he said when there was an answer. "Get dressed up in something fine. I'm taking you out to dinner."

"That's nice. What's the occasion, darlin'?" said his wife.

Chapter 14

THE LIGHTS FROM the docked fishing boats and motor yachts blinked across the dark channel like signaling fireflies. The view would have been idyllic, almost hypnotic, thought Blakely, except for the distraction of the traffic creeping along the freeway that spanned this out-of-the-way detour of the Potomac. Even at 10 p.m. the cars going into and out of the District were bumper to bumper.

Blakely watched as Sutton poured the clarified butter over his soft-shelled crabs and then shook the glass container to release the last few drops clinging to the lip. Blakely half expected him to lick his fingers. He had wanted to meet with Sutton for a while, and Sutton's trip from San Diego to DC to speak before the National Trial Lawyers' Association provided the excuse he needed. Blakely was beginning to worry about Sutton. He didn't want him too sure of their relationship, too complacent about his role in their arrangement.

The parents of two of the accused Marines had agreed quickly to have civilian representation at the trial of their sons. He had arranged the payment for their legal fees through a dummy group called, "Defend Our Defenders," or DOD, which was funded anonymously by trusted party contributors. Neither the group nor the funds could be traced to him. He had picked Sutton to represent the two Marines and wanted to make absolutely sure Sutton knew what he was supposed to do. However, the family of the third accused Marine had refused help.

"More wine?" asked Blakely. Sutton raised his empty glass as he leaned over his plate and stuck the glob of dripping flesh on the end of his fork into his mouth. Blakely poured the wine.

"Place isn't what it used to be, is it?" said Blakely.

"What do you mean?" asked Sutton.

"Not like when we were at Georgetown Law, DC glitterati at every table. The rich, the famous, the powerful," said Blakely. "The Flagship was really *THE* restaurant then. Now it's all tourists." Sutton had insisted on the Flagship in spite of Blakely's protests.

"You embarrassed to be here?" asked Sutton. Before Blakely could answer, he said, "We're doing our part for the glory days; you're powerful; and, I'm rich, and we're both here." Sutton chuckled and then slurped his wine.

"You're rich because of the cases I send your way. Don't you forget that," said Blakely.

"Oh, no worries there, pal. I know what side my bread is buttered on. Speaking of bread, pass me some will ya," said Sutton, cupping his hand and wiggling his fingers at Blakely.

"Speaking of cases," said Blakely, passing Sutton the basket of bread. "I trust there are no problems with the litigation involving the Marines."

"I told you not to be concerned. It's under control. I know what I'm doing. You just keep the money coming. I'll do my part." Sutton grabbed a roll from the basket and mopped his plate with it, swirling the bread in decreasing circles until the entire surface had been covered. In two quick bites, the roll was gone.

In spite of Sutton's assurances, it was clear to Blakely that he needed to tighten the leash he'd placed around Sutton's neck, and tonight he intended to make it very tight. The camera could not be detected from where it was hidden in the guest bedroom of the townhouse. Sutton would have no idea he was being video recorded. The film would be Blakely's insurance against any trouble from him.

He and Sutton had met their freshman year at law school and had become roommates in an apartment in Georgetown the next year. It did not take long before close quarters and a shared affinity for hard drugs led to a confession of each other's sexual proclivities: Sutton for pederasty and he for pedophilia.

"As I promised, dessert is waiting at a special place; foreign fruit, handpicked and newly-ripe," Blakely said. "Are you ready to go?"

"Yes, oh yes, I am," said Sutton, swiping the napkin over his mouth and rubbing his chubby palms together in glee.

Chapter 15

"Say that again, slowly this time," said Slidell.

"It was a mantra, sir," said Belmonte.

"A what?" asked Slidell.

"A mantra, a chant. The guys in the platoon said it all the time, especially before a mission."

"Say it again," repeated Slidell.

"You gotta kill who you gotta kill to save who you gotta save," said Belmonte.

Slidell wrote the sentence on the note pad in front of him. He then asked, "Did any officer hear this said in your presence?"

"Yes, sir," said Belmonte. "Pretty much all of them. They would even say it with us. Like I said, sir, it was like a unit mantra."

"What did this mantra mean to you?" asked Slidell.

"Same thing it meant to everyone, sir. If our guys were getting shot at, you shot back at anything and everything necessary to protect them and yourself. The rule was no Marine was allowed to die; no way, no how."

"Did that include shooting unarmed civilians?" Slidell asked.

"Like I said, sir, you shot at anything and everything, didn't matter who or what was in the way. No Marines were allowed to die, period."

"Is that why you shot the girl?" asked Slidell.

"No, sir. I told you before, I tried not to shoot her. She was trying to get away. I wanted her to. I thought I had a clear shot, but she was moving all over the place, kicking at the sniper and scrambling backwards. She must have got back in the way," answered Belmonte. "That's the truth, sir. I know it doesn't sound like it, but it is."

"Who shot the old man in the house?" asked Slidell.

"Don't know, sir. Could have been any one of us in the assault team. We were spraying bullets everywhere. He was probably upstairs on the second floor with the kids and the woman. Never saw him. I didn't even know about him until you went over the investigation report with me," answered Belmonte.

"He was shot at an angle through the forehead. The report concludes that the trajectory of the round and the entry and exit wounds are consistent with a pointblank, execution style gunshot," said Slidell.

"I can't say anything about that, sir. Like I said, I didn't even know about him until you told me," said Belmonte.

Belmonte sighed deeply. For the last hour he had sat erect in his chair with his feet flat on the floor. He'd barely moved a muscle. The boy refused to relax in Slidell's presence; refused to betray any sign of emotion. He had adopted a flat affect to his speech and had muted his body language to that of a statue. Only his sighing gave him away. Slidell was sure that Belmonte was not aware of his deep breaths and long exhalations after answering certain questions. Slidell had tried to keep his interviews with Belmonte short. It was time this one ended.

Slidell knew from Belmonte's military file that his parents were both alive, so he tried to steer the subject to a pleasant topic. "Have you heard from your parents?" he asked.

"Got a letter when I first arrived back in country," said Belmonte.

"Just the one?" asked Slidell surprised.

"Yes, sir."

"Are they coming to visit you?"

"No, sir. Don't think that's likely," said Belmonte.

"Why not?" asked Slidell.

"My mom's not in the best of health, and my dad has to stay home and take care of her and the farm." Belmonte said simply.

"That doesn't have to be a problem," said Slidell. "I can make whatever arrangements are necessary to have them come and see you. You have that right as a soldier."

"No need, sir. My folks weren't exactly happy about how I joined up." Belmonte sighed again. "And this trial isn't helping to set things right. My dad's a very proud man."

Slidell wanted to tell Belmonte that his relationship with his parents could be salvaged; that having them come to see him could be the first step. But he couldn't. He was unable to articulate such pap. His own experience had taught him that the wounds of some relationships could never heal, that some relationships were better off dead.

Slidell's mother gave birth to him in Baton Rouge when she was fifteen. She had given him to her older sister and her husband to raise. He was told that she was his aunt. She would take him to his favorite places, buy him his favorite foods and candies, spoil him in all kinds of ways. He adored her. When she was twenty-two she got married to a man with two kids and moved away, first to New Orleans and then to Portland, Oregon, before she finally just disappeared. He never saw her again. He was eight when he was told that the couple he thought were his parents weren't. He held out hope for years that his mother would come back for him. He imagined every knock at the door to be her, every telephone call the news that she was on her way to him. Now he didn't even know if his mother was still alive. He didn't know if he cared. Slidell became aware that Belmonte was staring at him.

"You okay, sir?"

"Yeah, sure, I'm fine," said Slidell, pulling himself back into the present. "Is there someone else I could contact for you? Someone you'd like to see, a girlfriend maybe?"

"Don't get a chance to meet many girls in the brig, sir," said Belmonte.

"Yeah, I guess not," said Slidell, embarrassed. "Well, if you think of anything you need, let me know," he quickly offered.

"Yes, sir," said Belmonte, his voice flat, his eyes staring straight ahead.

Chapter 16

IT HAD BEEN a long and busy day, and as Slidell drove down Route 5 toward San Diego and home he realized that he had not eaten breakfast or lunch and that the nagging tiredness he felt was hunger. He couldn't bear eating alone at a restaurant, and he was too tired to fix himself dinner, so he set his internal compass for the southeast corner of Clairemont Mesa Boulevard and Ruffner Street. A chili cheeseburger and chili cheese fries from Tommy's were just what he needed, comfort food to beat all comfort food.

Slidell sat down at his dining room table, pushed a dirty paper plate and silverware to the side, and put the brown paper bag in their place. He opened the wrinkled sack, removed the chili double cheeseburger inside, and peeled back the wax paper. As he did, grease coursed in rivulets and spread out on the dark cherry wood, where it began to congeal. Then he took out the chili cheese fries and shook them from their container so that they flopped onto the wax paper and surrounded the burger. He looked at the mélange of food in front of him. In the culinary arts, presentation was every-thing, he said to himself. He picked up a fry and dangled it over his open mouth so that chili slid down the cheese and onto his tongue. Prior to a feast, the palate must first be stimulated. He then dropped the fry into his mouth.

As he chewed, he thought of the woman at the bar, Candice. He had refused her offer of coffee; but she had stayed a while anyway, and they had talked. She had an easy way about her. She was comfortable in her skin, as they say. He liked that. He hadn't felt relaxed around a woman in a long time. It had been a while since he felt relaxed around anyone. She had given him her card before she left. Candice McNeil, MSW, with an office at the University. The card contained both her work and home phone numbers. So she was a social worker. Perhaps her easy manner was merely professional, a practiced persona she used with clients. He wondered. He ate one more fry and then bit into the burger, chili squirting from the sides and splattering his cheeks. Delicious!

*   *   *

Slidell had not slept well. His stomach had troubled him all night. It was the burger or perhaps the fries or maybe both he thought. His stomach was still queasy when he walked into his office, so he had skipped the usual three cups of coffee. Now he was having difficulty getting moving on the day without his usual kick-start of java.

"General Maxwell is pissed, Chuck, extremely pissed." Startled, Slidell looked up. Stubblefield had walked into his office unnoticed and silent as a cat. He could not understand how a man so large could move without making a sound.

"You mean he didn't like getting the subpoena for his deposition," said Slidell when he recovered from the shock of Stubblefield's presence.

"He didn't like it at all, according to his arrogant shit of an aide who called me." Stubblefield pushed a stack of papers out of the way and sat on the edge of Slidell's desk. "Apparently he's planning on contesting it. Says he's got better things to do. We're just wasting his valuable time there at the Pentagon."

"He was the commander of the Fallujah district when this incident occurred," said Slidell. "He was the one responsible for enforcing the rules of engagement for the troops he commanded. I want to put on the record what his orders were concerning the rules of engagement and how he enforced them."

"Well, he sure as hell isn't going to say they were to kill anything that moved," said Stubblefield.

"No he isn't, but I intend to show that he had to know the rules that his troops were

following and that he permitted and encouraged those rules," said Slidell..

"You gotta kill who you gotta kill to save who you gotta save," said Stubblefield.

"Yes, sir, the very same," said Slidell.

"You're treading on dangerous ground here, Chuck," said Stubblefield.

"How do you mean, sir?" asked Slidell.

"Two reasons. First, according to what you told me, Belmonte didn't follow those rules. He tried to avoid shooting the girl."

"The other Marines may have," said Slidell, interrupting Stubblefield.

"They're not your clients. And second, General Maxwell is not some old, broken-down soldier fading away in a dusty corner of the Pentagon until the day of his retirement. He's a rising star who is being groomed for the Joint Chiefs of Staff. He's not going to let you fuck with him without a fight. You do what you say you want to do, and this could derail his career," said Stubblefield.

"You saying I should back off?" said Slidell.

"You know me better than that Chuck. I'm just saying you may be picking a fight you don't need to get into," said Stubblefield.

I don't understand, sir?" said Slidell.

"Do you need the general to establish that the rules of engagement the Marines were actually following were known up through the chain of command? Like I said, he isn't going to admit he explicitly or tacitly approved of his men killing anything that moved if they were shot at. All I'm saying is that his testimony may make it more difficult to prove what you want to prove and that the time you spend fighting him may be better spent on other issues. Think about it."

Stubblefield slid off the desk and stood looking down at Slidell. "Listen, Bella and I are having a barbeque at the house on Sunday. She misses you. She'd like you to come. And this time she wants you to bring someone with you. Can you make it?"

Slidell was taken aback both by the sudden shift in their conversation and by the invitation itself. Without thinking, said, "Sure, that would be great."

"Good. There better be a lady hanging on to your arm. Bella insists." Stubblefield left the office as silently as he had entered it.

Chapter 17

"Ask him what I should bring. No wait, don't ask Colonel Stubblefield, ask his wife. He'll just say 'nothing;' she'll be honest. Find out and call me back."

Slidell had agonized for two days about calling Candice McNeil. He had picked up the phone a dozen times but had set it down without dialing her number. When he finally got up the nerve and allowed the phone to ring until she answered, he was stunned that she said "yes" when he asked her to come with him to the barbeque. It was only after he hung up that it dawned on him she hadn't said "yes." She hadn't said "no" either. She just asked him to find out what she should bring. And he had obliged her.

When he arrived at her house, she was sitting on the porch steps waiting for him. Next to her was a large, colorful platter covered in clear plastic wrap. Bella had said that a salad would be nice. She grabbed the platter and stood up when he waved to her. She was wearing a lime green, tight-fitting tank top and a diaphanous skirt made of layers of light silk in different hues of pale yellow that flowed down to her ankles. As she walked to the curb, Slidell couldn't help but notice the slight tremble of her breasts with each step she took and the shape of her long, slender legs beneath the silk that whirled over them. When he stepped out of the car and opened the door for her she smiled, and Slidell realized for the first time that Candice McNeil was beautiful.

At the barbeque, Bella made over Candice, saying how chic her clothes were and asking her where she got her stylish sandals, complimenting her on how delicious her salad was, and crowing about how she couldn't believe the dressing was homemade; it was just too good to be true. And several times during the evening, Stubblefield gave Slidell a huge conspiratorial wink. Slidell could tell that Candice was having a good time and liked Bella. Sitting together in the backyard, Candice had taken his hand and held it as they chatted. When he took her home, she leaned across the front seat of the car and kissed him on the lips; but before he could kiss her back, she opened the car door and disappeared into the house.

*   *   *

Candice bent over the sink and splashed warm water from the tap over her face. As she washed off her makeup, a toxic corkscrew of reproach wormed its way through her chest. "Damn," she said to herself. Her adult life had been a string of bad, sometimes dangerous, choices in men. In most of these relationships she had been the aggressor, pursuing men whose lives and character meant only one outcome to her efforts. They had demeaned, abused, debased, and exhausted her. Yet, she continually rummaged for damaged goods, slashing herself on their broken, jagged edges when she found them. These men were beyond repair. She knew that from the start, but lied to herself that she, only she, could fix them. For Christ's sake! She had gotten a degree in social work and become a psychologist and couldn't even heal herself.

It had been a long time since she had been in a relationship. She thought that she had finally overcome her penchant for self-destruction. But here she was again on the verge of another futile and damaging coupling. She hated herself for her weakness. She tried to convince herself that Chuck Slidell was no different from the string of other men she'd been with. She suspected he was a drunk. Shanahan's was not the place for casual drinking. And she had not missed the way Stubblefield and especially Bella glanced at him every time he passed the cooler of beer by the grill. But the giveaway was his not drinking at all. She noticed the subtle signs of a tight control and was convinced he wanted to drink but was holding back, holding back with difficulty. She was too old now for another dead-end relationship.

She dried her face and then went to the bedroom to undress. She took off her tank top and folded it neatly before putting it in the second drawer of her dresser. She removed her skirt and hung it up in the closet. Her underwear she tossed into the clothes basket in the corner of the room. She looked at herself in the long mirror hung on the wall to the side of her bed. She could no longer fool herself that she was young. Her breasts had started to sag, slightly, and probably only noticeably to herself; but the evidence was there before her eyes. And her stomach that had once been flat now had a small but tight bulge. She knew some men liked that and found it attractive in a woman, but she hated it. No amount of dieting and exercise seemed to make it go away. Time was running out for her. She told herself that she could not afford to take another risk.

But there was another reason she could not place a losing bet on a relationship. She had given all her heart once, unconditionally, blissfully. He had been her whole world. It seemed hackneyed to her now, thinking back on it in those terms, but it was true. He became the center of her universe, and she had thought that she was the center of his. But then she had gotten pregnant. His reaction was blunt. "Get rid of it," was all he said. When she wouldn't, he left without even saying goodbye; and she never saw or heard from him again. But now she had Anna, eleven years old and beautiful. Anna, who had taught her what to love and be loved meant. Most of all, it meant never making a decision that would hurt or harm her.

Candice put on her pajamas and then got into bed.

When she and Slidell had parted earlier in the evening, he had asked if he could see her again. She had said yes. The party, the warm welcome by the Stubblefield's, and Slidell's relaxed charm had seduced her; and she had let her guard down. Now she regretted it. She decided it was best she avoid any temptation to continue seeing Slidell. Just then the phone rang.

"Hi, Candice, it's Chuck. I hope I didn't wake you."

"No. No, you didn't; but I was just going to bed."

"I wanted to tell you how much I enjoyed this evening with you. I, well, I was hoping we could get together tomorrow--perhaps for lunch."

"Listen, Chuck, I had a good time too. I really did, but I don't think we should see each other again. I don't expect you to under-stand; it's just that it wouldn't be a good thing for me right now." Candice was surprised by her forthrightness and held her breath waiting for a response.

"You're right, I don't understand. But I'd like the chance to prove you wrong. It's only lunch, and if you still feel the same way tomor-row, then I'll respect that. Please. I'll pick you up at the University at noon. What do you say? You gotta eat."

Candice knew the answer she should give; any other and her life could spin down a path she could not afford to take. "All right, but just a quick lunch. I have an important meeting I have to attend in the afternoon."

"Fine. See you at twelve," Slidell said, and hung up.

"Shit! Shit! Shit!" Candice spit the words in a rasping whisper before she was able to stop herself. She hung up the phone and walked quietly down the hall to Anna's room to make sure she hadn't awakened her. She opened the door just enough to spill a little light from the hallway into the room. Anna lay in her bed on her side, the covers in a rumpled pile at her feet. Candice smiled. Here she was eleven years old and still wearing super-hero pajamas. She was seven when she got them, insisting on two sizes too big because she wanted big-girl pj's. They had hung on her like loose overalls. Now they were at least a size too small, but she wouldn't give them up. Candice eased through the crack in the door and stepped into the room. She looked down at Anna for a moment and then pulled the covers up to her shoulder, bending over and softly kissing her on the cheek.

Chapter 18

SHANAHAN'S WAS ALL but empty when Slidell arrived. Two men of indeterminate age sat alone at different tables along the wall. Slidell took his usual seat at the bar. He'd been on his best behavior at the barbeque, drinking only iced tea; and now he wanted a real drink. He also thought that he may have done something stupid. He didn't know how he felt about the evening, how he felt about Candice—her touch and her kiss. Yet, after he had dropped her off, he had called and asked to see her again. A mistake? He needed some neutral ground to escape to and think.

"It ain't Thursday," said the bartender after Slidell had sat down.

"Your meaning in that remark?" said Slidell.

"Whata ya doin here?" asked the bartender, ignoring Slidell's sarcasm.

"I just missed the ambiance of this establishment; couldn't stay away for four more days."

"Ain't that sweet. I'll write that down and put it under my pillow tonight," said the bartender, and poured Slidell a drink.

After the bartender left, two men sat down on either side of Slidell. He sensed that a third person stood behind him.

"Hey," said the man to his right. He was young, somewhere in his twenties, and well built. Although he was dressed in jeans and a tee shirt and wore a close cut beard, Slidell had the immediate impression that he was military. The man to Slidell's left was older, shorter and stockier than the man on his right, but the muscles of his arms bulged under the sleeves of his shirt. Slidell noticed that he had a tattoo of a dagger on his right forearm.

"Do I know you gentlemen?" Slidell slowly and calmly asked the man on his right. As he said this, the man on his left picked up Slidell's drink and drained it in one gulp.

"Not a chance," said the younger man, turning his head toward Slidell and squinting up at him. "But we know you, and what we know don't make us very happy."

"What do you mean?" asked Slidell.

"Seems like you get a hardon messing with heroes."

"I don't know what you're talking about," said Slidell, starting to get up. The man behind him now joined the action, shoved him back onto the stool and held him there, his hands gripping Slidell's shoulders.

"This country needs heroes, real ones. When one comes along, seems like shits like you always try to pull them down, destroy what they built," said the younger man.

"I told you I don't know what you're talking about," Slidell said and tried to shake off the man's grip with a twist of his shoulders.

The older man to his left reached into his back pocket and pulled out a crumpled piece of paper and smoothed it out on the bar in front of Slidell.

"Look familiar?" he said.

It was an article torn from a newspaper. The headline had been circled in red ink. It read, 'General Maxwell Subpoenaed for Deposition in Trial of Marines.'

"Fuck you," said Slidell.

"Don't say we didn't try to be nice," said the man behind him. The two on either side of Slidell grabbed his arms, pulled him off the stool, and spun him around. The third man slammed his fist into Slidell's face. Slidell felt the bones in his nose shatter and splinter into his sinuses. His knees buckled, but the two men, still holding his arms, pulled him up and the third man made two quick and powerful jabs to his chest. Slidell heard his ribs crack, and pain tore through him. Then came the explosion and a scream like a cornered cat. Slidell dropped to the floor.

When Slidell opened his eyes, he saw that the bar was empty and that the bartender was standing over him. He was holding a sawed-off shot gun. There was blood on the floor that trailed to the door.

"I shot the big guy in the foot," said the bartender. "Think I blew some toes off. The other two dragged him out of here. Those motherfuckers ain't coming back."

"Thanks," said Slidell.

"You're welcome," said the bartender.

"Why did you do this? I thought you hated your customers," said Slidell.

"I do, but that's love compared to how I feel about them that comes in here and tries to hurt 'em. Now get the hell out of my bar and never show your face in here again. Understood?"

"Understood," said Slidell through the pain that nearly blinded him.

Chapter 19

SUTTON TURNED OFF the lights and then closed the vertical blinds that hung the length of the window along an entire wall of his office, overlooking San Diego and the Bay. But he did not close them all the way, not quite. Thin strips of black sparkled with the lights of the city and the distant glow from the hotels along the Coronado shore, even at this late hour. The rest of the offices in the firm were empty, and no one would be arriving for several hours. This was his time, a twilight when all movement seemed suspended and silence filled every space. He was alone and untouchable. He took the DVD from his briefcase, went to his desk, and sat down. "A souvenir from your visit to Washington," Blakely had said that night before they left the townhouse together. He slipped the disk into his computer. As the first images floated onto the screen, he leaned back into his chair and unzipped his pants. He pulled his dick through the flies of his underwear and trousers and held it in the palm of his hand, feeling the weight and length of it increase as he watched himself begin to reach for the delicate boy. Semiconscious now, the boy offered no resistance to Sutton as the DVD continued to play. Slowly at first and then faster, Sutton began to stroke himself.

Chapter 20

STILL HALF ASLEEP and trying to untangle himself from the strap of his laptop case without spilling the cup of coffee in his hand, Anderson nudged opened the door with his shoulder and took one step into his office. The lights were already on, and someone was sitting in the chair behind the desk. Anderson stared into the black, close-set eyes of a stranger. They were pushed into a pasty face that would have resembled a cauliflower if it weren't for jowls that hung down on either side of a huge neck. Anderson thought that he had entered the bastion of Jabba the Hutt. He leaned his body back through the door and craned his head to check that it was his name on the wall. This early in the morning it was possible to make any kind of mistake, even entering the wrong office. He saw his name.

"Nice of you to show up today," said Sutton.

Anderson's addled brain connected the familiar whine with its owner, and Jabba morphed into Sutton. This encounter was so unexpected that Anderson hadn't recognized him.

"Surprised?" Sutton twitched his lips so quickly that Anderson could not tell if he had smiled at him or simply grimaced.

"I stopped to have breakfast at an all-night diner on the way here," said Anderson. "I'm not late am I?"

"You're late if you could've gotten here earlier, and you could've gotten here much earlier if you didn't stop at some greasy spoon on the way. Why do you think this firm provides a dining hall where breakfast, lunch, and dinner can be had by the associates at no cost whatever?" said Sutton.

When Anderson didn't answer but just stood in the doorway, Sutton said, "It's so we can have your sorry ass on the premises whenever it's needed; 24/7 if that's what's required. From now on eat your breakfast here, Anderson," Sutton barked.

"Yes, sir," responded Anderson.

"Sit down. I need you and Patterson to meet with the Marines today. This morning," said Sutton.

When Sutton didn't get up from his chair, Anderson sat in one of the two client chairs in front of his desk and waited for Sutton to explain why the meeting was so urgent.

"I've talked to the prosecuting attorneys, trial counsel as the military insists on calling them, and they are willing to cut a deal. Most unusual in a case like this; but my powers of persuasion are as sharp as they ever were, maybe even sharper," said Sutton, and his lips twitched again.

"What's the deal?" asked Anderson.

"Are you deliberately trying to antagonize me, Anderson?"

"What?" asked Anderson.

"Are you deliberately trying to antagonize me?"

"No, sir. I just asked a question," said Anderson.

"No you didn't. What you did was interrupt me. Interruptions annoy me. They annoy the hell out of me. So keep your pie hole shut until I have finished speaking and it becomes beyond obvious to you that I have nothing more to say." Sutton's eyes reduced to pin pricks.

"Yes, sir," said Anderson who wanted to do more than antagonize Sutton. He wanted to pummel the gross bastard to death. Anderson had to shake his head to rid himself of the impulse.

"Are you mocking me?" asked Sutton.

"No, no. I'm just clearing my head. I'm not a morning person," said Anderson.

"Well wake up and listen carefully. If our clients admit their guilt and are willing to testify that Belmonte ordered them to kill the civilians, they will receive a fifteen-year sentence, five years of it at hard labor, and be dishonorably discharged. They are young men. In fifteen years, they will still have most of their lives ahead of them. And they avoid the death penalty. It's a good deal."

The hell it is, thought Anderson. He had to say something to Sutton even if it meant pissing him off, yet again.

"It is a good deal if the Marines are guilty of the premeditated killing of civilians in retaliation for the deaths of their squad mates. But that's not what our clients are telling us. They say it didn't happen that way. And they have never said that Belmonte told them to kill the civilians. They say…"

"Now you stop right there, you snotty-nose little shit," Sutton bellowed. "You listen to me. Don't ever fall in love with the clients." Anderson started to protest, but Sutton cut him off again. "Criminal clients are lying, manipulative animals. They will say or do anything to make you believe they are innocent. They will feed on each other to save themselves. And they will turn on you in a nanosecond if they think it might help their case. They are not to be believed, and they are not to be trusted. So don't go thinking in that bone head of yours that you know better, because you don't."

Sutton got up, wobbled around the desk and stood behind Anderson. He bent toward him until his lips brushed against
Anderson's right ear. Anderson flinched and instinctively turned his
head away. The acrid smell of Sutton's breath made his stomach
lurch. In a whisper Sutton said, "You go grab Patterson by the dick,
and the two of you get your asses over to the brig at Pendleton. You
are to convince our clients to take this deal. You're young; they're
young. They'll trust you, and they'll do what you say. You'll be doing
them the greatest favor of their lives."

Then Sutton straightened up and shuffled to the door where he
stopped and turned around. "One more thing. I want to know what
Slidell is planning on doing. I need to know if he's going to plead his
client or if he is contemplating trying his case. If he's going to trial, I
want to know in advance what his defense will be. Start dating that
corporal again, in earnest this time. I want pillow talk, Anderson. I
need that info," Sutton said. "Oh and don't worry about the costs.
Take her wherever you want as often as you want. The firm will
cover your expenses." Sutton then left without waiting for Anderson
to reply.

*   *   *

The red Ferrari F430 sped north along Route 5 toward Camp
Pendleton. At nearly 100 miles per hour, the signature yowl of its 4.3
liter, V8 engine was an audible smirk at the lumbering heaps it
flashed passed. Patterson was in the pilot's seat, assured, totally in
control, and experiencing maximum enjoyment.

"The sun, the sea, and your very own rocket ship," he said to
Anderson. "It doesn't get any better than this."

"You think you might want to slow it down a bit? A speeding red
car is a ticket magnet," said Anderson.

"Look, relax and enjoy the ride. You're too uptight about this," said Patterson.

"You're going too fast," said Anderson.

"Don't act like a prick. You know what I'm talking about," said Patterson.

Anderson watched out the window as the exit sign for Solana Beach flashed by them.

"Don't go wobbly on me, buddy boy," continued Patterson. "We need to present a united front to our clients. No equivocations," said Patterson. Then he laughed. "Equivocation, great word isn't it? It was one of the words I learned in the LSAT prep-course. Still remember it. It means…"

"I know what it means," said Anderson.

"Well, excuse me, Mr. Maxed-the-Law-School-Admission-Test," said Patterson.

"Look, I'm sorry. It's just that what Sutton is telling us to do doesn't feel right. I think Sutton put it in their heads that if they turned on Belmonte and agreed to a guilty plea, he could get a deal for them. The bastard is guilty of suborning perjury and selling those Marines down the river. And he is trying to make us a party to it all. Don't you find this a bit troubling?"

"Ours is not to reason why; ours is but to do and die," said Patterson. "We don't question the higher ups, pal. You know that, so get with the program."

"Come off it. You really want to be a part of this, convincing those guys to go to prison for fifteen years when they're telling us that the Naval Crime Investigation Report is bullshit and before now haven't even hinted that Belmonte ordered them to murder the civilians?" asked Anderson.

Patterson looked over at Anderson. Anderson was his friend.

During their time at the firm together, Anderson had even become his best friend.

"I'll tell you what I want to be a part of, buddy boy. I want to be a part of a firm that gives me a salary of over two hundred thousand dollars a year with a bonus of fifty thousand. I want to be a part of a firm where, right now, I can afford a Ferrari and a condo in the best part of town. I want to be part of a firm where, if I make partner, I am set for life; the big house, the beach property, the yacht, the trophy wife, and the mistress. That's what I want to be a part of. And I want that for you too, pal. So what I don't want is for you to fuck it up for us," said Patterson. "Capisci?"

Chapter 21

HER LEGS STIFF and pressed so close together that her ankles touched, Debra Fallon stood by the table set with silver, china, and crystal. The waiter slid a chair out and grandly beckoned her to sit. She did. Not the way she had once seen Princess Di do it, with the tiniest bend of the knees, her torso tilted ever so slightly forward as the chair was floated beneath her so that she came to rest on its plush surface with the lightness of a feather. No, not like that at all. Instead, when the chair bumped the back of her knees, Debra Fallon pitched backwards like a felled Northern Pine and bounced onto its seat with a thump that nearly toppled the chair and set the glass chandelier above pinging like a burst of hail on a tin roof. "Timber," she imagined the waiter saying to himself.

"Are you okay?" said Anderson, as he rushed over and helped the waiter move her to the table, the two of them on either side of the chair.

"Oh my god," she whispered to herself, looking into her lap to avoid the stares of the other diners in the four-star restaurant.

"What?" asked Anderson, leaning closer to her face to hear her answer.

She looked up at him and, embarrassed as she was, had to fight the impulse to kiss him full on the lips. He was so beautiful, long jet black hair parted down the middle, dark eyes shining with concern for her, his face like a movie star's. How had she gotten so lucky? And now she was about to blow it on their second date.

"I'm fine, just lost my balance is all," she finally managed to say.

"Good," he said, sitting down with athletic grace.

The waiter immediately handed each of them a menu with a flourish that reminded her of a magician pulling a rabbit from a hat. She began to giggle at the thought of the image; a chubby, startled rabbit, its huge feet pumping the air; an oversized, upside down top hat rocking on a folding table; a triumphant magician, the tails of his tux dancing. Robert Anderson smiled back at her and chuckled.

"Did I miss something?" he asked.

"No. I'm sorry. It's just that I'm a little nervous. I've never really been in a restaurant this nice before." And rarely out with someone as gorgeous as you, she added silently.

"Would you like something to drink before you order? " said the waiter, yanking her out of her reverie. She had forgotten about him and was startled by the question. Her mind went blank. What sort of drink did you order in a restaurant like this? It certainly wasn't beer. The only fancy drink she knew of was the one she drank on the cruise she had taken with her girlfriends to St. Croix before she enlisted in the Marines—a Virgin's Last Stand. She didn't dare order that.

"Madame?" he asked again, his pen poised over his pad.

"I, I, uh, I," she stammered.

"Tell me, Frederick, do you still have that delicious 2003 Rioja?" said Anderson, coming to her rescue.

"Yes sir, we do."

"Fine, bring us a bottle please. If that's all right with you?" said Anderson, looking expectantly in her direction.

She managed a weak smile of assent as she wondered what the hell kind of drink Rioja was.

"Very good, sir," said the waiter, who clicked his pen, pocketed it, and turned toward the alcove marked, 'Wine Cellar.'

"I like your hair that way, Debra." Debra, not Debbie or Deb, but Debra. Somehow 'Debra' sounded right coming from him. She liked it. It made her feel older in a good way, more experienced, even elegant. He was Robert. That's how he had announced himself when he had come to the base to see Captain Slidell. "Robert, Robert Anderson, here for my appointment with Captain Slidell," he had said to her. Very formal. He was a civilian, a lawyer with the firm of Boswell, Noonan, and Clark, one of the best in the city. She couldn't stop looking at him. She knew she had made a silly fool of herself. Yet, he had asked for her number and, a week later, he called her and invited her to a movie. Robert had been all excited about seeing it. He told her it had won some award at a festival or something. She had been too nervous sitting next to him in the theatre to concentrate. Afterward, when he asked her what she thought of the movie, she couldn't remember a thing about it. She was certain he would never ask her out again. But now, here they were on their second date.

"Thank you, Robert," she said as she smoothed the long strands of blond hair that followed the curve of her neck, flowed over her right shoulder, and came to rest on the rise of her breast. Her black dress was low cut and short and showed off her best assets, long shapely legs and a pert, perfect cleavage. "Not bad," she had said to the mirror earlier that evening, except for the freckles that sprinkled her face and a dimple she didn't want. Farm girl dressed for the city. Oh well, she had thought.

"You realize don't you Debra, that even before you and I first met we were not really strangers," he continued.

She searched his face for any sign that he may be toying with her. Was this one of those lines she had heard so much about from other women, women more experienced that herself?"Really?" was all she thought it best to say.

"Yes. We shared something in common. Two things in fact," he said.

She knew now that he was playing a game with her, but she didn't know how to respond because she didn't know the rules. Was she supposed to guess what they had in common or deny that such a thing was possible?

As if he had read her mind he said, "I'm serious. We both represent Marines in a legal case, and we both will be working with Captain Slidell. We'll be seeing a lot of each other, so I thought it couldn't hurt for us to become better friends."

Big block letters like the ones that filled the TV screen on Sesame Street marched across her vision. They spelled F R I E N D S. Friends? Her heart began to wither. Just then the waiter arrived with their drinks.

"Do try some of this wine. I think you'll like it," said Anderson and gulped the splash of ruby red liquid the waiter had poured into his glass.

Anderson nodded, and the waiter brought the bottle to her. He tipped it over the top of her glass, and she watched as the wine swirled higher and higher toward the rim.

"Go ahead, have a sip," Anderson insisted with a smile.

Fallon lifted her glass and gently eased it to her lips. She drew in just a bit of the wine, balancing it on the tip of her tongue. Then she tasted it. It was like no drink she had ever experienced. Within the smoothness of plum, the tart pinch of cherry played tag with the mellow sweetness of vanilla, while the faint musk of clove cheered them on. They were there for her palate to chase down separately and linger over or to herd together and savor. Surrounding all was the essence of time; the gentle tug of the past. She sighed and immediately took another sip.

"See, I told you you'd like it," laughed Anderson.

"It's wonderful," Fallon said, and her face began to glow.

"So tell me, how do you like working for Slidell? He seems like a nice enough sort from what I've seen of him, if not a tad distracted," asked Anderson, restarting the conversation.

In fact, Debra Fallon adored her superior officer. She had been his legal assistant for over a year now; and in that time, he had transformed her from a near high school dropout to an eager legal researcher and nascent brief writer. How he had managed to do it was still a mystery to her, but she was grateful for it and for the corporal's stripes he had placed on her sleeve. She had come to see herself as he saw her from the beginning, not as the plump, small town girl hiding her shyness and inadequacies behind a shower of giggles, but as the slim, young, competent female soldier she now was. She had made a firm resolve that she would do anything for him, anything he asked. She thought carefully before answering. In spite of the wine, she was becoming wary of Robert's questions, especially since Captain Slidell had asked her to remember them.

"He's not easy to get to know, but you can trust him," she said.

"Well, shall we order now?" asked Anderson, reaching for his menu.

Chapter 22

CANDICE HAD CANCELLED all her client appointments for the afternoon. She knew she was being foolish. In fact, she was being doubly foolish. She should never have agreed to have lunch with Slidell in the first place, and now she had cleared her calendar in the silly expectation that lunch might go better than she expected. Was she hopelessly romantic or neurotically obsessive about getting into bad relationships? Slidell had said he would be at the University at twelve sharp. He apparently had believed her when she said that lunch would need to be quick because she had an important meeting in the afternoon. It was ten to twelve; she took a small mirror out of her desk drawer and inspected her makeup. She decided to lighten her lipstick and then changed her mind. She put the mirror back and checked her email. She was scrolling down her list for the third time when the phone rang.

She answered by pressing the hands-free speaker button. "Hello?"

"Hello," said a female voice. "Is this Candice McNeil?"

"Yes. Who's this?" she asked.

"Ms. McNeil, I'm Corporal Fallon. I'm calling about Captain

Slidell. He's in the hospital. He asked me to call and tell you he can't make lunch today."

"Hospital? What happened? Is he okay?"

"He'll be fine in a few days. He's rather banged up," Fallon answered.

Improbably, Candice began rummaging through her drawer looking for the mirror she had just used but couldn't find it. She became irritated and her voice acquired a shrill edge.

"What hospital is he in?"

"The military hospital here on base, room 25B." Fallon's tone was crisp and professional.

Candice stopped looking for the mirror and picked up a pen from her desk. She pulled the cap off with her teeth and held the pen over the notepad by her phone, preparing to write. Having something in her hand calmed her.

"Do you know if he is well enough to see visitors?"

"He would probably like to see you. Visiting hours start at 1400 hours. I'm sorry, I mean two o'clock," said Fallon.

Candice dropped the pen and got up from her desk, forgetting to hang up the phone.

* * *

Fallon's description of Slidell as "rather banged up" did not prepare her for what she saw in the hospital bed when she walked into room 25B. Slidell was propped up in a sitting position with three pillows behind his back and his head turned away from her, looking out the window. When she announced her presence with a tentative hello, he turned toward her. She almost fainted. His eyes were sunken and the skin around them the color of ash. His nose, which was swollen to more than three times its normal size, was draped in surgical gauze and bandages that displayed the recent seepage of blood. His smile was faint, tight, and strained.

"My god, what happened to you?" she said before she could stop herself.

"If I said I was in a bar fight, would you still be my friend?" said Slidell, in an obvious but lame attempt at humor.

"You're kidding?" she said, her worst fear about this man seemingly realized.

"No, but it's not what you think," said Slidell. "I was beaten up by some thugs who don't like my style of legal representation. However, it did happen in a bar, the bar where we first met, as a matter of fact."

Candice hadn't moved from where she stood after her few steps into the room. She walked over to metal folding chair that was leaning against the wall and opened it. She then dragged it to the side of the bed and sat down. The chair let out a metallic creak as she sat down. They both laughed or she laughed and Slidell attempted a smile that became a grimace of pain.

"You want to tell me about it?" said Candice.

"Yes I do. But first, how 'bout some chow? It's military fare but edible."

*   *   *

Over pork chops, mashed potatoes and gravy, applesauce with cinnamon, and milk so cold that shards of ice floated in it, Slidell told Candice about the Belmonte case. He began with Belmonte himself, his demeanor as a detainee and as a client. He explained to her how Belmonte's story held up under questioning, and how it squared with what he knew of combat and how soldiers sometimes react when civilians are killed. He also told her of his doubts about the criminal investigation into the deaths of the civilians and his plan to create doubt about that investigation at trial. Finally, he puzzled through with her the possible sources of the pressure being put on Stubblefield to rush the case and the reasons behind the assault. At first, as she listened to him, she felt flattered that he would confide in her, charmed by his attention. But the more he spoke, the more she realized that he was not trying to impress her. He was not engaged in any prelude to seduction. A sea change in her view of the relationship was taking place. She had never had her intelligence trusted or her judgment sought. She had never before been approached as an equal in a matter of importance by a member of the opposite sex. The shallow feeling of flattery was giving way to a deeper more substantial emotion; one of intense gratitude. She began to think that maybe it was possible to be with a man and not be physically and emotionally diminished. She stayed with him until she was ordered to leave by a nurse who announced that visiting hours had ended long ago.

As Candice walked out the hospital doors, she made a decision. What might be beginning between her and Slidell would either end or grow, and it would all depend on him. Tomorrow she would bring Anna with her to the hospital.

Chapter 23

SLIDELL LAY PROPPED up in the lumpy hospital bed covered from his waist down by a sheet so thin and worn that it was good neither for modesty nor warmth and sipped the strong, rancid coffee that had just come in a chipped plastic cup on the breakfast tray. The tepid, acidic liquid stung his torn sinuses as it hit the back of his throat; but he continued drinking it with equal measures of self-punishment and self-pity. He tried to look out the window, but the low morning light projected the dust and grime on the glass, blocking the view outside. He shouldn't be here, he shouldn't have a broken face, and he damn well needed a drink.

"I've brought someone to see you."

Startled, Slidell turned his head toward the voice, and a bolt of pain shot through his skull and down the back of his neck, tensing his body and making him spill coffee down the front of his hospital gown.

"Sorry," said Candice. "This is Anna."

Slidell's vision cleared as the pain subsided; and he saw, standing in the doorway, Candice and a young girl, tall, with long, thin blond hair tied in a pony tail. She wore faded jeans torn at the knees, a kelly-green t-shirt that looked new, and pink flip flops with glittered straps. Candice and she were holding hands. Only the girl was smiling.

"My daughter," said Candice.

It took Slidell a moment to process what he had just heard and then another moment to decide how to respond. In those moments his emotions rolled like the ball on a spinning roulette wheel, bouncing over 'shocked,' 'confused,' 'angry,' and finally landing on 'curious but cautious.' He wondered what else he might not know about this woman he had met in a bar.

"I wish I could say I've heard a lot about you," said Slidell, reaching out his hand as an invitation for them to enter the room and as an offering to Anna. He attempted a smile even though it hurt.

Anna stepped forward and took his hand and shook it.

"You didn't know about me, did you?" she said.

Slidell shook his head and looked past her at Candice who still stood in the doorway as if she were afraid to come into the room.

Anna turned around and also looked at her mother.

"I'm the deal killer; that's why she didn't tell you about me," she said with her back still to Slidell.

"Anna," said Candice.

"The what?" asked Slidell.

"The deal killer," Anna said, turning back around. "When my mom's boyfriends learn about me, then it's sayonara, adios, arrivederci, goodbye."

"That's enough, Anna," said Candice.

"Mom, if you didn't have the guts to tell him yourself, then you can't stop me from doing it in my own way," said Anna.

"I'm sorry," said Candice walking into the room and up to the bed.

"Are you apologizing for what I said, Mom, or for my existence?"

"What's happened to you? Why are you acting like this?" said Candice, moving to embrace Anna by the shoulders.

Anna jerked back, pulling from her mother. She turned away and strode to the window where she stood looking out, her arms folded across her chest.

"Look," said Slidell, "I'm obviously not able to go anywhere. Not right now anyway. So I can't leave the two of you alone, and I don't want either of you to leave. Why don't we all just sit down and get to know each other. Or know each other better, as the case may be." Slidell directed these last words at Candice. "I hear the best thing in the cafeteria is the vanilla ice cream. Why don't we buzz the orderly and have some brought in?" he added.

Neither Candice nor Anna replied, and neither smiled.

Chapter 24

SLIDELL SIDESTEPPED DOWN the stairs holding the railing with both hands while the house seemed to spin, and pounding jackhammers split his sides. An hour earlier, he had literally rolled out of bed to lessen the pain in his ribs and had had to crawl to the bathroom because of the waves of dizziness that overwhelmed him when he tried to stand up. He sat in the bathtub to shower and shave, and the consistent stream of warm water over his body had eventually made him feel good enough to make his way back to the bedroom and dress himself.

Now, halfway down the stairs, he wondered if he would be able to make it to the kitchen before he collapsed. His eyes were almost swollen shut, and his bandaged nose felt as if it were the size of melon. Most of the cartilage in his nose had been removed by the doctors who had worked on him in the ER. Those same doctors had told him there was nothing they could do about his ribs except wrap his chest. Try not to laugh, sneeze, or cough, they said. They had sent him home with a prescription for a pain killer that was having no effect. Victims of bar fights weren't getting preferred treatment at military hospitals.

Slidell took another step down, hesitated for a moment, and then resolved to push through the nausea and pain and get to the kitchen. He made it. After coffee and some dry toast, he shuffled his way to the driveway and slowly worked himself into his car. The drive to the base was an agony of hidden bumps on the highway and sudden stops in the heavy traffic.

*   *   *

Stubblefield paced back and forth across the floor in Slidell's office, his head down. He hadn't spoken for several minutes, as he seemed to measure off the length of the room with slow, even strides. He thought better when his body was in motion, and he needed to think to catch up with events that were moving beyond him. Never before had anyone physically intimidated one of his attorneys. Never before had a superior suggested he adopt a particular trial tactic in a case under his jurisdiction. Yet, in the Belmonte case both had happened. Finally, he slowed down and then stopped. Still looking at the floor, he said, "You think it was Maxwell who unleashed those pit bulls on you? If he did we might have a case for unlawful command influence."

"Anything's possible, but I don't think so. He would have too much to lose if an investigation proved he tried to influence the case by getting me to back off taking his deposition. Anyway, there are a lot of crazies out there, even ex-military; and news of Maxwell's deposition was printed in the paper. Anyone could have read it and thought we might be going after a hero-general to get Belmonte off," said Slidell.

Stubblefield lifted his head and turned toward Slidell. He was again shocked by his appearance. In his concentration, he had momentarily forgotten what Slidell looked like after his beating. He tried not to show his revulsion. "Perhaps," he said. "However I got a call from General Hammond recently, and he rather inelegantly recommended that I push for an early trial date."

"What did you say to him?" asked Slidell.

"Nothing yet," said Stubblefield. "I wanted to talk to Bella about it first. She believes he's trying to protect someone—someone important—who may get burned if we start mucking out the barn and piling up the manure."

"She didn't really say it that way, did she?" asked Slidell.

"She most certainly did," said Stubblefield. "She was a Georgia farm girl long before she was a military wife. Do you think she's right?"

"She might be, but General Hammond is your superior and has the prerogative to discuss trial tactics in a high-profile case. That's a far cry from unlawful command influence," said Slidell.

"Granted, but he's never done it before. And there's another thing that has aroused my considerable suspicion. That civilian law firm has filed a motion to expedite the trial. Usually those civilian attorneys try to delay a trial until everyone from the judge to the youngest witness is dead and buried." Stubblefield removed a cigar from his shirt pocket, started to put it in his mouth, but then stuffed it back in his pocket. "So what gives?" he asked. "Is this all just a coincidence or a concerted effort among Maxwell, Hammond, and Bozo, Numbnuts, and Fart or whatever the hell is the name of that firm?"

Slidell peeled the foil cover off a Vicodin and spilled the tablet into his palm. Stubblefield watched as Slidell tossed the pill into his mouth and dry swallowed it.

"I'm not sure, but if General Hammond is trying to protect someone by pushing for a quick trial, then it certainly isn't Maxwell.

He and Maxwell are working at cross purposes. If Maxwell wants to fight having his deposition taken, then that means that I can use his objection to protest any motion to set an early trial date. I can argue that we need his deposition before the trial starts, and we must have time to take it and investigate any new facts that arise from his deposition testimony. He is giving us exactly what we need," said Slidell.

A grin spread across Stubblefield's enormous face as he reached again for the cigar in his pocket. He put it in his mouth this time. "Forget what I said about not taking Maxwell's deposition. That punch in the face certainly didn't addle your brain. You still look like shit though."

Slidell grinned involuntarily and then his face contorted in obvious pain. Stubblefield winced.

Chapter 25

JUDGE TIBB'S STATURE was diminutive, her physique slender, her features fine and delicate. In her Marine Corps uniform, she looked like a porcelain doll displayed in the window of some small toy store on the main street of a Depression Era town. She appeared fragile and inanimate. Until she spoke. Slidell knew that her looks, as the saying goes, were deceiving. Colonel Gladys Tibbs was a dynamo, and she was not a person to be trifled with. The defending attorneys from the law firm of Boswell, Noonan, and Clark knew it, as did the trial attorneys for the military. She had made that perfectly clear when she had gathered all the lawyers in the case together in her chambers at their first conference.

"I don't mince words," she had said. "So I'll tell you straight in advance. I set the schedule in this case, not you; and I enforce it. I expect the court procedures I have established to be followed to the letter. And I expect my pretrial orders to be considered written in stone. If any of you choose to ignore this warning, even once, I will cut you off at the knees and do it in a way that will make the record look like a model of judicial restraint and decorum."

Slidell suspected that not a single attorney in her court room doubted her sincerity. They were all familiar with her record and reputation as a military judge. She was rarely overturned on appeal.

They were all gathered again for the hearing on Boswell, Noonan, and Clark's motion to advance the case to trial; and Slidell wasn't sure what to expect from the judge as she ascended the three steps to her bench in the front of the court room. This would be her first ruling in the case. Anderson and Patterson were seated at the second defense table; and Slidell thought they both looked nervous, especially Anderson.

"Please be seated everyone. Now, does anyone have anything to say in addition to what has been argued in the briefs?" asked Judge Tibbs.

"Judge, I would just like to reiterate that…" Patterson rose from his chair.

"Reiterate means that you are repeating a statement that has already been made, Mr. Patterson. Are you about to tell me something you have previously stated in your brief on this motion?"

"Yes, Judge, I know. It's just that I wanted to stress that…"

"I ask you once again, Mr. Patterson. Are you repeating something you said in your brief on this motion?"

"Yes, Judge."

"Then don't waste my time. Sit down."

"Yes, Judge." Patterson sat. Judge Tibbs allowed her stare to linger on Patterson for a few moments longer and then continued.

"I must say first that it is refreshing to see a motion to advance the date of trial, especially from the defense. For that reason alone I am inclined to grant the motion; however, I have received an objection to Mr. Patterson's motion from Captain Slidell. In stating his objection, Captain Slidell asserts that he has requested the deposition of a General Maxwell and that General Maxwell is seeking to delay the deposition for several weeks because he is currently involved in planning joint US and Japanese naval maneuvers. Mr. Patterson counters Captain Slidell's objection by arguing that General Maxwell's deposition is unnecessary and need not be taken. However, Captain Slidell maintains that General Maxwell's deposition is necessary. I agree with Captain Slidell. General Maxwell was in the chain of command at the time of the civilians' deaths; he may have information concerning the rules of engagement that the soldiers under his command followed. That information may have a bearing on this case. Captain Slidell may need the information to prepare his defense. I am also sympathetic to General Maxwell's need to have the deposition delayed because of his schedule. Therefore, I am denying the motion to advance the trial date. Thank you gentlemen, and good day." Judge Tibbs rose, descended the steps, but stopped at the door in back of the bench and turned to the courtroom.

"Captain Slidell. I couldn't help but noticing your nose. May I ask if you are OK?" she asked.

Slidell instinctively touched his nose. He suspected that what she really wanted to know was what had happened to him. "I'm fine, Judge. I was involved in an accident. Fortunately, there were only minor injuries." All true, but he hoped from the wording of his answer that she would think he had been in a traffic accident.

"I'm glad to hear it," she said, and disappeared through the door.

"Me too, Captain, and congratulations," said Patterson walking over to Slidell with Anderson and extending his hand.

"For what?" asked Slidell, shaking Patterson's hand.

"You did good. You drew first blood," said Patterson.

"I didn't know we were fighting each other," said Slidell.

"Oh, we're not. Of course we're not. I was just complimenting you on winning the motion," said Patterson, attempting to correct himself.

Slidell ignored Patterson, and, turning to Anderson, asked, "What was that motion of yours all about anyway?"

Before Anderson could speak, Patterson answered for him. "Just like we said in the briefs, we will be ready for trial and don't want our clients to remain any longer in the hell they're caged in. It's that simple," said Patterson.

"Sure it is." Slidell grabbed his briefcase from the table and walked out of the courtroom.

Chapter 26

H E HAD BEEN told that it would work this way. He would be visited by someone and given the word. It would not come directly from the source, not yet. First, an emissary would bring the news to him. Not quite the tap of the sword upon his shoulders as he knelt in supplication, but close enough. The rumors in the Pentagon and in the press had him pegged for the top spot, the one he had coveted almost since his days at the Academy. Now it was to be his. He received the call yesterday from the White House telling him that a James Arndt would like to speak with him, and did he have time at 10 a.m. tomorrow? Of course he did. The appointment would take place in his office at the Pentagon, on his turf. He would let nothing interfere with this meeting. He would let nothing prevent his appointment to Vice Chairman of the Joint Chiefs of Staff.

Maxwell surveyed his office to make sure everything was properly displayed. He had placed the items in his office to have the maximum effect on visitors. His intent was to impress and subdue. He arrayed his medals in gold frames on the wall to the right of his massive desk. Citations and awards covered the opposite wall. On the wall behind him hung battle flags, crossed swords, and photographs of him with soldiers in full battle rattle, politicians in full grin, and celebrities in full character. On his desk he had arranged numerous photographs of his five daughters taken at their graduations from various Ivy League colleges and one of his son at his graduation from the Naval Academy. A carefully posed, professionally taken photograph of his wife stood in the middle of his desk. She looked demure yet inviting, vulnerable yet strong. Everything sat ready and waiting.

Arndt arrived exactly on time. Maxwell stood when he entered his office.

"Good morning, Mr. Arndt," said Maxwell, walking out from behind his desk to shake hands.

"Good morning, General. Please call me James. It is an honor and privilege finally to meet you. I have been following your career with interest for many years."

"Really?" said Maxwell, genuinely surprised. "Please, sit down."

Arndt sat in the large winged-back chair, beautifully upholstered in silk, that Maxwell had motioned him toward.

"Believe it or not, that chair was owned by General George Washington," said Maxwell, seating himself behind his desk.

"You don't say. How interesting," said Arndt, gently stroking an arm of the chair.

"I literally had to wrestle it away from a retiring army general here at the Pentagon. I think he wanted to take it with him when he left," said Maxwell.

Arndt smiled. Maxwell smile back.

"General, the President appreciates your loyalty and your service. You are a great patriot, and both he and this country owe you a debt of gratitude," said Arndt.

"Mr. Arndt, I mean James, it's not necessary..."

"General. No need to be modest. I speak the truth," Arndt interrupted him. "I am here today to ask you to be of service again to your country."

"Certainly," said Maxwell, instinctively leaning over his desk to be closer to Arndt.

"General. You are to drop any objection to your deposition and testimony at the trial of the Marines accused of the murder of the civilians in Fallujah, Marines who were under your command," said Arndt.

"What? I thought that...I mean, I was led to believe that this meeting would be about my..." Maxwell stopped short of finishing the sentence.

"Your future?" said Arndt. "It is, General. But first you must make this small sacrifice. That is all I'm asking you to do right now, and then we will meet again, soon." Arndt stood. "It was a pleasure to have met you, General. I will give your sincere regards to the President."

As Maxwell watched Arndt walked out of his office, the muscle below his right eye began to twitch uncontrollably.

Chapter 27

PATTERSON'S VOICE ON the phone had been conspiratorial and excited at the same time. It was after 1 a.m. when he called, late, but not unusual for Patterson. Anderson had received calls much later from him, most of them virtually incoherent. But not this one; Patterson sounded cold sober.

"Buddy boy, have I got something that you won't believe. I'm bringing it over now. Throw out any broads you've got in the house. You gotta be alone when I get there. I'm leaving right away. Oh, and is your laptop working?"

Patterson had hung up before Anderson had the chance to ask him any questions. He wished now that he had not answered the call, or had told Patterson to "fuck off" and hung up and gone back to sleep. He wished now that he had never seen or heard what Patterson had brought him to view.

When Anderson opened the door, Patterson immediately grabbed him by the shoulders, spun him around, and pushed him into the small room he used as an office. "Sit down buddy boy; and buckle your seat belt, you are in for the ride of your life," he said, and then had placed the DVD in the laptop with great ceremony.

Anderson watched as two out-of-focus figures, one small and one large, seemed to dance in place together in a small room. Then, as the figures slowly came into focus, Anderson began gradually to comprehend what he was seeing.

The smaller figure was a boy in his early teens, thin, almost stick-like, with long dark hair. He was nude and feebly struggling, bracing himself with boney legs, and tugging against the grip of the larger figure. The larger figure was a male, also nude, and gross, covered with slabs of fat; his penis hidden under a flap of blubber. It was Sutton. The room was a bedroom, and he was pulling the boy to the bed.

"God, no," said Anderson turning his face away from the screen. "What the shit. Turn it off."

"Don't worry; you don't have to watch what comes next. It ain't pretty. But you have to hear what's at the end." Patterson advanced the DVD. Anderson felt as if he were going to be sick.

"Where did you get this?" he asked.

"Stella. Remember I told you I was screwing her. Well, I didn't lie. She found it in Sutton's laptop when she went in this morning to straighten up his office. He's a slob, but demands that his office be spotless when he arrives. You wouldn't believe the crap she finds, rotting food, soiled clothes, that sort of shit. But this, this was a real discovery. She brought it to me. I think it turned her on in a way. God, was she great in the sack tonight. "

"Did she steal it?" asked Anderson.

"Hell, no. Well, not technically. This is a copy. The original is still in his computer in his office. Sutton's computer was still on when Stella came in. He likes everything turned off and everything put away. She thought the disk was from a file, so she opened it to find out which file it should be returned to and saw what you just did. She wisely made a copy."

"I'm not so sure that was wise," said Anderson.

"You just wait, buddy boy, until you hear this. You will change your mind about that." Patterson started the DVD again.

Sutton was now in the bedroom with another man. The boy was gone, and Sutton sat on the bed, his legs and lap covered by a towel. The other man was fully dressed and standing by the door.

"Get some clothes on. Before you leave, I want to give you something to remind you of tonight. Something to keep you warm on those cold nights in San Diego," said the man in clothes.

"You always know what I want, don't you, Jake?" said Sutton.

"Yes, and I hope you know what I want. You make damn sure those Marines are found guilty, or cop a deal that leaves no doubt about their guilt. And do it fast. Is that clear?" said the other man.

"Perfectly," whispered Sutton, looking down at the bed and methodically stroking the wrinkled, stained sheets. Patterson stopped the disk.

"Well?" said Patterson with a huge grin, holding out his arms wide.

"I don't believe this," said Anderson.

"I said you wouldn't, didn't I? But believe it, buddy boy."

"No. I mean the bit with the kid just confirms what I have always suspected. Sutton is a twisted pervert. It's the part at the end I can't believe. He's agreeing to sell out our clients. But why, and to whom? And why would something so incriminating be on the disk?"

"Stella asked the same question. She thinks it was a mistake, that it was supposed to be erased, leaving the disk with just the evidence of Sutton's little peccadillo for his future viewing pleasure. Apparently, he hasn't seen the whole thing," said Patterson. "Or he is so confident that no one else will ever see it that he didn't bother to get rid of that part."

"Or he wants it on the disk," said Anderson. Isn't that Congressman Blakely Sutton is talking to? I've seen him on TV several times."

"Don't know. Don't care," said Patterson, taking the disk out of the laptop.

"Have you thought about what we should do about this?" asked Anderson.

"What we should do? Are you crazy? We got the goods on Sutton—double the goods. Our hugely profitable futures at the esteemed firm of Boswell, Noonan, and Clark are now guaranteed."

*   *   *

Sleep was out of the question. Anderson had argued with Patterson, tried to convince him not to approach Sutton with his knowledge of the DVD, not yet, and never in a way that amounted to blackmail. He implored his friend to calm down and think about how they should handle this situation, short of committing a crime; but Patterson wouldn't listen to him, and instead became angrier and angrier, until he finally told Anderson that he was a limp dick who just blew the greatest opportunity he'd ever get in his life.

After Patterson left the condo, Anderson, on a whim, had gone back to his computer and Googled, "Blakely." He wasn't sure of the spelling, but the third return after the Blakely Hotel, New York, and the city of Blakely, Georgia, was, "Jake S. Blakely, United States Congress, Colorado, Majority Whip." Anderson then searched Google for an image of "Congressman Blakely" and found several. The internet photos showed a man who looked like the person

Anderson remembered from the DVD; however, he could not be certain without seeing the DVD again. He was not ready to accept the possibility that Congressman Blakely was the man with Sutton on the DVD and all that might mean. He was exhausted and did not trust his judgment. Still, he thought it best to let Patterson know what he had found. He picked up his cell phone and dialed Patterson. He got Patterson's voicemail three times before he decided to give up calling. He did not leave a message. Perhaps he was becoming paranoid, he thought; but he wanted as little record of the calls as possible. He would try and talk to Patterson in the morning when he arrived at the firm.

Chapter 28

PATTERSON AWOKE BEFORE the alarm. Stella still slept, her face resting on his chest, her arm lying across his body as if she were trying to shield him from something. He felt her breath wash over him in gentle, rhythmic waves. She slept nude, and he liked that. He watched her as she slept. She was almost old enough to be his mother; yet she couldn't get enough of him nor he of her. She was like a teenager on prom night, only with the moves of a veteran pole dancer. She was asleep when he had returned to her house after his argument with Anderson. He tried not to wake her when he slid into bed beside her.

Stella opened her eyes and smiled at him.

"How did it go?" she asked.

"Great, couldn't have been better. He's in," he lied. He did not want to repeat for her what had happened. Anyway, he had put his argument with Anderson behind him, certain that Anderson would eventually come round to his point of view.

Patterson slipped two fingers into Stella's armpit and wiggled them.

"Arghh," she yelled and rolled off his chest. "What the…"

"Come on Princess, it's the big day. Let's get to it."

Stella sat up and rubbed her eyes. "What time is it?"

"Five-thirty, but we've no time to waste. You shower first."

Stella turned to him and grinned as she put her hand in his crotch. "How 'bout we shower together," she said.

* * *

Patterson stood outside the door to Sutton's office and reached into the inside pocket of his suit coat. He felt the disk. Walking down the hall from his office to Sutton's, he had compulsively checked several times to make sure it was still there. He withdrew his hand, feeling the smooth silk of the jacket lining slide over his fingers, and knocked on the door. He opened it when he heard Sutton order him to enter. Sutton expected him. Patterson had made the appointment as soon as he got to the firm, leaving a message on Sutton's phone that it was of the utmost importance that he see him right away. He had waited anxiously until Sutton's arrival, unable to work on any of his files in the interim. He and Stella had decided that he shouldn't wait to approach Sutton about the disk, but should act quickly before he discovered he had left it in his office and before he suspected that it may have been viewed by someone. They both wanted Sutton off guard, and surprise and shock would give them the advantage over him.

Sutton looked up from his desk as Patterson entered and smiled at him. In spite of the urgency of the message, Sutton appeared unconcerned. Good, thought Patterson, he suspects nothing.

"You have something important to tell me?" Sutton was still smiling at Patterson as he motion for him to sit down.

"Yes," Patterson said when he was seated. He almost addressed him as Mr. Sutton but stopped himself. He wanted to be on an equal footing. "It is important to both of us."

"Really?" Sutton grasped the edged of his desk with both hands and pulled his chair closer, sitting up. "I'm intrigued. What might it be?"

For a second Patterson thought that Sutton might be toying with him, but rejected the idea. Sutton couldn't possibly know why he was there or what he was about to show him.

Patterson slowly reached inside his suit coat, took out the disk, and placed it gently on Sutton's desk. He said nothing, waiting for Sutton to speak.

"And what it that?" Sutton asked, as if Patterson had placed a foreign coin or some valueless trinket on his desk.

"It's a ticket. Your ticket," said Patterson, watching for Sutton's reaction.

"Is that so?" And what is it a ticket to?" Sutton was still smiling, looking almost as if he were enjoying himself.

Patterson now smiled back at him. Excellent, he thought, the door was open for him to lay out what he wanted from Sutton. This was going so smoothly. Much more smoothly than he and Stella had imagined.

"For the price of this ticket you get to watch a very special show that no one else can ever know about or see, except me. And I will never tell," said Patterson.

"And what will this ticket cost me?" asked Sutton, his smile gone and his attention now focused fully on Patterson.

Chapter 29

PATTERSON TURNED ONTO the highway and let the Ferrari have its way. In seconds the speedometer read 100 mph. Stella's laugh was hearty and rough as she and Patterson settled back to enjoy the cruise to LA and a night away together. They both were relieved. Earlier, they had dissected every moment of his meeting with Sutton as if it were a lobster they were dining on at an outdoor restaurant in Paris. They were ecstatic at how well things had worked out. Their future at Boswell, Noonan, and Clark would now be one of wealth and security. As Stella put it, they were set for life.

Just past the Oceanside exit on I-5, Patterson had to slow down to weave around a car in the far left lane; he was about to speed up and maneuver back into the left lane, when a dark shape filled his peripheral vision on the left. He turned and saw a diamond blue Escalade looming over the Ferrari. The driver motioned for him to roll down his window, leaning over the passenger seat and extending his arm toward Patterson. When Patterson lowered his window, the driver of the Escalade started pointing frantically to the front of the Ferrari. Patterson yelled, "What?" but the driver only looked at him with an odd, lopsided smile and continued to point, stabbing his hand toward the car. It was then that Patterson noticed the Escalade begin to drift toward him. He instinctively shoved his arm out the window and held up his palm, both as a warning and in an attempt to push the SUV away. The driver continued to smile. Then Stella screamed.

Patterson was still thinking of the strange smile when the Ferrari glided off the road and hit the tree, splitting in half, and sending two bodies whirling through the air at ninety miles per hour.

Chapter 30

S LIDELL WAS LATE. He was asleep when the phone rang, dreaming that he was asleep, a deep sleep purged of all exhaustion and untroubled by dreams. He could see his dreams huddling far away; agitated and fretful, denied their rightful place in his slumbers. He was not afraid and watched them as a spectator might watch a ball game in the dog days of summer, high in the stands of a stadium, lazily and unfocused, the warmth of a late afternoon relaxing the muscles of his body. Then the sound of blaring sirens, and they began to rush toward him, like boulders released down a chute, tumbling and clattering over one another. From the sleep that was his dream, Slidell, frightened now, jumped to his feet and turned to run, the noise of their onslaught closing in on him. From the disappearing sleep that was not his dream, Slidell reached for the phone and knocked over the empty whiskey bottle beside it, sending it rolling angrily across the glass coffee table beside the couch.

Fallon's words had entered his brain through the phone like rusty nails pounded through a cedar two-by-four. His presence was needed at the base, she said. Judge Tibbs had called and wanted all the attorneys to meet with her at eleven.

It had taken him longer than usual to shower, shave, and dress in his uniform. The alcohol had its claws in his back, pulling downward, still trying to overpower him. He had to will his hands to stop shaking before he could hold his razor, and again before he could handle the buttons of his uniform shirt. He almost passed out bending over to tie his shoes and had to wait several minutes until the room stopped spinning. There was also a long trail of cars in the drive-thru lane at Dunkin' Donuts, where he had stopped to get the coffee needed to brace himself for the drive to camp. He should have pulled out of the line when it hadn't move for five minutes, but he didn't. The coffee was too important. By the time Slidell arrived at Pendleton, it was 11:20.

The staccato click of his heels echoed off the walls of the corridor of the Legal Affairs building as he headed for Judge Tibbs' courtroom, and the four people at the counsel table had already turned and were looking at the door when he entered. Slidell recognized Anderson and the two trial counsel, but the third person was someone Slidell had never seen before. The stranger ponderously rose to his feet and thrust a hand toward Slidell, a gesture Slidell sensed was more of a challenge than a greeting.

"Captain Slidell, it's good to meet you finally. I'm Sutton, Jeffrey Sutton, senior litigator at Boswell, Noonan, and Clark. My presence here is due to a very sad circumstance. James Patterson recently died in a tragic automobile accident. The entire firm is in mourning."

Slidell took his hand and shook it quickly. He was surprised and genuinely saddened by this news. He had seen many young men die and knew the cost to others. "I'm sorry to hear that. I heard he was a fine lawyer."

"Yes. Yes, he was. He will be missed," said Sutton.

Slidell glanced over at Anderson, who was still seated at the counsels' table, to offer him his condolences but was stopped by the way Anderson was staring at him. Slidell knew that look. It was controlled fear.

"Good morning, gentlemen, I'm glad you are all here now. Please, come in." Judge Tibbs stood in the doorway just to the side and behind the bench in the courtroom. The three men walked past her into her small office. Please sit down," she said, and motioned to the round table in the far corner. There was barely room for the four of them, and they sat almost shoulder to shoulder. The window air conditioner on the other side of the room rattled and whined; and although it succeeded in sending cool air vaguely in their direction, Slidell noticed that Sutton had begun to sweat.

"I wanted to meet with everyone today because I have received an email from General Maxwell's attorney informing me that he will no longer contest the subpoena for his deposition. He intends to cooperate fully with all parties in this case. Therefore, I have reconsidered the motion to advance the case to trial and have decided to grant it. Trial in this case will begin eight weeks from today unless I hear a compelling argument against it."

"That's fine with us, Judge; we'll be ready," said Sutton.

Slidell had expected Sutton to argue against the judge's decision. A key defense attorney in the case had just died. If ever there was a valid reason to delay a trial, this was it. Another attorney had to come into the case and get up to speed. That would take time. Slidell couldn't believe what he had just heard from Sutton.

"Wait a minute. Are you serious?" Slidell blurted out.

"As serious as a heart attack. We intend to go to trial in eight weeks as the judge has ordered," said Sutton.

"In spite of Patterson's death?" Slidell persisted, still incredulous.

"What?" asked Judge Tibbs.

"I'm sorry, Judge. Tragic, we are all still in mourning. I intended to inform you. Jim Patterson died in a traffic accident. However, we will not use that as an excuse to delay the trial. Boswell, Noonan, and Clark is a large law firm and can absorb the loss of Mr. Patterson, as good a lawyer as he was, without harm to our clients. In any case, Mr. Anderson here is well able to continue as lead counsel, with my assistance of course."

"Are you sure?" asked Judge Tibbs.

"Very sure, Judge. We owe our clients nothing less," said Sutton.

"Mr. Anderson, are you of the same opinion?" asked Judge Tibbs.

Slidell saw Sutton's body tense. It was clear that Sutton was not used to having his judgment questioned.

"Of course he is, Judge," said Sutton quickly.

"I would like to hear that from Mr. Anderson, if you please, Mr. Sutton," said Judge Tibbs. "Mr. Anderson?"

Anderson had had his head bowed since first sitting at the table. He now raised it but did not look directly at the judge. Slidell, who was sitting next to Tibbs, noticed that he focused his gaze in the distance behind her.

"Mr. Sutton speaks for the firm of which I am a part. If he says we will be ready, then we will be ready."

"There, you see," said Sutton.

Judge Tibbs turned to Slidell. "Captain, do you have any objections?"

"Yes. I can't possibly take General Maxwell's deposition, complete discovery, and finish my investigation in eight weeks time."

"Captain, you've had the time since I denied the original motion to advance the trial to investigate this case and initiate discovery. I assume that is what you have been doing. You should be able to depose General Maxwell in plenty of time before the trial. The trial date stands. Good day, gentlemen."

As Slidell stood, Judge Tibbs said, "By the way Captain, you are looking much better. I hope you are feeling better too."

"Thank you for your concern, Judge. I do feel better," said Slidell, less thankful for her concern than for her mistaking his bloodshot eyes and swollen face as the lingering effects of his broken nose.

*   *   *

Sutton caught up with Slidell in the parking lot as Slidell was opening the door to his car. The short walk from the Legal Affairs building had made Sutton breathless, and he was perspiring profusely. He stood with his hand on the car door, supporting himself. Slidell waited until Sutton had caught his breath.

"Listen. There is a way out of this for you," he finally said.

"What are you talking about?" asked Slidell.

"There doesn't have to be a trial in this case. My Marines have been offered a deal. They're considering it now. We've advised them to take it. Your boy could do the same. Presto! No trial."

"What's the deal?" Slidell closed the door and Sutton, his support gone, lurched forward almost losing his balance.

"Just hear me out before you say anything," said Sutton.

"What is the deal they're offering?" Slidell repeated.

"My guys get fifteen years if they plead guilty and agree to testify that your guy ordered them to murder the civilians," blurted Sutton.

Slidell took a step toward Sutton and grabbed the lapels of his suit coat.

Sutton tried to pull back, but Slidell twisted the cloth and yanked him closer.

"Wait. Please. I can help you and your client," Sutton wailed.

"How can you help me? You son-of-a-bitch," Slidell hissed in his face.

"Just let me go for god's sake," pleaded Sutton.

Slidell slowly loosened his grip and then completely released his hold. Sutton looked ready to collapse.

"Listen. I can make my clients' pleas contingent on Belmonte being given a deal that would require a life sentence." Slidell turned away from Sutton and reached for the car door. Sutton stepped to his side continuing to talk, his words urgent and quick. "It would avoid a trial and a possible sentence of death. It's what my guys want. I've already talked to the prosecution about such a plea. It wasn't rejected out of hand."

Slidell pulled on the handle of the door of the car; but Sutton clapped his large, sweaty hand over Slidell's preventing him from opening it.

"Don't be a fool, Slidell. This could be good for all of us."

"Get your hand off me before I break your arm," said Slidell.

Chapter 31

THE DRIVE FROM San Diego had taken almost three hours and, for the whole trip, Anna had sat in the back seat listening to her iPod and sending and receiving texts on her phone. She had not said a single word to the people nearest to her. Candice too seemed caught up in her own world, staring out the window as they droned north along the lengthy stretches of I-5, her conversation with Slidell turning moribund. The nascent suspicion that the day was turning into a mistake had become a fully formed conviction for Slidell well before they arrived at the botanical gardens of San Marino's Huntington Library.

The idea seemed right, to get the three of them away together for the first time. He thought the gardens were the perfect choice. He had guessed that neither Candice nor Anna had been there before, and he was right. Also, the drive was long enough that he, Candice, and Anna would have time to relax and get comfortable together before they arrived, but not too long for them to become bored or exhausted. He had planned out the day in his mind: they would go directly to the Chinese Gardens and start there, then wander through the Lily Ponds, work their way over to the Australian Gardens, skip the Subtropical Garden, and then spend some real time in the Japanese Garden.

Perfect.

Except as soon as they entered the grounds, Anna had immediately stepped ahead of them, setting the pace and taking control. He wanted Candice and Anna to savor the beauty and serenity around them, but Anna was rushing through the gardens. Candice made no effort to slow Anna down or make her walk with them. Anna was like a young, untrained dog on a leash, tugging her stumbling owner along the sidewalk. Why didn't Candice just jerk her back and make her heel? Finally, he'd had enough.

Slidell halted and waited for Candice to notice that he wasn't at her side. She finally stopped. "Anna wait a second," she called.

"What's wrong?" she said, walking back to Slidell.

"Let's just slow down, OK?" he answered. "How 'bout we pick the nearest garden and just stroll through it. We're sprinting past everything."

"Why don't we take a detour to the café and sit down for something cool to drink instead?" she said.

Somehow her answer just made him angrier, but he tried not to show it.

"We practically just got here; and, if we stop now we may not see much of the gardens before closing time. The café's way out of our way. Let's wait until lunch to take a break? We'll be nearly at the café by then," he said.

"The café will be crowded at lunchtime. Look at all the people here. We'll have to wait for a table. This will actually save us time. I could go for a snack now. I left the house without having breakfast, and eleven-year-olds can eat anything any time of day," pressed Candice.

"Let's just take a tour through the Australian Garden. It's not far ahead. You'll love the trees there. Then we'll head for the café." Slidell deliberately measured his words and moderated his tone. He had now lost all patience with both Anna and Candice and was within a hair's breadth of losing his temper.

Candice took a deep breath. "Look around you Chuck. Do you see many children here, other than infants in strollers?"

Candice's abrupt switch in topic confused Slidell, and he struggled to get her point. Then he understood. "Anna doesn't want to be here, does she?" he said.

"Well, let me put it this way, if we had to drive as far as LA for an outing, then Paramount Studios might have been a better choice for an eleven-year-old."

"What about you?" he asked.

Candice took his hands in hers. "Look at me," she said, "and listen carefully. I'm only going to say this once. I am not her."

Slidell pulled his hands out of hers. "You think I want you to be Mary? Is that why you think I brought you here?"

"She loved coming here, didn't she?"

Slidell shook his head. "Look, you've got it all wrong. We shouldn't even be having this conversation."

"She loved coming here, didn't she?" Candice repeated.

"That's a ridiculous question. Its answer proves nothing."

"Just ask yourself this: Did you ask me if I liked gardens? Did you ask me if I wanted to come here? Did you even ask me if there was somewhere else I might like to go?"

"Why didn't you just say you didn't want to come, you and Anna?"

"It was your enthusiasm. You couldn't stop talking about how great it would be, how much we would love it. We didn't want to disappoint you."

"And now you both feel shanghaied?" he said.

"Something like that."

"I'm sorry I brought you here." Slidell didn't know if he was apologizing or expressing regret.

"You needn't be. It was a very human thing to do. But, if there is going to be an us, then we have to find our own special places. Understood?"

"Understood," said Slidell just to put an end to the conversation.

Candice held out her hand and waited for Slidell to take it. He did. "I wasn't kidding when I said I was hungry. Can we go to the café, please?"

Slidell nodded.

"Great," said Candice. Then she called to Anna. "Anna, we're going to the café. It's back the way we came. Follow us."

Anna was far ahead of them and showed no sign of hearing her mother.

"Anna, we're taking a break for a snack. Follow us to the café," Candice called out louder.

Anna raised her hand and waved. She began walking toward them. Slidell and Candice then headed back along the path.

"If we leave the path and cut across the grounds, we'll get there quicker," said Slidell. "Sounds like a plan," said Candice. "Lead on."

As they walked, Candice did all the talking, chatting about nothing and everything. Slidell knew she was trying to move on from their last conversation. He was grateful for it, and it gave him time to think. He resented having to confront the genesis of his feelings. He hated doing it, but he grudgingly admitted to himself that he may have wanted Candice to be a stand-in for Mary. Had he been using her to recreate certain moments that he and Mary had shared? He loved the grounds of Huntington because Mary had loved them.

Is that why he had brought Candice to the gardens, because he wanted her to be Mary for him, if just for the day? And is that why he had become so upset, because Candice obviously did not love the gardens as Mary had? If so, Candice was right. It was unfair. And cruel.

When they finally reached the café, Candice announced with a tone of triumph, "We're here."

"Well, two of us are," said Slidell, looking behind them. "We're missing Anna."

"What? Oh my god? Where is she? I can't see her." Candice looked around her with what Slidell thought was the beginning of panic.

"I saw her just a few minutes ago. I'm sure if we wait here she will catch up with us in a minute," said Slidell, trying to calm her.

"No, you don't understand. She's only eleven; anything can happen to a girl that age when she is alone. We have to find her." Candice began jogging back the way they had come.

Slidell caught up with her; and together they retraced their steps, hunting for Anna and shouting her name.

Candice became more frantic as they raced down the hill to where they had started their trek. Her shouts for Anna had turned shrill. They frightened Slidell. Then he glimpsed the top of a blond head through the trees of the Jungle Garden. The head was wearing a ponytail.

"There," he said, pointing.

Anna was sitting on a large stone by the waterfall, one hand dangling in the pool at the foot of the falls. "It's so beautiful," she said, looking up at them. She lifted her hand from the water and pointed to the huge, gently swaying leaves above her. "Can we stay here awhile?" she asked, and then added, "Where were you guys? One minute you were in front of me on the path; and then, poof, you were gone. I thought I should just stay put until you came back for me instead of running around looking for you."

*   *   *

The drive back to San Diego was the happy opposite of the drive up to San Marino. They had stayed at the gardens until attendants in blue blazers had wandered the paths, announcing that Huntington was closing and directing visitors to the exit. Slidell listened, as Anna, the iPod and cell phone forgotten, chatted from the back seat about all she had seen, still in thrall with the artistry of the landscape and the beauty of the gardens' designs.

Chapter 32

THE LARGE INTERIOR room on the second floor of the Base Headquarters Building at Camp Pendleton looked like a military command center in the midst of a war. Computer stations sat on folding tables lining all four walls, their printers spitting paper, their screens glowing with the pages of websites, their keyboards manned by diligent naval paralegals. In the middle of the room, an island of copy machines snapped and rocked as they scanned, copied, collated, and stapled. A carillon of phones jangled. Uniformed JAG officers darted into the room from their offices to retrieve documents or issue instructions to the Navy legalmen at the computers. Brisk vocalizations and the scuffle of polished shoes on hard floors added to the noise in the room. Everyone seemed intent on accomplishing a single mission, the conviction of three Marines for murder; and it was obvious to Slidell that money and manpower fueled that mission.

Slidell had been waiting for forty minutes in the outer office to meet with the two JAG officers who headed the prosecution team. He had met with them twice before, and on both occasions they had kept him waiting. It pissed him off then, and it pissed him off now. He knew that was their intention—to unnerve him and establish their superiority, to make him feel he wasted their valuable time. He hated the bastards with their Ivy League law degrees, their condescension, and attitudes of entitlement. Navy assholes, he thought to himself. This was all a game to them with tallies of put-downs and one-upmanship, an amusing detour on their road to the high paying and prestigious law firms that awaited them. Take two hundred dollars and a lot of chuckles and pass *Go* to get your millions.

"Sorry, sir. They said to tell you they'd be with you in a couple of minutes."

Slidell looked up at the E-3 standing in the doorway but did not reply.

"Can I get you anything, sir? More coffee?" asked the E-3 when Slidell's silence became awkward.

"You can get me the two officers I came here to see," said Slidell.

"Yes, sir," the E-3 stammered as he quickly stepped back through the doorway, did an about-face, and disappeared.

Slidell regretted taking his ire out on the kid and thought of just saying to hell with the meeting and leaving. But he had to find out if Sutton was telling him the truth about being offered a deal and if that deal included his clients' fingering Belmonte as the one who ordered the killing of the civilians.

"Chuck. Sorry to keep you waiting. I really am. My scheduled got backed up. Couldn't be helped, unfortunately." Stan Reynolds, one of the two lead trial attorneys, seemed to jump into the waiting room exuding camaraderie and good cheer as he spewed his bullshit. As usual, his khaki uniform was crisp, the pleats razor sharp.

"I'm running a bit behind on my schedule too, Stan," said Slidell.

"Yes, of course. Then let's get started. Come with me," said Reynolds, dialing down the radiance of his smile.

Reynolds led Slidell into a small conference room where Cheryl Schmidt, the other lead trial attorney, stood along with three young naval lawyers whom Slidell did not know.

"Please sit down," said Schmidt, pulling out a chair from the conference table. "We hope you don't mind, but Stan and I thought some members of our staff could benefit from sitting in on our meeting. Good experience for them. Lieutenant Junior Grade Grant, Lieutenant Junior Grade Ellis, and Lieutenant Junior Grade Bell," said Schmidt, rushing on and introducing the junior officers.

The three attorneys said, "Good afternoon, sir," in unison and waited for Slidell to be seated before they sat down.

Slidell knew why the other lawyers were there. This was to be a performance, and Reynolds and Schmidt wanted an audience to view their act. They were also there so that Slidell would be over-whelmingly outnumbered and appropriately cowed.

Reynolds closed the door, and the roar of the outer room became a purr. "So, you talked to Sutton about our offer to him," Reynolds said as he took the place left for him at the other end of the table.

"Why didn't I hear it from you first?" Slidell meant his question to be an accusation.

"Fair question," Reynolds responded. "The answer's simple. We wanted to be certain that this was not going to be a cutthroat defense."

"A what?" asked Slidell.

Slidell noticed the junior offices glance at each other and begin to smile.

"Oh. I'm sorry," said Reynolds. "A cutthroat defense is part of the lexicon of the British criminal bar. It is when each defendant in a murder case accuses the other defendants of doing the killing. They all defend themselves by incriminating each other. I thought you knew the term."

The three lieutenant j.g.s now sported full-blown grins.

Even Reynolds had the trace of a self-congratulatory smirk.

The prick, thought Slidell. Reynolds had succeeded in humiliating him. He had demonstrated his intellectual superiority over a dumb fucking Marine. Slidell felt like dog shit but wasn't about to show it. He also wondered what the hell a 'lexicon' was.

"Is Belmonte going to accuse the other Marines of doing all the killing?" Schmidt's question immediately changed the atmosphere in the room. The junior officers' grins vanished, and they became alert, waiting for Slidell's answer.

"The simple answer is that the civilians died in the cross-fire. This wasn't murder. I think you know that," said Slidell.

"What we know is what Sutton says his Marines will testify to and what the NCID investigation and autopsies show," Reynolds shot back. "The civilians were beaten and shot, proof that they were killed by the three Marines in a rage over the deaths of the other Marines in their squad. Belmonte instigated and encouraged the killing of the civilians. Sutton's clients confirm that. That kind of evidence doesn't leave your client with much wiggle room for a defense."

"Fingering Belmonte is a recent invention of the Marines or their lawyer to work a deal with you and save their necks. It's pure bullshit," countered Slidell.

Reynolds started to speak, but Schmidt signaled him to be silent.

"Gentlemen, there's no point in arguing this way. The reality is that in a death penalty case stories change. And sometimes you have to go with the flow, Chuck," said Schmidt.

*　　*　　*

When Slidell returned to his office at Defense Counsel Offices, Fallon greeted him with and anxious look on her face. She pointed at his chest and said, "Sir, you've been bleeding."

Slidell looked down and saw dark stains dotting the front of his uniform. His nose had been dripping blood during his conference with Schmidt and Reynolds, and they hadn't uttered a word about it.

Chapter 33

BELMONTE HAD LOST weight, even more weight than when Slidell had last interviewed him. His health was now clearly a concern, and Slidell wondered if Sutton was right about pushing so hard to advance the trial date and pressure the prosecution to settle. Slidell had asked Belmonte several times if there was anything he wanted, but all he had requested were some books to read, mostly novels by Steven King and Dean Koontz. Slidell had purchased them for him. Today he had brought Belmonte a cup of cappuccino with a double shot of espresso, his preference in boutique coffee. Belmonte sipped the coffee slowly and with obvious relish.

"Thanks for the coffee, sir. It's great," said Belmonte.

"You don't look good. I'm worried," said Slidell.

"I'm fine, sir. Truly, I'm good to go, no worries," said Belmonte.

"There is something I need to tell you," said Slidell. "It looks like Alvarez and Conroy have been offered a deal in return for a guilty plea. I heard this from their attorney. They will receive a long prison term but escape the death penalty. He also told me that as part of the deal, his clients are going to testify against you." Slidell paused and waited for Belmonte's reaction.

"No way. No way they would do that. Somebody's lying to you," said Belmonte.

"I don't think so. I confirmed what their attorney told me with the lawyers for the prosecution. Alvarez and Conroy are going to say that you ordered them to shoot the civilians and that you started the killing."

Belmont took another slow sip of the coffee, never taking his eyes off Slidell. Then he put the cup down on the table and wrapped both hands around it as if warming them. The window unit air conditioner was too small to bring the humidity in the room down enough to cool it. Belmonte's gesture somehow made Slidell suffer even more discomfort from the heat.

"They wouldn't do that, sir. I just don't believe they would. And if they did, they would have to lie. Those civilians didn't die the way that report says they did. It didn't happen like that."

"Your buddies no longer care about the truth or care about you. They're scared and are thinking only about saving themselves. I believe that their attorneys are fueling their fears to get them to accept the plea bargain. They are trying to frighten them into it," said Slidell.

"They won't accept it, sir."

"Yes, they will," said Slidell. "That's the way it usually works when some defendants are given an opportunity to control their future and others are not. We haven't been given a choice."

Belmonte released his grip on the coffee cup and pushed it to the side, out of the way. He was silent for a moment and then released a quick, short breath, a barely audible chuff that Slidell interpreted as either the punctuation to a resolve or resignation. He hoped it was the former.

"I have to ask you this," said Slidell. "Do you want me to try and strike a deal for you?"

Belmonte's answer came immediately. "No way, sir. No fucking way."

*　　*　　*

Belmonte sat on the floor of his cell, his knees up with his back against the wall, and looked out through the bars of his cell. He imagined he could see through the wall across the narrow hallway out onto a beach, the waves rolling over the white sand, the fronds of palm trees shuttering in the breeze, bikini clad women strolling by smiling at him seductively. Then he imagined reaching over the breasts of his prone girlfriend, his arm brushing against them as he pulled a beer from the cooler next to her. He smiled to himself, not at the daydream—he was convinced it would someday soon be real for him—but at the gullibility of Slidell. Slidell thought he was a stupid kid, an ignorant grunt. But he was wrong. He knew what Slidell was up to. It was all bullshit about his buddies being willing to turn on him and make a bargain with the prosecution. They had agreed that no matter what happened they would cover each other's back. They had been in shit together worse than this. Slidell was just trying to scare him into a plea of guilty so he could get the case over with as easily as possible. Besides, they had all expected the prosecution to probe like an enemy seeking to penetrate their perimeter defense. What was that expression he had heard, 'Divide and conquer?' That was not going to happen. He, Alvarez, and Conroy would all stick to their story, and it would be they who conquered.

He wondered again about his choice for a defense counsel. He had thought a lawyer with combat experience would have a set of balls. Maybe he had thought wrong in the case of Captain Charles Slidell.

Belmonte stepped back into his daydream and imagined the girl beside him on the beach without her bikini.

Chapter 34

THE HUGE ANIMAL corkscrewed through the water toward them, becoming larger as it came closer, its gigantic paws shoving the ice-blue liquid behind it in a roiling wake of bubbles. Just before it reached them, it reared up against the Plexiglas window, eyed them for an instant, and then shot away.

"Do you suppose it was looking at us?" asked Debra Fallon.

"I'm sure it was," said Anderson. "I'm also sure that one look at me scared it away."

Fallon smiled. Anderson had called her the day before and had asked if she would like to meet him for lunch the next day at the zoo. She had said yes far too quickly and was now trying to hide her enthusiasm for the invitation by keeping things low-key between them. It had not been easy. She found Anderson charming; and he made her laugh, a deadly combination.

"My favorite place in all of San Diego is this zoo," said Anderson. "I come here a lot; and, whenever I do, I always wind up spending the most time with the polar bears."

"They are amazing animals," said Fallon, more to keep the

conversation going than out of any real conviction.

"I guess what I find most fascinating about them is the incongruity of their captivity here; bears in a place that has no bears, polar animals where there is nothing but heat," continued Anderson.

"That's sad in a way," said Fallon.

"Yes, I suppose it is," said Anderson.

There was silence between them for a while, and then Anderson spoke again.

"Are there any bears where you come from?"

"Wisconsin? Sure, black bears, not as big as these guys though; but we have lots of them."

Since they had met at the zoo, Anderson had been all over the place with his conversation. He jumped from one topic to another, each topic seemingly unconnected to another, his discussion of each topic cut short before its finish. Fallon thought he seemed to be finding his way to what he really wanted to say by first eliminating every other subject. She decided she would help him. She took Anderson's hand and led him to the exit of the underwater viewing room. When they got to the stairs, she stopped. She knew she was about to take a risk, one that she might regret; but something told her it was worth it.

"Look, call it intuition—just don't call it feminine intuition—but it seems to me that you've got something on your mind, something that you need to say. Would you like to tell me what it is?"

Anderson turned toward her, and she saw the surprise in his eyes and also that he could not meet her gaze.

"Is it that obvious?" he asked.

"It's pretty obvious," Fallon said.

A loud thwack startled them, and they both jumped. They laughed along with the children who were squealing and pointing at the bear swimming away from them.

"That happens all the time," said Anderson. "The bears love to scare the viewers by smacking the Plexiglas with their paws. Don't let anyone tell you animals don't have a sense of humor."

Anderson started to climb the stairs, but Fallon pulled him back.

"There was something you wanted to say to me," she said.

"Let's go get some ice cream," he said.

*   *   *

They found a small table on an upper deck of the Tree House Café that overlooked the gorillas. Anderson had Fallon sit in the chair facing outside, and then he pulled the other chair around next to her so they could both enjoy the view. At first Fallon felt awkward sitting next to Anderson instead of facing him; but when his thigh nudged hers as he scooted his chair to the table, she liked it just fine. She decided that she would let Anderson speak first. He was taking his time getting settled, adjusting his chair, spreading the napkin on his lap, and examining the menu; so she occupied herself by watching the gorillas. She noticed them lumbering around their environment, moving from place to place with their rolling gait and a solemn, almost stoic, expression; and she was surprised when Anderson finally did speak.

"Debra, listen, there's something I want to tell you, something I need to tell you, and I want to ask you something too. I don't know how to put this, but just hear me out. Please don't say anything until I'm finished."

Fallon drew in a quick breath and held it. She didn't move a muscle. She wasn't going to blow this with her awkwardness and nervous babble. She hadn't dared to hope that he felt about her the way she felt about him. She was falling in love with him but couldn't imagine him falling in love with her. She was willing to settle for his affection or just a little more than his friendship, anything that would keep them together, anything that would keep him seeing her.

"You're the only person I can talk to," he continued. "There sure as hell is no one at the firm I can speak to, and I don't know anyone outside the firm who would understand what I am talking about except you. I'm not making sense, I know. I'm sorry. Let me start over."

Fallon closed her eyes and willed his words to say what she desperately wanted to hear. 'You're the only person I can talk to' was all that registered, and her heart leapt.

Anderson turned his chair slightly toward Fallon. "I'm under pressure. I don't feel right about what's happening. I have to know something. Has Belmonte been offered a deal? Is he planning on testifying against the other Marines?"

Fallon opened her eyes. Had she heard right? What was this about Belmonte? Wasn't he talking about their relationship? Slowly she began to comprehend what he had said. So this was what he thought of her. She was nothing to him except a way to get information he needed. There was no relationship between them and no hope of one. She was just a commodity to him, something to be used until it wasn't needed anymore and then thrown away. She hadn't expected this and wasn't prepared for it. She cursed herself. She really was just an ignorant hick, a love-sick fool. She felt about to cry. Damned if she would let him see her like this. Fallon pushed her chair away from the table and stood. Anderson grabbed her arm and tried to pull her back into her seat.

"Take your hand off my arm," she said, refusing to sit down.

Anderson loosened his grip but did not let go. "Please. I know we are not supposed to discuss our cases. I know you've been ordered not to say anything about Belmonte. But just listen. Please, hear me out."

"I said to let go of me."

Anderson released her.

"Don't ever touch me like that again. Don't ever see me again." Her words were between a hiss and a growl, and her eyes shone with hurt and anger. Fallon spun away from him and ran from the café.

"Please," Anderson's called after her. "Something is wrong, very wrong. I need your help."

*   *   *

Anderson sat at the table and tried to ignore the stares of the other patrons. He'd blown it—big time. He felt attracted to Debra. She was real, and she brought out the best in him by just being herself with no pretense or game-playing for advantage. It had been insane to think that he could ask her about the Belmonte case. Of course she would refuse, and how could he not have guessed she would take it the wrong way? He trusted her and needed to confide his fears about Sutton and what was going on in the firm. He couldn't talk to anyone else. He'd hoped to tell her what she meant to him, how much he needed her. But she had misunderstood. No, he had been a goddamn dunce to not know that she would misinterpret what he said. He was a lawyer. He should be an expert in communication, but he had failed with Debra. Now there was no one.

Chapter 35

THE DRAWN CURTAINS of the picture window glowed amber from the setting sun, hardening the shadows in the darkened living room and wrecking its symmetry. Anderson imagined himself under siege and wondered how long he could remain immobile and invisible. He sat alone, still and quiet, thinking. He had always trusted the workings of his mind, his ability to reason through a problem. But now he was stymied. His rational side was beginning to fail him. His undependable emotions now seemed to dictate his actions. If he had to rely solely on his emotions, he knew he would make mistakes.

Anderson felt like a dog chasing his tale. There was too much uncertainty. He struggled to bring order to the past few days, to make sense out of what had happened, to find meaning in motive and events. In spite of himself, his efforts at reasoning always began with the unthinkable.

Murder. Had such a thing happened? The newspaper article about Patterson's and Stella's deaths reported that their car was travelling at nearly 100 miles per hour when it crashed. It might well have been an accident. He knew Sutton was an amoral slime bag, but was he capable of killing? To believe Patterson and Stella had been murdered by Sutton, or by his order, he had to first assume that Patterson had approached Sutton about the DVD and had blackmailed him. But had this occurred? He had not spoken to Patterson after he left his condo that night with the DVD. With Patterson and Stella dead, he had no way of knowing. And what if Patterson had died before approaching Sutton? Then Sutton would not be aware that the existence of the DVD was known to others. If this were the case, then what, if anything, should he do with the knowledge? He wasn't even certain that the 'Jake' on the DVD was Congressman Blakely.

Round and round. Faster and faster. But the chase always ended with the same question: What if Sutton did know that Patterson had seen the DVD and had made a copy? Whatever Sutton may be, he was no idiot. He would suspect that Patterson had told him about it.

The room was now totally dark. Anderson tried to picture the layout of his living room, its dimensions, the placement of the furniture, the color of the rug, the art on the walls; but he couldn't. Instead, details of other rooms filled the darkness with a strange vividness, his bedroom when he was eight-years-old, a hotel room in Madrid where he had been for only a few hours. Then the darkness became complete as he drifted into sleep.

He awoke to the tone of his cell phone beside him on the couch. Anderson picked up the phone and pried it open with numb fingers. "Hello," he said, still half asleep.

Sutton's voice pierced through to his consciousness and shoved him fully awake. "I want that disk, Anderson, and I want it now."

"Disk? What disk? What are you talking about?"

"Don't start playing games, Anderson. Your friend Patterson was a clod, an unreasonable idiot. I couldn't deal with him. You're smarter than that," said Sutton.

"Is this some kind of sick joke?"

"If it is, no one is going to laugh at the punch line. Bring the disk to me now. I'm in my office."

"I told you I haven't got any disk. I've no idea what you are talking about," Anderson said, trying to sound irritated and sure of himself at the same time.

"Look, this doesn't have to be difficult. You either have the disk or know where it is. Give it to me and forget you ever saw it, and I'll make it worth your while," Sutton purred.

"I don't believe you," Anderson said before he could stop himself.

He waited for a reply but there was none. Sutton had hung up. As the silence swarmed over him, Anderson realized that he had just made a big mistake. He had stupidly admitted to Sutton that he knew about the disk.

*　*　*

Anderson packed quickly, throwing just two pairs of jeans, two sweatshirts, and some underwear, tee-shirts, and socks into a back pack. He then went to his bedroom closet, took down a polished, wooden box from the upper shelf, and opened it. Inside was a Glock 19 with one loaded clip. He tossed the clip into his back pack and nuzzled the gun between his belt and the small of his back. He hid the pistol by putting on a loose, soiled work shirt. Before he left the apartment, he thumbed through the phone book until he came to the page he was looking for. He tore it out and stuffed it into his pocket. Once on the street, he went to the ATM nearest his condo and withdrew the maximum amount he could in a single transaction. Then he walked the twelve blocks to the bus station in downtown San Diego, taking side streets and stopping often to check if he was being followed. He did not intend to use his credit cards, cell phone, or real name for a long time. His car was left in the basement garage of his building. He planned on flying under the radar and divested himself of all things through which Sutton could trace his location.

The Greyhound bus he chose was headed for Wyoming with a dozen stops in between. Trying to hide his destination even from himself, Anderson resolved not to pick the stop where the trip for him would end until after the bus had departed the station. As the bus rocked loose from the lock of its brakes and began to move, Anderson settled back into his seat and closed his eyes.

Chapter 36

Pushing across the continent through four time zones was like leaping hurtles in a foot race, irritating if not exhausting. Slidell's airplane touched down at Reagan National Airport at 7:43 p.m. local time. For him, it was actually 4:43 p.m., not a great difference, but one he could never get used to. He had tried to use the time on the plane to prepare for General Maxwell's deposition, but it was impossible. Two overly large gentlemen boxed him in and appropriated both armrests, an elderly woman reclined her seat over his knees, snoring the whole trip. The deposition was set for 9 a.m. the next day. He knew he wouldn't get to sleep before 3 a.m. DC time, and then he would have to awaken at 4 a.m. San Diego time to make the deposition. That meant about four hours sleep, max. But that was all he could afford; you did not keep generals waiting.

Fallon had booked him a room at the Holiday Inn National Airport in Arlington's Crystal City. This is where he stayed when his duties took him to DC. It was a mile from the airport and provided a private, reliable shuttle to the hotel. It was also a six-minute cab ride to the Pentagon. At least travel time would not be a serious factor in his scheduling.

When Slidell entered his room, the drapes were drawn. He still felt claustrophobic from the flight, and he pulled the drapes apart to open up the place and view the DC night. He smiled to himself. By chance or design, Fallon had reserved him a room on an upper floor facing north where he could look out over the sprawling mass of the military's ziggurat, the Pentagon. And to his right, broad swaths of light marked the monuments and memorials of Washington. Slidell took his cell phone from his pocket and dialed Candice's number.

She answered on the first ring. "Hi, how was the flight?"

"How did you know it was me?"

"I have my phone set to ring in a certain tone when you call. That way I will always be sure and answer it," she said.

"Or not answer it," Slidell added.

Candice laughed.

"I didn't know you could do that."

"Sure, I'll show you how when you get back," she laughed again. "I miss you."

"I miss you too. I should be finished by late tomorrow afternoon. Fallon has got me on the red-eye to San Diego. Keep your fingers crossed."

They talked awhile longer, saying nothing of consequence. Yet, in the way of lovers, telling each other everything, not by what they said, but in the way they said it. For Candice and Slidell had become lovers, easily and naturally, surprising both of them. After the death of Mary, Slidell had accepted the inevitability of a life devoid of joy. He had gone through the motions of living, anesthetizing himself against the pain and sleepwalking through his days. Why seek happiness, he thought, when it could be obliterated without warning or withheld without reason? When nothing was certain, why risk anything? But then Candice appeared and with Candice, Anna. As an adult, his experience of children had been nonexistent. He had no nephews or nieces, and his wife had died carrying the child they both had desperately wanted. Anna was novel to him, frustrating, even infuriating, at first, but then captivating. He began to experience the world afresh through her eyes, seeing the ordinary marvels to which he had blinded himself. Grace had come to him unbidden. He still was not sure how to react.

After he hung up with Candice, Slidell reviewed the notes he had made for the deposition. They covered the usual areas, Maxwell's education—civilian and military—his duty assignments, promotions, combat experience, publications in military journals, and command responsibilities. They also included the rumor that Maxwell was being fast-tracked up the Marine chain of command in anticipation of his being appointed as Vice Chairman of the Joint Chiefs of Staff. Slidell did not know what to expect but was certain of one thing; somewhere in his history Maxwell was hiding something. He was not appearing at the deposition willingly.

*   *   *

The conference room was enormous, impossibly long and wide, with a high ceiling and recessed lighting. A huge mahogany table dominated the chamber, spreading from narrow ends to a vast center. Circular tables, a black phone resting in the middle of each one, stood in the room's corners. Around the conference table were two dozen high-backed, black leather chairs on rollers. A thin-stemmed microphone angled from the table toward each chair like a scolding finger. There was not a single window. Instead, muscular oil paintings of military campaigns and battles—their importance accentuated by ornate gold frames—hung on the walls.

Except for Maxwell, Slidell was the last to arrive at the deposition. Positions had already been taken around the table by Maxwell's three attorneys, the two trial counsel, Sutton, and two court reporters. Slidell quickly surveyed the seating order and assessed Maxwell's strategy for the deposition. Maxwell's lawyers, one military and two civilian, had secured the end of the table closest to the door. From here Maxwell could control the dynamics of the deposition. He sat at the apex, the horizontal peak of the polished slab. This position constituted the psychological high ground; and, as all military strategists knew, those who possess the high ground hold the advantage. Behind their name plates, Reynolds and Schmidt sat next to each other near the center of the table, symbolically pushed to the side, as was Sutton who sat across from them. Slidell and the two court reporters were placed beyond the table's center, farthest from where Maxwell would sit. Maxwell planned to isolate him, separate him from the other participants, not only by distance, but by the physical barrier formed by the central width of the table. More game playing thought Slidell; but clever, very clever.

Before Slidell sat down, Maxwell strode into the room; and everyone, including the two civilians, stood to attention.

"Please sit down," said Maxwell, taking a seat in the chair between his two civilian attorneys and leaning forward to rest his elbows on table. "Are you ready to begin, Captain Slidell?"

"In just a moment, sir." Slidell took his time unpacking his briefcase and arranging his notes and legal pad and pencils. He then sauntered over to a metal cart against the wall arrayed with coffee, tea, juice, and rolls and poured himself coffee. He sipped it on his way back to the table. Maxwell had attempted to take over the deposition and rush it along. Slidell was not about to let that happen.

Slidell sat down in the leather chair behind the stenciled plaque containing his name and rank. "I'm ready now, sir. Would you please raise your right hand?"

Maxwell raised his hand. "Would one of the court reporters swear the witness in?" said Slidell.

"Please refer to the deponent by his rank and name." The civilian attorney to Maxwell's right was glaring at Slidell. He was not making a request but a demand. However, his tone of voice would not be apparent in the written record of the deposition.

"Certainly. Would one of the court reporters please swear in General Maxwell?" Slidell was not going to let this deposition be derailed by a barrage of petty objections. He would marshal his energies and choose his battles carefully.

After Maxwell took the oath to tell the truth and nothing but the truth, Slidell began the deposition by establishing the record. "Let the record show that this is the deposition of Major General Oscar Maxwell taken pursuant to subpoena…"

"Objection! General Maxwell is appearing here today voluntarily, and the record should properly reflect that fact," shouted Maxwell's other civilian attorney.

"If you wish to put that statement in the record, I have no problem with that," said Slidell and waited for the attorney's response.

"Let the record show that General Maxwell has withdrawn all objections to the deposition and is appearing voluntarily," he said, after whispering with Maxwell.

"Fine, now General, will you state your full name and rank?" said Slidell.

"Oscar J. Maxwell, major general, United States Marines." Maxwell stared directly at Slidell as he readied himself for the next question, adjusting his body as if he were playing a game of handball.

"General, would you tell me about your post-secondary education, where you went to school, civilian and military, and the degrees you obtained?" Slidell watched as Maxwell's body sagged and his stare softened and drifted away. He had judged Maxwell correctly. He was a hard-charger. He wanted the tough questions, and he wanted them now. But Slidell had decided that he wouldn't get them, not now and for a long time. First, he would ask the easy questions, the ones that could be answered almost without thought, the ones to which there could be no objections. Slidell wanted to establish a rhythm to the proceeding—easy question and easy answer, easy question and easy answer—one after the other, monotonous, nonthreatening, and pro-forma. He wanted Maxwell to get used to answering his questions automatically. He wanted Maxwell's attorneys lulled into a sense of complacency. He would appear to be what they thought he was, a washed-up military lawyer just covering his ass by going through the motions.

After three hours Maxwell was tired, frustrated, and ready for his deposition to end. His attorneys were obviously anxious to get back to their more lucrative cases and make some real money. Now was the time. Slidell had just finished a series of questions about Maxwell's overseas assignments.

"You knew that civilians had been killed in Fallujah by men under your command ten days before you ordered an investigation into their deaths, didn't you, General?"

"What?" Maxwell jerked his head back in surprise. His attorneys leaned forward, now alert.

"Would you like a court reporter to read back the question, sir?" said Slidell slowly, in the same lackadaisical tone he had been using throughout the deposition.

"No, I mean, yes, I would." answered Maxwell.

At Slidell's request, the court reporter nearest him read the question to Maxwell.

"I ordered an investigation as soon as I was informed of the killings," said Maxwell, getting his bearings.

"The report of the investigation states that it was initiated under your command on May 24. Is that when you learned of the deaths?" Slidell waited while Maxwell thought about how he should respond. But Maxwell's answer didn't matter because he had been snared by Slidell's trap. The firefight occurred on May 14. If Maxwell was not informed of the deaths of the civilians until May 24, then his chain of command had failed. It had not timely notified him of a matter that should have come straight to his attention. He, therefore, had overlooked a fatal weakness in the chain. This seemed unlikely with a commander of the caliber of Maxwell. On the other hand, if his staff had immediately informed him of the killings, then why had he waited ten days to do anything about it? Either way, he had been negligent in his duties as a commander. More importantly, his actions or inactions cast doubt on the creditability of the investigation. A ten-day delay in investigating the deaths meant that crucial evidence may have disappeared or been destroyed, and that those involved had ample time to establish and coordinate their testimony.

"I can assure you, Captain, that I ordered an investigation as soon as I was informed about the death of the civilians." Maxwell's answer was casual, almost off-handed.

Slidell could end the deposition now. Maxwell was locked into an answer that would help Belmonte. Still, Slidell wondered why Maxwell had waited ten days to investigate the killings. And then the import of Maxwell's answer became clear. Maxwell had just told him that he ordered an investigation immediately after the report of the civilian deaths. What if there wasn't a flaw in his chain of command? What if Maxwell had been timely informed of the civilians' deaths? Slidell weighed the possibilities. If he ventured on, he would be stepping off a cliff. He would be in a free fall, out of control. He would be at the mercy of Maxwell's answers.

Experience and judgment dictated that he should be cautious and not jeopardize what he had already accomplished for his client. But Maxwell's demeanor had shifted with Slidell's line of questioning about the timing of his knowledge. His last answer was almost flippant, as if he didn't care anymore what the questions were. Slidell had seen this reaction in other deponents. They sensed that the worst had been done to them and that nothing they could say could do them any further harm. This was when they relaxed their guard. Slidell decided to gamble.

"General, when did you learn that civilians had died in the firefight in Fallujah on May 14?" Slidell held his breath and waited for the answer.

"On May 14," said Maxwell.

Maxwell could not admit to waiting ten days to investigate the death of civilians by soldiers under his command without destroying his career, Slidell reasoned.

"And when did you order an investigation into the deaths?" asked Slidell.

"On May 14."

Slidell was stunned by the answer. He had no idea there was an investigation before the 24th of May. Trial counsel had not turned over information about any such investigation pursuant to a court order for pre-trial discovery. He looked over to Schmidt and Reynolds. They both were staring at him, and he could tell from their faces that they'd never been informed of the May 14 investigation either.

Slidell returned his attention to Maxwell. "Then was there an investigation prior to the one initiated on May 24?" he asked.

"Yes."

"Who conducted the first investigation?"

"Officers under my command. It was done in accordance with the Naval Judge Advocate General Manual."

"Did you make a report of that investigation?"

"Of course I did. I just told you the investigation was conducted in strict accordance with the Naval Judge Advocate General Manual. The report was sent up two higher levels of command and was approved and signed off on at each level."

"General, what was the conclusion of that investigation regarding the conduct of your soldiers in those deaths?"

"The soldiers were following the rules of engagement. The civilians were being used as human shields, and my soldiers acted in accordance with Standing Rules of Engagement regarding human shields. As they were trained to do," Maxwell added.

"Would you consider your investigation thorough, General?"

"Of course," answered Maxwell.

"The Judge Advocate General Manual requires autopsies as part of an investigation into the killing of civilians by troops, does it not?"

"It is my understanding that autopsies are not required. In any case we could not have autopsies performed because Muslims bury their dead immediately, and Islamic law forbids autopsies in most cases. We were not allowed to exhume the bodies to examine them."

"But in the second investigation the bodies were exhumed and autopsies performed by Iraqi doctors under the observation of our military doctors. Isn't that correct?"

'Yes, and I don't know how or why the Iraqi families got permission from their Mullahs to have the bodies exhumed and examined. It is almost never permitted and certainly not in these circumstances."

"General, then why did you order a second investigation?" asked Slidell.

"I was ordered to do so."

"By whom?"

"The order came from USCENTCOM," answered Maxwell.

"You were ordered by the Commander of US forces in Iraq to conduct a second investigation?" asked Slidell.

"That's what I just said, Captain. Only this time the Naval Criminal Investigation Division was to handle the investigation."

"Do you know why the second investigation was ordered?"

"No, I don't. I was not consulted nor informed." Maxwell's expression held its own question for Slidell. It asked, "If you find out, I'd sure as hell like to know."

Slidell had no idea what to make of this information.

"Did your officers keep records regarding the conduct and findings of their investigation?"

"Of course they did."

"Would you turn those records over to the prosecution and defense in this case?"

"I don't have the records, Captain."

Slidell had expected predictable responses to these last pro forma questions. This answer broke the pattern and caught him off-guard. "What do you mean you don't have the files?"

"The files were taken by the NCID team that was sent from stateside to perform the second investigation. What it may have done with them, I don't know. My requests for those files and for the report of my initial investigation have been ignored." Maxwell held his hands out, palms up, and shrugged as if to suggest that there wasn't anything more he could do about it.

Slidell asked a few more questions, attempting further to probe Maxwell's knowledge of the second investigation. He then curtly thanked Maxwell for his time and cooperation. The deposition lasted for another hour while Sutton, Reynolds, and Schmidt took their turns questioning Maxwell.

As Slidell packed his briefcase to leave, Sutton walked over to him.

"Well, congratulations, you got some nice bits of evidence there. The question is what are you going to do with them?"

Slidell did not answer Sutton and did not look up from his briefcase as he loaded his notes into it.

"Hey. I've got an idea," said Sutton. "Let's you and me meet for lunch at my club when we get back to San Diego. We need to make up. Whether you like it or not, we're in this together, and it wouldn't hurt if we got along. I meant it when I said I could help." As Slidell pushed passed him and headed out of the conference room, Sutton shouted, "By the way, good job today."

*   *   *

It was on the plane ride back to San Diego that Slidell came to a full understanding of what Maxwell had done. He had given Slidell a trophy, but it was actually the general who had won the contest. Slidell must now defend Belmonte by showing that Maxwell's investigation had exonerated him of premeditated murder, that Belmonte and the other Marines had followed the rules of engagement. Before Slidell discovered this first investigation and its results, he had planned to defend his client by proving that Maxwell had encouraged violations of the rules, permitting his men to "kill who you've got kill to save who you've got to save." He was going to argue that it was Maxwell who was responsible for the deaths of the civilians, that it was Maxwell who should be on trial, not his men.

But now he could not pursue such a strategy without admitting that the first investigation was a sham, a cover-up. That would only lend creditability to the second and much later investigation. Further, not only did Maxwell's first investigation clear Belmonte, but it also cleared him. If his Marines had actually adhered to the rules of engagement, then Maxwell could not be accused of encouraging the illegal killing of civilians by turning a blind eye to violations of the rules. Maxwell had successfully forced Slidell into a legal strategy he could not easily abandon. Slidell would have to argue that the conclusions of the first and timelier investigation were more creditable and convincing; that the second investigation was too remote from the incident to be accurate. Maxwell had used the deposition to protect his career.

It now appeared to Slidell that Maxwell's objection to the deposition may have been a legitimate complaint about the convenience of its timing and not a ploy to avoid it because he had something to hide. If this were so, then who had had him beaten up in the bar, and why did they want it to look like it was Maxwell?

Chapter 37

THE CAR DOOR opened and let in the noise of the street and a tall, extremely thin man in casual clothes so devoid of color that he seemed to blend into the upholstery. He angled himself awkwardly into the front passenger seat, bending his legs away from the dashboard in the cramped interior until his knees were almost level with his eyes. His movements, stiff and deliberate, reminded Sutton of a praying mantis. The door closed with a sharp metallic click, instantly silencing the sound outside the car. The man stared straight ahead, his profile obscured by the glare through the side window. He waited for Sutton to speak first.

"This is a very delicate matter. None but a very few at the firm know of it. I am to be your only contact. Do not call me at the office. If it is necessary to meet, we will do so in a place we are unlikely to be seen. You are not to mention this arrangement to anyone. Is that understood?"

The man nodded, and Sutton passed him an envelope. The man took it and stuffed it inside his shirt.

"Half your fee. You'll get the rest when you find him. He has to be found fast."

The man, still facing forward, nodded once and shouldered the door open. He methodically unfolded himself limb by limb and then was gone.

Sutton started the engine and listened to the guttural hum as he leaned back in his seat. The man would be quick. The firm had used him before in sensitive affairs, and Sutton knew his skill. He had supplied him with the numbers for Anderson's passport, driver's license, credit cards, and social-security account. He had also given him Anderson's cell phone number and the names of his banks. This would not take long.

Sutton sighed deeply and turned the steering wheel toward the street. As he edged the car into the late afternoon traffic, he realized that the man had not spoken a single word.

Chapter 38

THEY WAITED WHILE the children crossed the street, two-by-two, holding hands, the teacher and her aide shepherding them as they skipped, hopped, or dawdled over the zebra bands of the pedestrian crossing. One boy, his face scrunched and red, refused to step off the curb, as his partner, a little girl in pigtails, tugged his arm with both hands. The aide hurried over and scooped him up. She carried him half-bent over her shoulder, while he rubbed his eyes with his fists. His partner, her hair jouncing in rhythm with her strides, marched beside the aide, gripping her free hand. All the children wore powder-blue tee shirts stenciled in cinnamon letters that read, 'Kids' Power Day Care.'

Candice couldn't take her eyes off the children, even after they were safely across, and was startled when the driver behind her blasted the horn.

"You okay?" asked Slidell as the car lurched and began to gain speed.

"I should be asking you that question. You've hardly said two words since I picked you up from the airport. You want to tell me what's wrong?"

"I was outclassed. Maxwell blindsided me, and now I have to rethink this case. I thought I had him in a corner, but he got me on the ropes. Sorry about the boxing analogy."

"No problem. I actually like boxing. I had a boyfriend who fought professionally."

"You're kidding, aren't you?"

"Just watch your step; he still likes me." Candice turned to Slidell, smiled, and winked at him.

"What's one more pummeling?" said Slidell, but he too was smiling now. He reached over and put his hand on her knee. Then he moved his hand slowly up her thigh, pushing her skirt until he could see her crotch. She was wearing red panties that curved high on her hip exposing her cheek.

"Careful, cowboy, you're giving that truck driver next to us a thrill."

Slidell twisted to his right to look. No truck. No leering driver. When he turned back, Candice had pulled her skirt down.

"Patience, we're almost home," she said.

Candice had asked her mother to take Anna for the weekend. Her mother had driven down from LA and picked Anna up after school. The next two days would belong only to her and Slidell.

*   *   *

Slidell lay motionless on his back in the dark bedroom feeling the sheet across his chest gently tug and release in time to Candice's breathing. When he was sure she was asleep, he slid out of bed and shuffled into the kitchen, feeling his way along the wall. He was still unfamiliar with Candice's house. He found the stove and clicked on the bulb in the overhanging exhaust hood. Its pale, yellow glow barely illuminated the room; but he did not want to switch on the ceiling light and risk waking Candice. He sat down on a stool at the breakfast bar.

He wanted a drink, and he was unable to sleep. Candice did not keep alcohol in the apartment, so if he succumbed, it would require that he leave and drive Candice's car. They had come straight to her apartment from the airport. He might be able to dress and sneak out without waking her, backing her car silently in neutral out of the driveway. A couple of quick drinks at one of the local bars, and he would be back. A piece of cake, except that she would wake up, would know he was gone, and why. Or that she would not wake up, and he would not stop at a couple of drinks. Either way would be the end. He walked over to the stove and turned off the light. Blind and disoriented, he reached out for the wall.

Chapter 39

SUTTON HAD TAKEN care of the details. The waiter had been tipped generously beforehand, not to insure his promptness but to purchase his discretion and willingness to see to it that Slidell's drinks were doubles and that Suttons's were watered down. The dining room of his club was the perfect venue. It provided intimacy, a panoramic view of San Diego, and food prepared with panache, if not to the highest of epicurean standards. He was certain that Slidell would succumb quickly to the ambiance and easy refinement of the place.

Slidell had scored big at Maxwell's deposition, and Sutton was worried. The information that Slidell had extracted from Maxwell could be used in any number of ways at trial to cast doubt on the guilt of the Marines and undermine the investigation by the NCID. Maxwell's testimony had eroded the underpinnings of that investigation. Sutton saw the reactions of the prosecutors to Maxwell's admission. The sheen of confidence that covered them and reflected his own assurance that the case was a loser had melted away. Slidell was either phenomenally lucky or was proving to be a much better litigator than Sutton had thought. Either way, Slidell had to be removed from the case; he was now an obstacle to the end game Sutton planned.

Sutton pushed these concerns aside and began mentally preparing for his conversation with Slidell. He would say nothing that might put Slidell on the defensive. He wanted him relaxed and collegial. He must convince him they were both advancing toward the same goal, what was best for the Marines. Above all, he had to keep the conversation moving, control its pace, and make alcohol the weave of its fiber. To that end, he had scheduled lunch for two o'clock, late enough to insure an empty stomach and the stirring of cravings for that first drink of the day. Finally, he would be nursing a martini when Slidell arrived.

"Captain Slidell, sir." The waiter stood by the table, Slidell beside him. Slidell was in uniform; and as Sutton looked up and saw him next to the waiter who was also in uniform, he couldn't help himself and laughed. To Sutton, the two appeared as a parody of one another, the waiter in a pseudo tuxedo and Slidell in military garb, each seemly dressed for some part in a campy burlesque. Sutton quickly got control of himself.

"Chuck, it's good to see you. Sit down, please." Sutton partially rose and nodded toward the other end of the table, where the waiter was pulling out the chair, and then plopped back down. "Would you like something to drink? I'm afraid I have a head start on you. Couldn't wait; after all, the sun is over the yard arm—somewhere." Sutton let out a throaty laugh.

"Can I get you anything, sir?" asked the waiter when Slidell was seated.

"A dry red wine would be fine," said Slidell.

"No, Chuck, no. You need something with a bit of meat on it. We have a lot to discuss. Come on, how about joining me in a martini, vodka very dry with an olive stuffed with blue cheese. Nothing better," urged Sutton.

"No thanks," said Slidell.

"What will it be then?" queried Sutton.

Slidell thought for a moment and then said, "I'll take a whiskey, Irish, with just a splash of water, no ice."

"That's more like it," hooted Sutton, pumping his fist in the air.

"Will that be Bushmills or Jameson, sir?" asked the waiter.

"Jameson," answered Slidell.

"Is the 18 Year Old acceptable, sir?" asked the waiter.

Slidell was about to pass on this top-shelf and very expensive brand of Jameson's when Sutton said, "Go ahead, it's on my tab, I insist."

"That would be fine then," Slidell answered the waiter. "And forget the splash of water," he added.

"Say, did you hear the one about the old man on his first day in the senior citizen's home?" Sutton did not wait for an answer. "This aide puts him in a wheel chair and takes him to the dining room for lunch. He leaves him at the table, but before he goes he tells the old man to watch out for this old lady who's always hitting on the men in the home. Well, sure enough, before long this old broad comes walking over, and when she is right in from of him, she reaches down, grabs the hem of her dress, yanks it up over her head, and yells, 'Super Cunt!' She's wearing nothing underneath. The old guy looks, hesitates, and then says, 'I'll take the soup.'"

There was a second of silence, and then Slidell roared with laughter. Before he stopped, he reached for the crystal tumbler of whiskey that the waiter slid in front of him.

"Another," said Sutton, holding up his martini glass and tapping its rim. "And keep them coming every twenty minutes until I pass out; then every thirty minutes after that."

"So what did you want to discuss?" asked Slidell, slouching back in his chair and watching the liquid coat the inside of his glass as he gently swirled it.

"Whoa. Not so fast. We've got plenty of time for that. First, how 'bout we get to know each other a little bit. I like to know who I'm working with. Tell me something about yourself," said Sutton.

"Sounds like truth or dare," said Slidell. He turned sideways in his chair, facing away from Sutton, and crossed his legs.

"What?" asked Sutton.

"It's a kids' game; never mind," answered Slidell.

Sutton wondered where to go from here. He wanted to keep the atmosphere convivial, relaxed; but it was clear that Slidell did not want to talk about himself. He watched as Slidell took a sip of his whiskey and then decided not to change tack.

"Why the Marines?"

Slidell tilted his head slightly and eyed Sutton. He observed him that way for a moment as if appraising him and then said, "Youthful impetuosity or arrogance."

"How do you mean?" asked Sutton.

"I joined when I was eighteen. I thought I was tough and wanted to prove it."

"Did you?" asked Sutton.

"Did I what?"

"Did you prove you were tough?" explained Sutton.

Slidell smiled. "No. I was wrong. What about you?" He was looking straight at Sutton now.

"You mean how I got into the law?" asked Sutton, not really understanding Slidell's question.

"No, I meant are you tough?"

Sutton jerked back in his chair, his eyes wide in surprise. And then he started to laugh. It began as a snort, morphed to a guffaw, and escalated to full blown hysterics until he was hooting madly, his body wobbling and shaking, flab rolling in great waves under his clothes. The other patrons of the club began looking his way in alarm. "God, that was a good one, Slidell. I haven't heard anything that preposterous in a coon's age," he said when he could breathe again. "That calls for another drink. One more before we order."

*   *   *

Slidell was a drinker. Even on watered-down martinis, Sutton was beginning to feel the effects of the vodka; but Slidell appeared impervious to the whiskey. He matched Sutton drink for drink; yet his speech remained cogent, his hands steady, and his demeanor anything but belligerent. Sutton searched for signs that the liquor was taking hold: unfocused and drifting eyes, slurred and halting speech, a laugh too loud, a slide into moroseness. But Slidell betrayed none of these markers of inebriation. Impossible, thought Sutton; he must be drunk by now. And even if he somehow weren't, he surely had enough alcohol in his blood to make him legally intoxicated. That was all that mattered. Sutton decided that it was time for the next step in his plan for Slidell. They had finished dessert, and Sutton signaled for the waiter.

"We're done here. Just put everything on my tab, and give yourself a twenty-percent tip," he said when the waiter had drifted over to their table.

"That's very generous of you," said Slidell. "You sure I can't throw something into the pot?"

"No, of course not. My treat. I'm sorry, but I must get back to the office. The coffee is excellent here. We'll have to try it next time.

This has been most enjoyable. Thank you for coming." Sutton rose from his chair. "Let me show you out. I assume you used the valet parking?"

He and Slidell rode the elevator down to the lobby and walked together out to the sidewalk in front of the entrance to the club.

A young Hispanic man in black trousers and a red vest rushed up to Slidell.

"Your ticket, sir?"

Slidell reached back and pulled his wallet from his rear pocket; but as he did, it slipped from his hand and corkscrewed to the ground. He bent down to pick it up, tipped forward, and fell on his knees.

"Jesus Christ," he said as he tried to push himself up off the concrete. He managed to get one foot under him, but then listed, stopping his sideways fall with an outstretched arm.

Sutton held out his hand, offering his great frame as an anchor; and Slidell grabbed it, pulling himself to his feet like a baby learning to stand at the rail of its playpen, all wobbly at the knees.

"You okay, sir?" asked the young man.

"Yeah, yeah, no problem," said Slidell, fumbling for cash from his wallet. He handed the valet a five-dollar bill.

Sutton put his arm around Slidell shoulders, holding him steady. As he propped up Slidell, he searched the line of parked cars across the street until he found what he was looking for. One of the cars, a grey Toyota, was occupied, the man in the driver's seat staring intently at Sutton. Sutton nodded and the man turned away and started the engine.

A car pulled up to the curb, and the young man who had taken Slidell's ticket jumped out and handed Slidell the key. Sutton stepped off the curb with Slidell, his arm still around him, and walked to the open driver's door.

"Don't be a stranger. Let's stay in touch on this case."

"Yeah, sure, good idea. Thanks again," said Slidell.

Sutton pushed the door shut as Slidell put the key into the ignition.

As Slidell lurched the car into the street, the Toyota did a U turn and eased behind him. Sutton watched them coast toward the intersection until the blue and red Mars lights inside the rear window of the Toyota began to flash.

Chapter 40

IN THE HEAT, the road seemed to undulate over the low crests of the land like a dark ocean serpent. On and on the animal swam through the inland sea of Nebraska's western prairie straight to Wyoming and the far horizon. Anderson waited for over an hour for the bus, watching. In that time, only three cars had passed him, all heading west. He stood by the side of the road next to the bent pole that supported the faded sign for the Greyhound bus stop. He was the only person there.

He checked his shirt pocket again for the envelope and the fifty-dollar bill clipped to it. He had debated with himself for days about the person he should send the letter to. His account of what he believed had happened to Patterson and the danger he himself felt read like the ranting of someone on the verge of a nervous break-down. It appeared preposterous. But it wasn't. He had seen the DVD, had heard the words of the man at the bedroom door admonishing Sutton about the necessity of the Marines being found guilty. He hadn't dreamed it, of that he was certain, although his life was beginning to seem like a dream, or like a nightmare. If what he had written were true, then he was placing in danger the person he had written to. He had agonized over this.

Anderson swiped his face once with his bare hand and then rubbed the leg of his jeans to get the sweat off his palm. The bus should have arrived, and Anderson began to worry that he may have gotten the time wrong and missed it. He tried to visualize the schedule he left on the table in his small motel efficiency, hoping to recreate the destinations and times. But he couldn't. A horsefly landed on his ear; and he swatted at it, but not in time to stop the sting. It hurt like hell.

"Fuck," he yelled in frustration; and then the bus came into view.

Anderson waved for the bus to stop; and as it approached, he began to hear the sounds it made on the road, the hum of its wheels and the strain of metal twisting and bending to bounce over unseen ruts. As the bus pulled onto the shoulder, the flash of the sun off its blue metal skin momentarily blinded Anderson; and then it wheezed to a standstill, enveloping him in an angry swirl of dust. The door swung open.

"Hop in," said the driver in a thick southern accent.

Anderson climbed the stairs into the cab. "I'm not a passenger, but can you do something for me?" He handed the driver the envelope with the fifty-dollar bill. "When you finally get to where you're going, would you mail this from there?"

The driver pulled the bill off the envelope and shoved it into his pocket. "Consider it done, friend," he said and then dropped the letter into a dirty canvas bag hung on the side of his chair.

"Thanks," said Anderson and backed down the stairs, steadying himself with the hand-rails. He stood watching the bus until it was almost out of sight. He wondered if he was doing the right thing.

Chapter 41

STUBBLEFIELD'S MASSIVE FRAME filled the doorway and obscured the outside world. Slidell searched his face for signs of anger, or worse, disappointment. His bulldog mug registered only curiosity and a certain level of intensity that Slidell could not connect to any emotion. He hoped it might be concern.

"Are you going to ask me to come in or are you just gonna let me stand here like I'm some no-account Jehovah's Witness trying to rustle up more souls for heaven?"

Slidell stepped out of the way and motioned for Stubblefield to enter. Stubblefield walked past him into the living room and sat down on the couch. The couch looked like a chair with Stubblefield in it. Slidell tried mentally to accommodate Stubblefield's size to the scale of the room and failed. He felt as if he were in a museum exhibit where everything had been shrunk to allow visitors to feel what it's like to be a giant.

"Sit down, shit-for-brains," said Stubblefield.

Slidell sat in the recliner, opposite Stubblefield, the coffee table between them. Stubblefield leaned forward, making the couch groan and creak. "I'm not here looking for excuses," he said.

"I know this looks bad, but…"

"Bad! This ain't *bad*. This is two alligators up your rectum chewing your fucking innards out after they bit your balls off. That's what this is. You're in a whole mess of trouble."

The vehemence of Stubblefield's words startled Slidell. There was even a shade of violence to them that frightened him.

After his arrest for DUI, Candice had posted bail and taken him home. She had not said a word on the drive from the police station to his house. When she pulled into his driveway, she had waited in stern silence, her hands clenched to the steering wheel, for him to get out of the car. Now she refused to answer his calls and ignored his messages to her.

Stubblefield telephoned that evening and told him to take a couple of days leave and that he would come by soon to see him. The call was ominous in its brevity. And now here he was.

Stubblefield slowly shook his head from side to side. "Did you have to take your miserable peccadillo public? Couldn't you have kept it on the base where we could have handled it within the Corps?"

"I'm sorry," said Slidell.

"You ain't half as sorry as you're gonna be. I got a call from a lawyer by the name of Kowalski. He's with a small firm in San Diego. Belmonte no longer wants you as his attorney so Kowalski is filing a motion to have you removed as his lawyer. It seems Belmonte's parents have hired him to represent their son after they heard about your arrest."

"Shit," said Slidell.

"It gets worse. The base commander wants something done about you, and fast. It doesn't look good for the Corps to have one of its officers arrested for DUI, especially one defending a soldier in a trial that is in the media weekly. I have been fielding questions from the press almost from the moment of your arrest. Hell, I found out about it from the press."

"Are you going to Ninja Punch me?"

"You should be so lucky; a non-judicial punishment may be out of the question. You more likely will face a court martial for conduct unbecoming an officer."

"What happened to the presumption of innocence?"

"Don't get smart with me," said Stubblefield. "I'm not in the mood for it."

"I'm not. I haven't been convicted of anything. In any case, I wasn't on duty when this happened. I was having dinner at a private club," explained Slidell.

"Bullshit. You were in uniform. You were meeting with the lawyer for two of the defendants in this case, a case in which you are the defense counsel. You sure as hell were on duty, no matter what place you were at," continued Stubblefield.

"Well, I may have been drunk, but I wasn't disorderly. I cooperated fully with the police," Slidell continued to argue.

"That defense just won't fly. Your actions seriously compromised your standing as an officer and as defense counsel," said Stubblefield, shaking his head again. "And stop thinking only of yourself. Shit also rolls up hill in the Corps. I'm about to have a case yanked away from my jurisdiction because of the conduct of an officer under my command. That's humiliating as hell, as well as a career buster."

"You're right, and I'm sorry; but nothing snowballs this quickly. This is all happening too fast," said Slidell. He wasn't bemoaning his fate. He meant what he said, literally.

Stubblefield seemed placated by this foray in contriteness. He leaned back and spread his arms out along the back of the couch.

Then he placed the sole of his shoe on the edge of the coffee table and, with his foot, gingerly pushed the table across the floor so that he could fully stretch his legs.

Slidell wondered if Stubblefield had understood him. "Don't you think it's odd that the press found out about this so fast?" he tried to explain.

Stubblefield thought a moment. "No, I don't. Reporters check the police blotters daily."

"And what about Belmonte's parents, how did they find out?" Slidell pressed.

"The reporter who discovered your arrest, he or she could have found out their telephone number and called them before the story was filed," answered Stubblefield.

"Assuming it was the reporter who contacted them," said Slidell.

It was obvious that Stubblefield was curious and interested in Slidell's suspicions. Slidell knew that for all of his bluster and the country boy facade, Stubblefield had a keen analytical mind that he exercised to the benefit of his clients and the Corps. And he couldn't resist using that mind at every opportunity.

"Are you thinking it was someone else?" asked Stubblefield.

"Yes," answered Slidell, slowly pronouncing the word.

"Who?" asked Stubblefield.

Slidell looked at Stubblefield and cocked his head as if to say, "Who the hell do you think?"

"If you think it was Sutton, then you just stop right there, pal. You got yourself drunk. Sutton didn't force those drinks down your throat. You've destroyed too many brain cells if you expect me to believe that he did. Maybe he's just taking advantage of a situation you got yourself into. Nobody forced you into that car," said Stubblefield, his demeanor changing.

"I know that. I wasn't thinking clearly at that point, obviously. But in a way he did get me drunk," said Slidell, trying to reengage Stubblefield in his speculations.

Stubblefield held up his hand, motioning for Slidell to stop talking. Then he shot to his feet and took a step toward Slidell. He loomed over him.

"This is bullshit, and it's making me sick. I told you I'm not going to play along in this." Stubblefield spit the words at Slidell.

Slidell felt physically threatened and confused by Stubblefield's reaction. He honestly didn't know what to make of it. He tried to explain himself.

"Look, it's hard to understand…"

Stubblefield interrupted him. "It ain't hard to understand. You are an alcoholic. You can't control your drinking. The DUI arrest was an inevitability."

Stubblefield's expression shifted from anger to puzzlement as if he were surprised at his sudden aggression. His body sagged and he slumped back down onto the couch. "You are a good lawyer Chuck. I think you could be one of the best, but you are destroying yourself and this case. And you're bringing me down with you. What the hell am I going to do about this?" he seemed to say more to himself than to Slidell.

Chapter 42

THE THIN MAN leaned against the wall and watched the crowd of people pour in and out of the bus station like the sands of an hour glass, those leaving emptying onto the busses, those arriving filling the station again, all a commotion of scuffle and rub. But the thin man was not searching the passengers. He was looking for those who did not come and did not go, the stationary grains of sand. He knew he would find them quickly because he could see what others refused to notice, what others conveniently ignored. The homeless were his greatest asset; for although they were not seen, they saw all that was going on around them. The public places were their homes. They knew their homes well and had remarkable memories for their many guests.

A middle-aged man in grey trousers and a blue sports coat sat in one of the molded plastic chairs bolted to the floor of the station. He had his legs crossed and stared down in front of him as if deep in thought. Occasionally, his head jerked to the side; but otherwise he did not move. The thin man waited until the seat next to the man was empty, and then he walked over and sat down. The thin man leaned close to him so that their shoulders were almost touching, but the man paid absolutely no attention to him. Up close, the thin man could see that the man wore wool trousers, worn thin and so frayed at the cuffs that threads of material hung down over his shoes, filthy white canvas high-tops. His coat, too large for his frame, had an irregular pattern of dark oval stains down the front.

"Did you see this guy in here recently?" said the thin man. He held a picture of Anderson in front of the man.

The man lifted his head slightly to glance at the picture and then dropped his head again. He said nothing.

"His wife's looking for him. He left her and the baby. She needs to find him. It's worth it to her to find him," said the thin man.

"I seen him, yeah. The other day. Came in here, stood around for a while and then bought a ticket to somewheres. He didn't belong here. I can tell you that," said the man.

"Why not?" the thin man asked.

"He was dressed in old work clothes, but it was the shoes what gave him away. He was wearing Alden American moccasins. They was worn some, but they was no hand-me-downs. People walkin' around in those kind of shoes don't belong here. You can tell a lot about a body from shoes. I know. Used to be a shoe salesman back in the day."

"You sure it was him?" asked the thin man.

The man slowly turned his head and looked at the thin man. "I told you it was him, didn't I?"

"Yes, you did. Here, this is for you from the lady with thanks." The thin man took twenty-five dollars out of his wallet and shoved it into the side pocket of the man's jacket.

The man turned his face away from the thin man and returned to staring out over the floor of the station.

The thin man got up from the chair and walked to the ticket counter. There he purchased the cheapest ticket he could and headed for the bus terminal. He was looking for drivers, those arriving and those departing. The first several drivers he approached and showed the picture either told him to get lost or said they had never seen Anderson. Then he got lucky.

The driver had been about to get into a bus when the thin man accosted him. He was carrying a large, to-go cup of coffee and had a donut in his mouth. At first, he was wary of the thin man.

"Why you looking for this guy?"

"His wife left him. Now she wants him back. You know how it goes?" said the thin man.

"Yes. Sure I remember him. That explains the letter. He gave me fifty dollars to mail it for him. You don't forget that. Hell, I'd have done it for free. Do it a lot for my passengers. You wouldn't believe how often I'm asked," said the bus driver.

"Do you know where he was going?" asked the thin man.

"Oh, he wasn't a passenger. He was waiting at a stop in Nebraska for the bus, but he didn't want to go anywhere. He just wanted me to mail the letter for him."

"What stop was he at?"

"Sidney. Sidney, Nebraska," the bus driver answered.

*   *   *

The drive to Sidney, Nebraska, from San Diego had taken nineteen hours; and the thin man had done it non-stop. He was tired but not yet ready to sleep. He had asked at a gas station about motels in Sidney and found that there were two. He was parked across the highway from the one on the western edge of town. There were no cars in the lot, and for the past hour no one had entered or left any of the twelve rooms. He had just made the decision to move on and was turning the key to the ignition when the door to room eight opened. He watched as Anderson stepped out and headed toward the motel office.

The thin man took his cell phone off the dash board and dialed the number Sutton had given him.

"Yes?" The one word answer was curt and bulging with impatience.

"I found him," said the thin man.

"Good. You know what to do. Make it clean," said Sutton.

Chapter 43

ODDLY, ANDERSON HAD come to consider the Fast Pitch Motel as home. Isolated on the edge of town, wrapped in the quiet of the prairie, and lying, vulnerable, under an enormous open sky, it forced its occupants into a kind of rough community, much like pilgrims come together, their journeys converging for a brief time. In his condo in San Diego, Anderson barely knew his neighbors well enough to remember their names. Every one of them was caught up in the rush of city life, himself included. An apartment was a place to crash, not to establish a life. There simply was no time for that. But at the Fast Pitch Motel, in spite of its name, time seemed to slow down enough so that he could take notice of the type of cars that passed by on the road, read the sky for the weather, or discern something of people's lives by the way they walked or smiled. The idle talk at breakfast among the sleepy travelers at the small motel café somehow warmed the spirit in the way coffee warmed the body. Anderson had discovered more about the lives of the motel's transient guests than he had in three years about the people at his condo. To his surprise, he was beginning to like the place more than he had any other.

Anderson was finishing his eggs, once over easy, as Katrina saun-tered over to his table.

"You want more, yes?' she said in a Polish accent, pouring coffee into his empty white mug before he could answer. Anderson learned that she and her husband, Michael, had bought the Fast Pitch Motel after seeing an ad for its sale fifteen years ago in the *Chicago Tribune*. They had come to Chicago from Poland, and Michael had worked as a floor sander for twenty years while Katrina had cleaned offices at night in the Chicago Loop. In that time, they had saved, in cash, enough to buy the motel outright. Neither had ever been anywhere in the United States outside of Chicago; but within two weeks after seeing the ad, they were in Sidney, Nebraska, cleaning and fixing their newly purchased means of earning a living.

Anderson looked up and was momentarily blinded by the light from the large picture window across the west wall of the café. "It's going to be a hot day, no clouds to block the sun," he said.

"Sure. No wind either." Katrina set the glass coffee pot down on the table and stood looking at Anderson, her hands on her hips.

"What?" said Anderson after she stood there a while in silence.

"Michael. His knees. They are no good now. Too much bending and lifting in Chicago, and here. He must go into town today and buy lumber and tools. He wants to build another room. He's crazy, I think. But he says business is that good we need another room. Will you go and help him?"

"Of course, I will."

*   *   *

Michael picked up Anderson at noon outside his motel room, and they headed into town in Michael's old truck.

"My knees are not so bad," said Michael after they pulled out onto the highway. "I think Katrina wants you to have a life. Get you someplace else besides the motel."

"I like the motel," said Michael.

"Bullshit, nobody like that motel after two days. Why you stay for so long? You commit crime or something?"

"No." Anderson was surprised by Michael's directness and by his questions. He just had not considered that his stay would create such suspicion. He had not even bothered to make up a cover story. Still, he had not used his real name to check in, of course, or his real address; and he paid for everything in cash. But in his conversations with Michael and Katrina and with those who passed through the motel, he had been honest about his life, except that he had avoided giving reasons for being at the Fast Pitch, other than to say he was taking some time off and traveling. Traveling to Nebraska? It did sound preposterous.

"Look. My life got a bit messy. That's all. I broke up with my girlfriend, or she broke up with me. Okay? Then things started to go south at work. I needed to get my head together. So I just got on a bus and ended up here. It's that simple," Anderson lied. "I'll go back when I'm ready."

Michael nodded his head but kept his eyes on the road and didn't look at Anderson. "The lumber center is at corner," he said, pointing. "We go there first. Pick up lumber ourselves. We must make several trips. They will deliver, but it cost too much. This way take more time, but cheaper."

It took them four trips to load and bring the lumber back to the motel, where they unloaded it and put it on pallets by the newly-poured cement foundation for the room.

"Must not cover lumber. It stay drier out in open, even if rain. If covered, it swell with water and no good to use. It shrink later when dry and twist and pull out nails," Michael cautioned.

During their trips back and forth to town, in answer to his questions, Michael schooled Anderson on the rudiments of framing and finishing the room and on how to extend the roof of the motel to cover it. Michael was building the room himself. Anderson was fascinated. And he liked the physical labor. It felt good to use his muscles for something more than lifting a latte or typing a brief. At the end of the day, he was exhausted, but also exhilarated. He felt alive.

*   *   *

The instant the door to the motel room shut, the thin man pushed himself away from the wall and shoved Anderson hard between the shoulder blades. Anderson shot forward and tumbled face down on the bed. The thin man dug a knee into his back, pinning him to the bed, and grabbed his hair, yanking Anderson's head to the side. The needle of the hypodermic entered deep into the back of Anderson's neck as the thin man pushed hard on the plunger. Anderson's body shivered for a second and then was still.

The thin man turned him over and lifted his torso, pushing him against the headboard so that Anderson sat propped upright in bed. He left Anderson there for a moment to retrieve a bottle of whiskey, a vial of pills, and a wooden tongue depressor from a brown paper bag he had left by the wall. He poured the pills from the vial into the bottle and shook it several times. He then returned to the bed. Tilting Anderson's head back, the thin man forced his mouth open with the tongue depressor and jammed the bottle into Anderson's mouth forcing the neck far down into his throat. As the bottle emptied, the thin man massaged Anderson's esophagus insuring that the liquid flowed into his stomach. When he was done, he placed the empty bottle and vial on the stand by the bed, and then waited for darkness to cover the Nebraska prairie.

Chapter 44

SUTTON ERASED THE one-word text message he had just received—*Done*—and mixed himself another martini. Then he turned his back to the bar in his living room, and standing as still as he could with his eyes closed, let the silence of his condo seep into his body. He craved silence; struggled to surround himself in absolute quiet. He had the walls and ceilings to his condo soundproofed before he moved in; and every inch of the floor was carpeted.

Sutton rarely watched TV and hated music, music of all kinds. Strange, since his mother had been a concert pianist, a promising one, until she had met his father and turned her life over to him, a gift he had squandered with his jealousy and meanness. She had eventually escaped his father. The authorities ruled her drowning off the beach of their lake home an accident, but he knew better. She had simply had enough abuse and wanted no more. Such beauty and talent wasted. Sutton had waited patiently while his father entrapped other women and then grew old. In the end it was easy. While his father slept, he put a pillow over his face and held it there until he stopped breathing. Sutton imagined it must have been much like drowning.

Sutton needed the silence to think. It was like the martinis. It stimulated his mind, greased the bearings. He walked over to the couch and sat down. The white, supple leather of the cushion rippled and stretched tight under his weight. It barely made a sound. He placed the Waterford glass holding his drink carefully on top of the end table and settled back to begin assessing his situation. He would not allow himself to think of it as a crisis, not yet.

That prick Patterson and his bitch had been eliminated, and now Anderson was out of the picture. Sutton was certain that they were the only people besides Blakely who knew of the disk, and there was no way the police could connect him to their deaths. Patterson's and Stella's deaths were reported as a tragic one-car accident—a thrill-seeking driver losing control of a speeding car. And Anderson's body would not be identified for months, if ever. Sutton suspected that Anderson was smart enough to erase all evidence of his true identity. He would become just another of the tens of thousands of perpetually missing persons in America.

But there was still one loose end, a troubling thread that could lead to the unraveling of the curtain that hid his connection to Blakely. The thin man had told him of a letter, a letter a bus driver had said that Anderson had asked him to mail. Maybe the letter was nothing, merely a note telling someone not to worry about him, that he would be gone for a while. Then again, maybe Anderson had unburdened himself and revealed what he knew about the disk. Sutton was ready to discount this possibility. If Anderson considered himself in danger because of his knowledge of the disk, then he was not likely to put someone else in danger by telling them what it contained. That would be contrary to what Sutton knew of him.

Still, Sutton could not shake free of the thought that Anderson might have acted against his nature. And if he did, then to whom had he sent the letter?

Sutton's eyes snapped open when he heard the noise. It was a low rumble, distant and muted, like an empty dump truck bouncing over a rutted road. Sutton wondered what it could be and from where it was coming. The sound seemed to fill the room. He cocked his head to better detect its location. It grew louder, and Sutton began to sense a slight tremor, a vague vibration. Then the sour imitation of a smile etched itself across his face as the rumble turned to a rolling growl in his midriff. It was time to eat.

Chapter 45

BOTTOM FEEDER, POND scum, the fly-infested crust of drying shit on the sidewalk, a yellow dog. In Slidell's mind there weren't enough epithets to describe Conrad "Connie" Kowalski's mendacity. Kowalski trolled the muddy depths of the criminal courts for clients, extracting from them an exorbitant fee for pleading them guilty to prostitution, drunk driving, possession of controlled substances, shoplifting, credit card fraud, check kiting, and the thousand other minor crimes that the poor commit to get through another day. He gamed an overcrowded court system and scammed the hordes of confused and frightened customers who were shoveled into it from the streets of San Diego. As far as Slidell could discover, Kowalski had never actually tried a case in his life. And this was the attorney Belmonte had picked to replace him, or the one that had been chosen for Belmonte. Slidell suspected that Kowalski was nothing more than Sutton's willing puppet. He imagined Sutton poised above a stage waiting to pull the stings that made Kowalski dance, pleading Belmonte guilty.

"I've checked up on Mr. Kowalski," said Slidell. "He is not familiar with the military justice system, and he has never tried a murder case. Are you sure you want this man to represent you?"

Belmonte, still in shackles, stood with his back to the door just a few steps into the interview room of the brig. He hung his head, looking at the floor.

"It's all arranged, sir. My parents handled it."

"You can tell them you want them to find someone else, someone with more experience, a former military lawyer."

Belmonte raised his head and made eye contact with Slidell.

"I can't do that, sir," he said and looked away again.

Slidell saw pain in Belmonte's eyes and understood what it meant. It wasn't that Belmonte couldn't ask his parents to find him an attorney other than Kowalski. It was that he couldn't risk a burnt-out drunk for a lawyer.

"I'm sorry, sir. I appreciate all you've done for me," said Belmonte. The look on his face told Slidell that there was no use saying more.

*   *   *

Emotionally drained after meeting with Belmonte, Slidell decided to drive home from the brig rather than return to the office. He drove on auto-pilot, feeling out of time, unconnected, a stranger to himself. Until now, magical thinking had protected him from the truth. He controlled his drinking, relegating it to an indulgence enjoyed privately and in innocence. It affected no one but him, and he could handle it. No harm, no foul. It was all just bullshit. Belmonte had made him see himself for what he was: a Marine officer accused of a crime, his addiction made painfully public, his disease a liability in a capital case, his weakness a disgrace.

As he pulled into his driveway, Slidell saw something dash between two of the toyon bushes that separated the far side of his house from his neighbor's. The darting movement resembled a nocturnal animal forced into the daylight, and its quickness caught his eye. Perhaps it was a coyote, he thought, or, god forbid, a skunk. He decided to take a look in case he needed to call animal control; he closed the car door quietly so he wouldn't startle the animal.

Slidell walked to the edge of his neighbor's yard and scanned up and down the row of bushes but saw nothing. He then examined the ground between the bushes looking for animal tracks. As he bent closer to the sandy soil, he saw where the dirt had been pushed into a small, uneven crater about three inches in diameter and about an eighth of an inch deep. To the side of the crater, and separated from it by an inch or two, was a scrape about seven inches long. It looked to Slidell as if some gardening tool, perhaps a trowel or hoe, had made the markings. But he had not done any gardening for some time, and his neighbor would not have been gardening either. His neighbor had built a high fence between the two houses, and the bushes did not belong to him.

Slidell puzzled over the impressions but could make no more of them, so he stood up to go into the house. He turned and glanced down at the ground one last time, and that's when their identity became clear. He had been looking at them as if they were side by side. But they weren't. One was in front of the other. Viewed this way, they were obviously the print of a shoe. The print was very shallow, but was too large for a child. It was either that of a woman or a very slight man, and it had just been made.

Slidell sprinted along the narrow passageway between his house and his neighbor's fence into his back yard, scraping his shoulder against the stucco as he ran. In one sweep of his head he surveyed the yard and noticed that stones from the pond he had built for his wife had broken loose as if kicked or stepped upon. Looking to the far corner of the yard, he saw the young cumquat tree by the stone wall shake, and he yelled, "Stop." Slidell leaped over the stone wall and landed on the roof of a dog house, twisted his leg at the knee, and fell back on top of the dog's water and food bowls. He heard someone shout, "What the hell's going on out there?" and he rolled over and tried to stand; but pain shot up his spine, and he dropped back to the ground. Looking up, he saw his neighbor holding a rifle over him and glaring down the barrel, the bushy grey eyebrow of his right eye arched high above the sight.

"Wait, wait. Hold on a minute, Pete. It's me, Slidell. I was chasing someone off my property. Did you see anyone jump my wall and run through your yard?"

"Only you, and you aren't running," said his neighbor, lowering the rifle.

"Mind if I look around over there by the cumquat tree?" asked Slidell, struggling to his feet. "Sorry about the dog house. If it's damaged, I'll pay," he added.

"Never mind, come on," said his neighbor, who signaled Slidell to follow him to the tree.

On the ground, by the stone wall, Slidell found envelopes, the colorful, decorated, annoyingly eye-catching flyers of junk mail; and they were all addressed to him.

His neighbor was looking over his shoulder as Slidell sorted through the envelopes. "Damn," he said. "Who would want to steal your mail, especially your junk mail? Hell, I'd a given it to them if I was you."

"I don't know," answered Slidell, shaking his head. "Funny part is that the only kind of mail I ever get is junk mail."

Chapter 46

CANDICE TUGGED THE thin, golden foil thread; and as it began to sever the crisp cellophane, it set free the aroma of tobacco from within the pack of cigarettes. The musty, sweet smell made her nostrils flare, and she tapped the top end of the pack against her left palm. She had not smoked in eleven years, not since she became pregnant with Anna. But she had bought a pack now and intended to smoke every cigarette. Her emotions had become a battlefield; the dwindling army of her resolve outflanked by battalions of anxieties and insecurities. The good guys needed relief even if it was illusory and physically dangerous. She lit up and inhaled her first drag. It burned her lungs, and she coughed. But as grey smoke funneled up her throat and out her nose, she felt the first rush of pleasure and release.

She wanted to be rid of him. She made that clear to Slidell when he called her after she had bailed him out. She told him then that she had had enough of alcoholic men. It was over. She had meant it at the time. First, there had been her father, then her brother. Then came the others, the men she wanted to forget. They all had promised to stop drinking. They all had stopped drinking, at least for a time. And in that time they simply turned to nonchemical addictions: thrill seeking or gambling or her.

At first she was charmed and flattered by their dependence on her, by their willingness to make her the center of their lives. But she came to realize that their dependence was a form of control and dominance. When she tried to pull away from their grasp, they cemented their hold with physical abuse and the threat of worse if she left them. And they always began drinking again, blaming her for their relapse. It had taken her years to twist free of the guilt they had inflicted upon her.

Candice absentmindedly plucked a fleck of tobacco from the tip of her tongue and wiped her fingers on the leg of her jeans. Damn it, she said to herself. From the moment she had hung up on Slidell, she waited for him to call her back. There had not been a day when she had not thought about him, had not checked her cell phone for missed calls, and had not been tempted to call him. She had even found herself staring outside her office window, searching the campus sidewalks for him. But Slidell had not called her, had not attempted to contact her in any way. And now she was losing all her resolve. Several times in the last two days she had actually started to dial his number. She had concocted a way to save face. She would pretend she was calling to see if he had found a pair of earrings she might have forgotten at his house.

She brought what was left of the cigarette to her mouth, drew on the filter as if sipping through a straw, and then flicked it into the air. She let the smoke swirl in her lungs before she exhaled. Then she tapped another cigarette loose from the pack, snatched it free with her lips, and lit it with the butane lighter from her hip pocket. She noticed the crinkle of the paper as it shriveled above the flame, and she felt the heat of the lighter spread against the lids of her closed eyes. Her first cigarette still glowed red in the grass as she began to smoke her second. The nicotine sharpened her thinking, helping her to focus. She was right to dump him, she told herself. She was getting off this train before it steamed, ever faster, down the track toward the ravine and the washed-out bridge. She knew she could not save Slidell from himself.

When the phone in her pocket vibrated, she tossed her cigarette on the ground and crushed it under her foot. Candice waited until the phone hummed twice more, pulled it from her jeans, and answered it, not bothering to check the caller ID.

"Hello," she said, her voice flat.

"Hi. It's me Chuck. I fell and hurt my back. I need some help. Can you come over?"

Chapter 47

WITH THE SOFT touch of her fingers, Candice gently guided him into her and began to rise and fall over him, bending her back so that the tips of her breasts stroked his chest in rhythm to the movement of her hips. The pain in Slidell's back faded to memory and then slid into oblivion as he matched her cadence, all sense of urgency abandoned as she took control, accepting him by turns deep and slow or shallow and quick until he felt her rock and heard her sigh; and then it was over.

They lay next to each other in bed, holding hands, not talking. Slidell felt as if he were awaking from a pleasant dream that is sensed but not remembered. He did not want the feeling to end.

"Your back feel better?" Candice let go of his hand and rolled over on her side toward him.

"Much."

"Sex is always the best therapy, and I say that as a social worker." Candice pushed her red hair out of her eyes, propped herself up on her elbow, and smiled.

"You got that right," said Slidell, smiling back at her.

"So what now?"

As Slidell looked up at Candice, he saw that her smile was frozen. Although her words were soft and sweet, Slidell knew damn well what she meant. This was an ultimatum, not a question. He would either shape up and stop drinking or lose everything—her.

"Dinner. That's what's up. Let's go for cheeseburgers," said Slidell. He swung his legs over the side of the bed and howled in pain as he tried to stand up.

Chapter 48

"Y OUR MAIL, SIR." Slidell grabbed the mail from Fallon's outstretched arm as he strode by her desk.

"Top of the morning to you, Fallon," he said over his back, holding the mail above his head in an ersatz wave as he entered his office.

As he threw the mail on his desk, Slidell caught the odor of dry paper and dust. He stood still and took in the smell. It was pervasive, and he wondered when it had filled his office. It somehow made him feel slow and heavy. He looked around. The feel of the room mirrored its odor: lifeless, colorless, dry, and brittle. It had taken on an atmosphere of staleness that verged on morbidity. Why wasn't he aware of it before? Slidell glanced down at his desk, the piles of paper, the coffee-stain rings decorating its wooden surface. He reached for the nearest mound of paper and attempted to form it into a tidy stack, when it slid over the edge of the desk toward the floor, rattling and flapping like a flock of Canada geese.

"Damn," Slidell yelled.

"What's going on in there?" Fallon hollered back.

"Why the hell don't you ever clean up this desk?" Slidell shouted.

"Because you told me never to touch it," replied Fallon, standing in the doorway with her arms folded. "Or don't you remember, sir?" The 'sir' being unmistakably stressed.

"Well at least get some flowers in here or something to brighten the place. It looks like a tomb. Smells like one too," said Slidell.

"I'm glad you finally noticed," said Fallon. "I'll bring you some coffee, or should I call the interior decorator first?" She offered Slidell a quick smile and walked back to her desk, completely ignoring the papers scattered over the floor.

Slidell sat down on his office chair and propelled himself with two quick thrusts of his legs to the front of his desk where the papers lay in confused heaps. He bent over and began grabbing handfuls, stuffing them into his lap. When he had as much as he could carry, he glided over to the wastebasket and crammed them in not giving a damn if any of the papers were important. Whatever was important would somehow reassert itself soon enough; and he would deal with it when it did. What wasn't important could just stay buried. When he was done, he pushed himself back behind his desk and grabbed the mail.

The first envelope came from California's Attorney License Division and was stamped FINAL NOTICE in red. Slidell made a mental note to himself to pay the annual license fee before the bastards put him on inactive status. The second envelope was government-issue, obviously sent out in bulk, and he trashed it without bothering to open it. The third envelope caught his attention. He turned it over, inspecting carefully the front and back. It was addressed to him in handwriting. That was unusual.

Slidell noted with chagrin that no one he knew might send him a personal letter. There was a time when an enlisted person would occasionally send him a letter seeking legal advice. But written correspondence had gone the way of the dinosaur. Today, young soldiers never wrote anything unless ordered to do so. They communicated by email and texting. The envelope also had no return address. Slidell tried to examine the post mark to determine the letter's origin, but it was little more than an illegible smudge. He wiggled the tip of his forefinger under the outer edge of the flap and pulled. Instead of tearing along the seam, the envelope ripped in half diagonally and three pages spilled to his desk. The pages weren't numbered; it took Slidell a few seconds to figure out their order.

The writing was neat and precise, the words progressing across the page in straight, even rows. Just the look of it reminded Slidell of a manuscript: weighty, authoritative. He checked the signature. Anderson had written the letter, and that surprised him. Why was this correspondence written and not typed on law-firm stationary? He turned back to the first page and began to read. Slidell stopped at the end of the first sentence, unable to read further. He felt as if he had just plunged into an icy lake without first testing the water. Anderson's words rippled in and out of focus as he tried to read them again:

Captain Slidell,

I am in hiding. I believe that my life is in danger because of information I possess about Sutton, others, and the case in which we are both involved. I also believe that my friend and law partner, Patterson, and his girl friend were murdered because they were in possession of the same information.

The letter continued in a straightforward, almost detached vein, recounting the discovery of the DVD, its contents, and Sutton's knowledge that Anderson was aware of its existence and what it contained. Slidell finished the letter and placed it carefully on his desk. He reached down and retrieved the torn envelope, which had somehow fallen on the floor by his chair. He put it beside the letter, thinking that later they both may be evidence, but for what he wasn't sure. Then he leaned back, rubbed his forehead and tried to analyze what he had just read.

At its core the letter was simply a statement—a statement of very disturbing facts, but still a statement. It asked for nothing. Anderson did not seek help from Slidell or even ask that Slidell do anything with the information. It did not elaborate beyond its crisp recitation, and it did not speculate. And it gave no hint of where Anderson might be or if, and when, he might return. Slidell tried to place this new information into some context. He struggled to recall details about Anderson, but had trouble even remembering what he looked like. He had virtually no memory of Patterson. He thought about Sutton and what he could remember of the interactions and conversations he had with him about the case in light of the letter; and as he did, his suspicions about Sutton began to change to certainties. Slidell was now convinced that his intoxication at Sutton's club had been aided and abetted by Sutton. Instead of a devastating coincidence, Sutton had arranged the DUI arrest to have him removed as Belmonte's attorney, paving the way for Sutton to plead Belmonte and the other Marines guilty.

Wasn't this what Anderson had said the man in the DVD insisted Sutton accomplish, the man Anderson believed was Jake Blakely, the majority whip in Congress? Before the DUI arrest, hadn't Sutton pressured him to convince Belmonte to enter a plea? And then there was the issue of Blakely. Why, Slidell wondered, would the majority whip of Congress instruct Sutton to make sure the Marines were found guilty? He could not yet begin to answer that question. And without Anderson, he could not even begin to legally prove the allegations it contained. Without Anderson, the letter was useless as evidence in the defense of Belmonte. It was just potential trash.

Chapter 49

"YOU GOTTA BE shitting me. I'm just not believing this." Stubblefield had thrown the letter on his desk. He was now striding back and forth, his heels pounding on the linoleum floor like the hooves of caisson horses on parade; his preferred method of attacking a problem. When Stubblefield was upset or perplexed, he was in constant motion; and motion generated heat, lots of heat, in this giant. With each turn, the sweat on his forehead became more pronounced; and Slidell knew from experience that perspiration would soon begin to seep through this big man's uniform, staining under his arms and blotching the back of his shirt.

"What are you, Chuck, the salt in the clouds of a shit storm? First you get arrested, then you lose your client, and now this…this…" said Stubblefield, waving his hand generally in the direction of the letter. "Hell, I don't even know what this is—a sick joke, a ploy, a…Christ, I'm tempted just to burn the motherfucker and forget about it."

"Sir, if it's real we have to do something about it. If…"

"Real? Hell, we can't prove a single thing in that letter. What exactly are we supposed to do, have Sutton arrested for diddling children, subverting the legal system, or worse, murder? You get real, Chuck." Stubblefield strode over to the door of his office, opened it, yelled, "Can we get some coffee in here ASAP?" and then slammed it closed before he heard the answer.

Stubblefield walked behind his desk, sat down, and became perfectly still, glaring at the letter. Slidell waited, aware of what was coming next. Stubblefield's commotion, his physical and verbal flailing, were a mental trick he employed, a means to help him arrange the pieces of a puzzle into a recognizable picture, to interconnect seemingly disparate concepts into a whole. After a moment, Stubblefield looked up from the letter and stared at Slidell.

"Okay, here's what's going to happen. You are to take this letter to a Ben Harrington in San Diego. He's with an outfit called Scientific Evidence Analysis (SEA). I used them before your time here to analyze some evidence in a murder case. They were very good. I get a Christmas card ever year from them, so I know they are still in business."

"What am I supposed to have them look for?" asked Slidell.

"Anything and everything. See what they come up with. Now take this letter and put it in a plastic bag. I don't remember SEA's address; you'll have to look it up."

"Thank you, sir."

"Don't thank me for anything yet. You may not like what you find out." Stubblefield swiveled around and opened the cigar humidifier on the credenza behind him, just below the no smoking directive posted on the wall. As Stubblefield leaned forward to reach for a cigar, Slidell noticed the dark circles of sweat covering his back.

∗ ∗ ∗

SEA was on the fourteenth floor of a high-rise, smoked-glass building just across East Harbor Drive from the Convention Center.

The lobby was small, containing only three chairs and a low table with magazines, but offered a commanding view over the buttressed façade and winged roof of the Center, along the east coast and southern curve of Coronado, past the Coronado Bridge and the Naval base, and down to the northern tip of Silver Strand State Beach. The bay was calm; and Slidell watched as the one o'clock ferry, white as a swan in the light reflected off the water, ghosted along the shore. The inner door of the lobby opened and a tall, young woman stood under the lintel smiling at Slidell. She wore a white linen jacket with the letters SEA embroidered in red script above the left breast pocket and held a glass vial in her right hand.

"May I help you?" She transferred the vial to her left hand, wiped her right hand on her jacket and then offered it to Slidell. Slidell hesitated a moment before taking her hand to shake it and resisted the urge to wipe his own hand afterwards. God only knew what was in that vial.

"I'm Tabitha. We all do double duty of some kind around here. No receptionist. What can we do for you?"

"Captain Slidell. I'm here to see Ben Harrington."

"Sure, right this way." Tabitha stepped aside and ushered Slidell through the door with a slight bow and low sweep of her left hand, still clutching the vial.

"That's him over there by the ultraviolet spectrophotometer." Slidell stared ahead, down rows of what looked like ovens, microscopes, refrigerators, computer screens, and blenders. Standing in front of this equipment were six white-coated men and women. "Oh sorry. Third guy on the left." Then she shouted down the aisle, "Ben. Captain Slidell. He's here to see you."

A grey-bearded, bald, late-middle-aged man looked up, waved, and walked toward Slidell. He had a limp, a slight drag of his right leg; and Slidell noticed that his left arm was held close to his side. When he reached Slidell, Slidell extended his right hand; but instead of shaking it, Harrington wrapped his hand over Slidell's and gave it a slow squeeze.

"Good to meet you," said Harrington. "Let's go in here and have a seat." Harrington pointed to a small cubicle off to the left.

Slidell sat down in a space where nothing seemed out of place. All compartments along the desk's surface and the cabinets and file boxes underneath were labeled, and the few papers next to the computer were stacked and covered by a sheet of heavy paper, marked Scientific Evidence Analysis. Like the lab, the cubicle was neat, well organized, and discrete.

"I'd take you on a tour of the lab, but you just had it," said Harrington as he settled into the chair opposite Slidell.

"I'm sorry?" said Slidell, confused.

"What you see through the door is what you get, but we got it all, including gas chromatograph / mass spectrometers, a gas chromatograph / Fourier transform-infrared spectrometer, an ultraviolet spectrophotometer, a pyrolysis-gas chromatograph, a Fourier transform infrared spectrometer microscope, a visible light microspectrophotometer, a polarized light comparison microscope, a robot for DNA extraction and purification, an automated DNA quantifier, and four genetic analyzers." Harrington rattled off the complicated names of the equipment as if he were reciting the alphabet. "Hell, we do DNA analysis, biochemical hazard and explosives detection, latent fingerprint identification, analyses of handwriting, and recognition of document alteration, counterfeiting, and forgeries. Plus, sixty-eight law enforcement agencies in twenty-four states use our services, not to mention private detective agencies, law firms, and, of course, the Marines."

"Impressive," said Slidell, not understanding a word Harrington said about the lab's equipment but daunted by the sound of the names.

"You bet it is. You've come to the right place."

"So, how's the big guy?" said Harrington changing the subject. Before Slidell could answer, he continued, "You said in your phone call that Stubblefield had recommended me. I remember his case very well. Our analysis helped get his client out of a murder charge, a Marine accused of killing his wife after he found out she was cheating on him while he was deployed. Turned out it was her boyfriend. We helped prove it." Harrington was quiet for a moment as a smile slowly spread across his round face, his grey-streaked eyebrows rising slightly, and then shook his head quickly as if clearing his mind.

"So, what brings you here?"

Slidell opened his briefcase and removed the plastic bag with the envelope and letter. He handed it to Harrington who held it up and began to examine it.

"I need as complete an analysis of that envelope and the pages of that letter as you can make, but one thing first," said Slidell. He took out another piece of paper from his briefcase and laid it on the desk top. I need you to sign this.

"What is it?" asked Harrington, still examining the letter through the plastic bag and ignoring the paper beside him.

"It is a document stating that, under penalty of federal law, you and your employees or agents will not disclose to anyone other than Colonel Stubblefield or me the contents of that letter or the results of any analysis of it."

"That's not really necessary," said Harrington looking around the bag and at Slidell. "Everything we do here is strictly confidential and protected. If it weren't, we wouldn't get a lick of work."

"Be that as it may, the document must be signed in the interests of national security," Slidell insisted. The document had been Stubblefield's idea. Neither he nor Slidell were certain it was strictly legal and could be enforced. Still, whether the contents of the letter were true or not, they were volatile and if leaked "a whole mess of trouble would come raining down," as Stubblefield put it. They both hoped the document would have a chilling effect on Harrington.

Harrington whistled. "Now I really am curious," he said, laying down the letter and taking a pen from his jacket pocket. He quickly signed the paper without reading it and slid it over to Slidell.

"Is there anything in particular I should be looking for?" he asked.

"No, just everything you can tell us about it," said Slidell.

"When do you need the report?"

"ASAP."

"I can get it to you in three days, two if you pick it up yourself."

"I'll pick it up."

"Fine, see you Thursday then," said Harrington, standing up and grabbing the plastic bag.

Chapter 50

SLIDELL'S CELL PHONE emitted a soft electronic chime, a noise he had not heard it make before. Curious, he flipped the phone open. The screen announced that he had a text waiting to be read. Another first. He had never received a text. He pressed the call button, not knowing any other way to retrieve the message; and, to his amazement, it appeared.

It was from Anna. It read, *3d movie. regal horton plaza. 6. meet us there?*

Those were the words that glowed on the screen, but the text was a puzzle to Slidell. There was no capitalization and little punctuation. The absence of capitals made the message especially cryptic. Was 3d a misspelling of 3rd, and did Anna want to see the third movie on a theater marquee somewhere or did Anna mean 3D as in three dimensional movie? Slidell knew of the Horton Plaza in San Diego, but was *regal* an adjective and was there a Regal Horton Plaza in addition to the just plain Horton Plaza? If there was, he'd never heard of it. Or was *regal* a noun and was Anna referring to a movie theater, the Regal at Horton Plaza? He'd never heard of that either. It was confusing.

Slidell thought of calling Candice and asking for clarification, but he backed away from that thought. Candice had not extended the invitation; Anna had. And Anna had chosen to communicate with him in the way she communicated with her friends, by texting. Maybe he was reading too much into a simple message, but he felt that it was important that he respond to her in the same way, not by calling her mother but by texting her back. Oddly, Anna choosing to text him—even more than the invitation itself—felt like a new link in their relationship, and he wanted to acknowledge and strengthen that link.

Now a new problem, how to do it.

Reply hovered on the bottom of the screen above the talk button on the keypad. Slidell pressed the talk button and the display screen blinked. In place of Anna's text was a blank screen with *Enter Message* above it and *Send* below it. Letters were on the keypad but arranged in groups of three or four on the same keypads as the numbers. He wanted to type *s* but *s* trailed at the end of *pqr* following the number 7. How in the hell was he supposed to single out the letters he needed? Slidell intuitively pressed the 7 button and the letter *p* jumped on the screen. He pressed 7 again and *q* replaced *p*. So that was it, keep pressing a number until you got the letter you wanted. If someone had explained to him that to type a letter you had to press a number, he would have rejected the idea of texting as bizarre and unworkable. Yet, he had discovered the technique on his own, and it worked. Tapping his thumbs over the keypad he managed to compose,

See you there.

Slidell hit the key below *Send* and watched a cartoon of a envelope flying from a mailbox and the words *Message Sent* flash on the screen. Instantly, his phone chimed. It was another text from Anna. He pressed the talk button and read, *great! cant wait* :-)

Pretty cool, he thought, Except that he still didn't know where in the hell he was supposed to go.

Rather than attempting another text or, worse, wimping out and calling, Slidell decided to leave the base now and drive to Horton Plaza. He'd arrive early enough so that if there was no Regal theatre there, he would have time to find out where Anna and Candice were and get to them by six. He was being stupid, he knew. It would be simple to call, but he just didn't want to risk embarrassing Anna or losing face with her by revealing he couldn't understand her text. She had become too important to him.

Chapter 51

THE SEA WAITING ROOM was empty when Slidell entered. Assuming that a signal sounded inside the lab when the outer door opened, he sat down and waited for someone to come and attend to him. This time it was Ben Harrington himself.

"Come in. Come in. I've been expecting you." He ushered Slidell through the inner door and directed him to the cubicle. On its otherwise bare desk surface sat a large white envelope addressed with Slidell's name and rank and Pendleton office location.

As Harrington seated himself, he said, "Go on. Open it. You might as well read it now and ask me your questions."

Slidell picked up the envelope, lifted the flap and removed the report. It was thick, written in single-spaced small type; and, if the first page was any indication, crammed with technical jargon. Slidell frowned and shook his head as he flipped through the pages.

"Or, if you like, I can summarize it for you; and you can read it in detail later," said Harrington.

"That would be great," said Slidell, setting the report back down on the desk, scooting his chair back, and crossing his legs to get comfortable.

"The letter paper is common stock found in any office-supply store. The fiber tells it was manufactured in Thailand. The envelope paper is from the Philippines, if you can imagine that. The ink used in the writing on both the envelope and the pages of the letter is from a late model Bic pen. An analysis of the handwriting shows that the writer was under stress or maybe inebriated when the letter was written. The writer was also male and probably from the Midwest."

Slidell wondered how Harrington could possibly have discerned that from the handwriting, but decided he would read the report later to find out rather than interrupting Harrington's summary.

"There are dozens of traces of finger prints on the envelope. By our calculations, over thirty people handled this letter before it was opened. That is about right for a letter posted in the United States. None of the prints are from anyone with a criminal record. According to a print analysis, only three persons handled the pages of the letter: you, Stubblefield, and the person who wrote it, whoever that might be. In case you are wondering how we know the two sets of prints belong to you and Stubblefield, the prints of all military personnel are contained in the data bases we search."

In fact, Slidell was wondering how Harrington knew the prints were his and Stubblefield's.

"The third set is not from someone who is or ever was in the military, and they have no criminal record." Harrington paused for a moment and then asked, Helpful so far?"

"Yes, very," answered Slidell.

Harrington smiled. "Isn't it wonderful living in the modern world? Now comes the interesting part, at least for me. Pollen. There is pollen adhered to the glue of the flap of the envelope. Corn pollen. That is very unusual."

"Why?" asked Slidell, curious.

"Because this pollen is not from genetically modified corn."

"And that's unusual?" Slidell was becoming even more curious.

"You bet it is," said Harrington. "The mega agribusinesses genetically engineer corn and then market it as being pest resistant and producing higher crop yields. So far the marketing strategy has worked. A majority of farmers in the US buy genetically modified corn seed. As a result GM pollen is everywhere. But here's the down side. The agribusinesses genetically control the germination of the seeds and the chemicals that are needed to grow them. They even engineer the destruction of their corn's resistance to disease which can only be recovered through the use of chemicals they alone own and distribute. That's so they can sell farmers their seed and chemicals every year, keep them financially chained, manipulate the price of the seed, and make mega bucks. But organic farmers are breaking free from the agribusinesses by growing organic corn. Hence, no need for the bastards. Right now there are only two farms in the United States that grow corn organically on a large scale and that have found a way to prevent the cross pollination of GM corn with theirs. One is in central Illinois. The other is in western Nebraska."

Slidell uncrossed his legs and leaned forward in his chair. "That is interesting," he said.

"You're looking for the guy who wrote the letter, right?" When Slidell didn't answer right away, Harrington added, "No need to be coy, I read the letter; had to as part of the analysis."

"Yes, we need to find him," said Slidell.

"In the report are the names and numbers of two law enforcement officials that I've worked with in the past, both good men. One is in central Illinois and the other is in western Nebraska.

Maybe they can help you find him. Sooner or later a new person in town comes to their attention in some way. It's worth a try."

"Thank you," said Slidell as he stood up. "This is very helpful."

"You're welcome," said Harrington. "Be sure and say hi to the big guy when you get back to Pendleton. Tell him I appreciate the business."

As Slidell walked to his car, he felt a breeze from the bay and heard the dry rustle in the tops of the tall palm trees that lined East Harbor Drive. He thought to himself how it must sound like stalks of corn blowing in the winds that sweep over the prairie.

Chapter 52

A S HE LOOKED at the picture of the young man on his computer screen, Slidell held the phone to his ear, waiting for the person on the other end to speak. Seated at a small table in a café at the San Diego Zoo, Anderson was smiling, his black hair the stylish tussle currently popular with men professionally on the make, his tee-shirt stretched tight over the muscles of his chest and biceps, and his long, handsome face tilted back as if he were about to laugh. The attitude of his body in relation to the table denoted a laziness at odds with his obvious vigor, much like a resting lion. Slidell had asked Fallon if she had any pictures of Anderson and when she said that she did, he had engaged in a ruse to get one from her. He did not want her to know about the letter yet. He had told her that he needed the photo because Candice's brother thought he might know Anderson from college, and he wanted to check it out. Fallon had acted suspicious of his request, but she had emailed him this picture from the photo gallery on her computer. She had taken it when she and Anderson had spent the day at the zoo.

When Slidell had returned to base from San Diego after getting the report on Anderson's letter, he had immediately called the two

telephone numbers Harrington had given him. The law enforcement official in Illinois had no information about anyone new in his
area who might be Anderson, but the call to Nebraska proved
promising. Sheriff Daryl Worth of Cheyenne County informed him
that the body of a young man had been in the morgue in the
basement of Sidney Nebraska's one and only hospital for almost two
weeks, and no one had any goddamned idea who he was. Worth had
checked several data bases for missing persons, including the FBI's
National Crime Information Center and the National Missing and
Unidentified Persons System, but found nothing. If a missing
persons report had been filed fitting the description of the body in
the morgue, it must have been in one of the hundreds of state and
private data bases available over the internet that he had not
searched. He asked Slidell for a picture and said that he would get
back to him. Slidell had emailed him the zoo photo of Anderson.

"Well, he sure as hell looks like the guy in the picture you sent me.
I've got the coroner's photographs right in front of me for comparison;
but he ain't smiling in them, that's for sure." The sudden sound of a
voice at the other end of the line startled Slidell, and he almost dropped
the receiver. "Anyhow, there can't be a positive identification unless
someone who knows him comes out here and verifies that the body is
that of Robert Anderson," said Sheriff Worth.

"I'm coming out there myself," said Slidell, "and I'm bringing
someone with me who knew him well. We can be there the day after
tomorrow. Is that okay for you?"

"It's more than okay. I could use the excitement. Last thing I did
that counted for much was serve a summons on my wife's brother
for child-support delinquency. She ain't spoken to me since; him
neither. Course, that's been rather a good thing. See you when you
get here."

*   *   *

Slidell wrestled with a dozen different ways to tell Fallon that a body resting in a morgue in a remote part of Nebraska may be Anderson's and why it was necessary that she identify the body. He finally settled on the incremental method, slowly giving her just a little bit of information at a time, and letting her digest it before telling her more. When he felt she was ready, Slidell called Fallon into his office. He had placed a chair at the side of his desk and motioned for her to sit in it. He did not want his desk to be a physical barrier between them. He began by telling her how he had received information via letter that Anderson believed his life was in danger and had gone into hiding. Without revealing too much detail, he then told Fallon about Anderson's knowledge of a DVD that was damaging to Sutton. Explaining how the letter had no credibility unless they could question Anderson about it, he summarized his efforts to find him. Finally, he revealed to her as gently as he could his conversation with Sheriff Worth. Fallon had at first appeared confused. As Slidell progressed, her confusion turned to an intense curiosity. But with the news from Worth, she broke down.

"Oh my god no, please no." Fallon stood up and looked around as if searching for something she had misplaced. Then she collapsed into her chair, her head down and her arms hanging limp. She began to cry.

"Sir, he tried to tell me something was wrong; but I wouldn't listen. I thought he was using me to find out things about our case with Belmonte. I shut him up, sir, before he could tell me. I broke it off between us. I should have heard him out." Fallon's arms began to tremble, and Slidell instinctively reached out to comfort her but caught himself, fearing that professionalism and the relationship between a male officer and a female enlisted person would not permit such an overt act. He felt helpless.

"The body may not be Anderson's. There's a good chance it isn't. But we have to find out." Slidell's words to Fallon did not sound comforting, even to him; but he didn't know what else to say. "I need you to be strong so that we can do this."

There was a long pause, and then Fallon took a deep breath and said just above a whisper, "Yes, sir."

Chapter 53

THE IDENTIFICATION HAD been difficult. The flight to Lincoln, Nebraska, was cramped and boring and made long by the connecting flight Slidell and Fallon had to catch in Denver. Sheriff Worth had picked them up at the airport, holding a placard in his hands with Slidell's name on it. The placard wasn't necessary. Worth wore his uniform with silver badge, hand-tooled western boots, and a large white Stetson. He couldn't be missed. Worth was older than Slidell had expected, lanky, with a weathered face that Slidell suspected he might have earned as a farmer before he was a Sheriff. He drove them directly to the hospital in Sidney. He had called ahead, and an orderly waited for them when they arrived.

The orderly led Slidell, Fallon, and Worth through the lobby and then down a metal staircase to the basement. They entered a grey, unmarked metal door at the end of a cement block corridor lit by dim, hooded neon lights that hung from the ceiling. The orderly searched his pockets looking for the key to the door and, when he couldn't find it, left the three of them alone while he went back upstairs.

Slidell could tell that the wait was having a bad effect on Fallon. He hoped that the entire procedure would be over quickly and that he and Fallon could get back to the airport and on the familiar ground of Pendleton. Now Fallon stood perfectly still, barely breathing, once again mouthing the prayer she had repeatedly murmured in the seat next to him on the plane, "Don't let it be him. Don't let it be him." The three of them simultaneously looked up to the top of the stairwell when they heard the orderly's steps echoing off the metal stairs.

"Sorry about that folks. This should work," said the orderly as he tried the key in the lock. He pulled the handle down and pushed on door with his shoulder. The door opened. "Yep, that's the one."

The room was dark and smelled of must and a sharp chemical tang. A light flickered and then held its glare, revealing a small empty space except for large, burnished-metal double doors along the left wall.

"He's in here," said the orderly. He pulled opened the doors, and the room instantly became cooler. Inside the refrigeration unit, Slidell saw three metal stretchers, arranged length-wise, one on top of the other. The middle stretcher contained a body covered by a white sheet. The orderly reached for the middle stretcher and slid it out. The vibration of its rollers made Fallon jump, but she did not take her eyes off the stretcher. The orderly bent over the corpse and grasped the top of the sheet with both hands. He then looked up at Slidell. Slidell gave a slight nod and the orderly gently pulled the sheet off the face of the body.

Fallon turned, doubled over and threw up on the floor of the morgue, heaving until there was nothing left in her gut.

*   *   *

On the way back to the airport, Fallon sat huddled in the back seat of Worth's car, a small ball of grief, while Worth and Slidell talked.

"So why were you looking for this guy, if you don't mind my asking?" Worth made a quick sideways glance at Slidell.

Slidell did not want to answer his question. But he recognized and respected the curiosity that all law enforcement officials have for everything that occurs within their jurisdiction, and he also recognized that if he didn't give an answer that satisfied Worth, then Worth would not tell him anything he knew about Anderson. And there were some things that Slidell wanted to know from him. Information was a commodity, and its exchange was the currency that purchased it.

"He was a lawyer in a case I'm involved in. He represented two Marines accused of murdering civilians. I represent the third. He suddenly disappeared." Slidell waited to see if this answer flew with Worth.

"And?' said Worth.

"What do you mean?" asked Slidell knowing exactly what Worth meant.

"And so why were you looking for him?"

"He wrote me a letter, no return address, saying his life was in danger and he had to hide. Why he felt he was in danger has to do with the case, so I can't tell you what it was because I'm bound by attorney/client privilege. But it had to do with something he knew about, something he discovered. Sorry."

"No problem, I understand. You told me enough to be very helpful. Thanks," said Worth.

"It was clear from the body that an autopsy wasn't performed. Why not?" Now it was Slidell's turn.

"When a body is found dead in Nebraska, the county coroner has jurisdiction; and if there are no relatives to authorize an autopsy, then it's his decision. In this case, because it appeared that the deceased had taken enough pills and booze to kill Big Foot and because there were no signs of a struggle or any visible injuries or trauma, the coroner decided an autopsy wasn't necessary. He declared the death a suicide." Worth shook his head.

"But you don't believe it?"

"Let me show you something I brought with me for you to see." Worth leaned over and opened the glove compartment in front of Slidell. He withdrew something wrapped in cloth. "Here, take this."

Slidell took the cloth and knew immediately what it was.

"Unwrap it," ordered Worth.

Slidell unfolded the cloth and exposed the gun in a plastic bag. It was a Glock 19.

"We found that in the deceased's motel room under the mattress. It's been my experience to a certainty that if someone is going to commit suicide and has one of those, they use it. They don't take no goddamned pills."

Chapter 54

STUBBLEFIELD HADN'T FELT this energized in a long time, which was a pleasant surprise to him. His career as a Marine and as a JAG officer was coming to an end. Although he had thought about retirement off and on for the past several years, he had imagined it as some sort of catastrophe that befell others or a rare disease that others caught, like contracting Ebola. You read about it in the papers. You heard it on the news. It never happened to you.

But now he realized that retirement was like the common cold, everyone got the virus, including him. Time had somehow sped up; the years flashing past like a film on fast forward. And he was caught unprepared. An emotion he was unfamiliar with began to take hold of him—fear. He had never been afraid before, not as the center for a championship football team in college, not as a candidate in Marine officer training, not as a combat officer, not as a law student taking the dreaded California bar exam (he'd passed the first time), not even as a trial lawyer defending capital cases. But now he was afraid. Afraid of the beginning of the end, of getting old, of that slide into uselessness and then, god forbid, helplessness.

Who the hell coined the term 'The Golden Years?' He could see they wouldn't shine like precious metal. Instead they would be like the spreading rust on the surface of corroding steel. Stubblefield was not just depressed, he was damned depressed.

But they had found Anderson, found him dead; and he may well have been murdered, which put his letter in a new light, which put Belmonte's case in a new light, which put Stubblefield in a very fine mood. Life was looking good again. Stubblefield leaned back in the black leather chair in his den and raised his arms high into the air, feeling the muscles in his forearms and shoulders tighten as they stretched into hard, solid bands. The cracking of the chair gave sound to the silent power of his exertion. Old? Hell, he thought, he was still strong. And there was another muscle in his body that had not weakened. Viagra was not on his shopping list. He had a few good years left yet before his decline.

Stubblefield relaxed back into his chair and took a sip of strong, black coffee from the ceramic mug on the table at his side. The colorful emblem of the last combat unit in which he had served decorated the cup, and years of repeated washings hadn't dimmed it a bit. Relaxing, drinking coffee before his morning jog, he had let his mind wander over everything Slidell had told him about identifying Anderson; and as he strolled this mental landscape, he began to make connections and reach conclusions. With the discovery of Anderson dead, the Belmonte case had turned into something far beyond the defense of murder.

If it were true that Blakely was on the DVD, and if it were true that he had directed Sutton to make sure the Marines were found guilty, then the stakes in this case must be unimaginably high for someone in a position several notches above Blakely, high enough to have Anderson, and maybe Patterson, murdered to protect that information. Who that might be or why they wanted the Marines found guilty didn't matter a whit to Stubblefield right now. What mattered to him was that the tactics in the case would need to be adjusted. The playing field had changed. It was now a battlefield; and, as Stubblefield well knew, when the stakes get high in battle, the rules of engagement didn't mean shit—for either side.

Stubblefield reached into the pocket of his jogging suit and took out his cell phone. He dialed information, and got the number for the office of the San Diego police chief. He was automatically connected.

"Good morning," said a cheerful, female voice, "Office of the Chief of Police. How can I help you?"

"Would you connect me with Chief Wall?"

"I'm sorry. He's busy right now. Could I have your name and number?" said the voice, still chirping like a happy finch.

"Would you tell him that Colonel Stubblefield from Pendleton is calling. I'm sure he'll want to talk to me."

"Just a moment, sir"

A moment was all Stubblefield had to wait.

"Bernie? Is that really you?"

"In the flesh," said Stubblefield.

"How are you? It's been a while. Too long. I should've called first."

"Listen Al. Would you call me back on your cell phone?

"Sure, I guess, what's up?"

"Just call me back." Stubblefield gave Wall his number, snapped his cell shut, and waited for its familiar ring tone. It rang almost immediately.

"Al, I've never asked you for a favor, have I?" Stubblefield began talking without the preliminary of even a "hello."

"No. No you haven't, and I owe you one, big time. Hell, man, you saved my life."

"I need a favor."

"Anything, Bernie. Shoot."

"An officer of mine, Captain Charles Slidell, was picked up for DUI by one of your finest. I can't tell you why, but I think now that it might have been a set up. Can you arrange a vacation for the police officer who arrested Slidell, one that would mean he wasn't at the next court hearing. As you know, if the arresting officer isn't there in court to testify, the case against Slidell will be dismissed."

"I gocha. It's as good as done," said Wall without any hesitation. "And Bernie."

"Yes?"

"This conversation never took place."

"What conversation?" said Stubblefield.

The second number he dialed was Slidell's.

"Hello." Although it was early, Slidell sounded alert, his voice crisp.

"Chuck. It's Bernie."

"Yes, sir," said Slidell.

"You are to stay on board as Belmonte's attorney. That's an order. Find some way to beat Kowalski's motion to have you removed."

"Yes, sir," was all Slidell said before Stubblefield hung up, but Stubblefield had detected the elation in his voice.

Stubblefield eased himself out of the chair and opened the den's sliding glass doors that led out onto the deck. He stepped outside, took a deep breath and began his stretching exercises, warming up for his jog. It was a fine start to the day. He was in battle again.

*   *   *

When Stubblefield was at camp and in his office, his jog over and the last bite of his cream-filled donut swallowed, he shouted down the hall from his desk to Fallon. She eventually appeared at his door.

"Sir, you only just passed my desk a few seconds ago, and the phone also works as an intercom," she said with a quick smile.

"Don't be a smart ass Corporal. I'm fully aware of that, as you know; but I love the sound of my voice, and you need the exercise. Now get me the number for the FBI in San Diego." He dismissed her by turning his attention to the work on his desk.

"The FBI, sir?" Fallon stood at the door waiting for an answer.

Stubblefield lifted his great head and glared at her. "We're giving them Anderson's letter," he said. Fallon was gone in an instant, and he listened to the rapid clatter of her footsteps as she sped down the hall.

Chapter 55

THE DRIVE FROM San Diego to Camp Pendleton along Highway 5 was an elixir for Slidell, a visual tonic that he drank in with his eyes. The gradual rise of the Santa Ana Mountains on his right contrasted with the expanding panorama of the Pacific Ocean on his left giving him a sense of confinement and freedom, challenge and ease, a Yin Yang that opened his mind and freed his thoughts. He watched as long waves materialized on the blue surface of the water, streaking toward the beach, and imagined a brush in the hand of an invisible artist, its bristles daubed in white paint, swept over a cerulean canvas. Then he thought of swimming. He had not swum in a long, long time, not since his honeymoon. He had hardly exercised at all since Mary's death, and it was beginning to show. His stomach bulged over his belt, and his uniform fit tightly, especially under his arms and across his backside. Either vanity or laziness prevented him from buying a larger-sized uniform; he didn't know which.

Until now, his body had needed very little maintenance. He was blessed with a lithe physique and a hearty constitution, and he had taken them for granted. He lived as he wanted to live. He ate and drank anything he wished and as much as he desired. And he, when working, paid little attention to the need for sleep or regular hours. Now it was all catching up with him. He felt like shit most days. But today was different.

The phone call from Stubblefield was an awakening. It opened a road to a future for him he thought had been closed, and it provided a way to erase the specter of a past filled with failure and regret. It also made him see the selfish life he had been living. He despaired for only himself, felt only his own pain, believed he hurt only himself by his behavior. But Candice and Anna had come into his life. And with them came the budding realization that hurting himself hurt them. Stubblefield's call had transformed that nascent awareness to a wrenching, physical reality.

Slidell turned off the air conditioner and rolled down all four windows. The hot, dry air blasted into the car, before settling into a steady stream that washed over him. He felt renewed. As he drove, he began thinking of how he could prevent his removal as Belmonte's attorney and what he could do to atone for the hurt and disappointment he had caused to Candice and Anna.

Chapter 56

*H*E IS BOTH *a part and not a part of the dream. He watches as it unfolds before him like a play on a stage while he performs upon the stage, a character in the play.*

He walks on a smooth, white surface toward two figures in the distance. He is having trouble keeping his balance. He slips, falls. When he stands again, the figures are closer. He can see now that one is short and the other tall. He tries to run toward them, but the surface beneath his feet changes from white to the color of drying mud, and the smoothness turns rough and grainy. Running becomes difficult, exhausting. He feels an overwhelming urge to reach the figures. He struggles but falls again. He tries to get up but can't. The figures come toward him, slowly at first and then faster. As they approach, he sees they are a woman and a young girl. Just before they get to him, they stop. The woman is crying. They begin to speak, but he does not understand what they are saying. The woman starts screaming, and then the girl. The ground beneath them falls away, spiraling down. A vortex of sand is swallowing them. They reach out to him. He lunges and grabs their hands. He holds them tight. They hang from his arms above a black pit. And then, he lets them go. He watches as they fall, their screams improbably becoming louder as they disappear into the blackness.

Belmonte opened his eyes. He was in his cell, lying on the bed, but he could still hear the screams of the woman and the girl, piercing and primal. They were louder than even in the dream. He covered his ears with his hands to shut them out, but they drilled through his head. He tried to drown them with his own screams and realized that he was already screaming, that the screams he heard were his own and that he could not stop them.

Chapter 57

"ALL PERSONS PLEASE rise. A general court-martial convened by Lieutenant General Jonathan Wiederman, commander First Marine Expeditionary Force, Camp Pendleton, is now in session, Military Judge Gladys Tibbs, Colonel, U.S. Marine Corps, presiding." The words of the bailiff brought the court officially into session and everyone to attention.

"Please be seated. Corporal Belmonte."

"Yes, Ma'am," said Belmonte, jumping back to attention as Judge Tibbs called his name. The grating scrape of his chair along the wooden floor knifed through the small courtroom. Slidell stood up with him.

"Is it true that you do not want Captain Slidell to be you attorney?"

"Yes, Ma'am."

Judge Tibbs shifted her gaze from Belmonte to Slidell and continued to stare at Slidell as she spoke again to Belmonte.

"And is it true that you now want Mr. Kowalski to be your attorney in this case?"

"Yes, Ma'am."

"Then what is the meaning of your motion, Captain?"

"My thoughts exactly, Judge," blurted Kowalski.

The judge looked at Kowalski as if she had just noticed that he was in the courtroom. "Mr. Kowalski, when it's your turn to speak I will let you know. Until then you are to sit quietly and not interrupt me."

"Yes, Judge." Kowalski's jack-o-lantern smile slowly faded.

Judge Tibbs turned her attention back to Slidell. "Captain, before you speak, let me warn you that if I decide that you are trying to delay or derail these proceedings or are attempting to trick this court into making an appealable error with this pleading, you will be sanctioned. Is that clear?"

"Yes, Judge," answered Slidell.

"Okay, then once again, Captain, what is the meaning of this motion?"

"Judge, until your ruling on the motion for substitution, I am still Corporal Belmonte's attorney. Therefore, my duty to protect his interests continues, regardless of the motion or Belmonte's request for a new attorney." Slidell felt his confidence grow as he heard his own voice. His early uncertainty faded as he moved toward the core of his argument.

"We believe that Corporal Belmonte is not presently capable of making decisions in his own interest in this case. We believe he is suffering from Post Traumatic Stress Disorder."

"I'm not crazy, Judge," Belmonte shouted. "He's trying to say I'm crazy."

"Precisely Judge, this motion is just so much hogwash," interjected Kowalski, jumping to his feet.

"Quiet, everyone," said Judge Tibbs, raising her gavel but then quietly lowering it again when order returned to the courtroom. "Do you have any evidence for that assertion, Captain?"

"Corporal Belmonte was admitted to the hospital three days ago. He was diagnosed as suffering from a severe panic attack. Apparently this was not his first," said Slidell.

PTSD had been Candice's idea. Slidell talked to her about his concerns for Belmonte, including his loss of weight, the stress of confinement, his long silences during the client conferences, and his flat affect. She told him how his observations of Belmonte mirrored her observations of those clients she counseled who had suffered from PTSD, observations such as emotional numbing, self-destructive behavior, hopeless, and even mental paralysis. Most of the symptoms seemed to fit Belmonte.

"I have also spoken with a social worker about Corporal Belmonte's deteriorating emotional and physical states. She has informed me that they are consistent with a person suffering from PTSD. Judge, Belmonte was taken from combat to pretrial incarceration as a defendant in a capital murder case. That is more stress than most twenty-year olds could stand without trauma. I'm asking that the court appoint a psychologist or psychiatrist to examine my client and inform the court on this issue. I want to confirm that Corporal Belmonte is capable of making the important decision to seek another attorney to represent him at this stage of the litigation. I am not trying to remain as Belmonte's attorney nor am I objecting to someone else ultimately becoming his lawyer."

Slidell sat down, and, as his did, he noticed how comfortable his new uniform felt. Absent was the dread that his pants would rip as the fabric tightened around his backside when he bent over to sit down. He had tried on a size larger, but that was also too tight. He had to go up two sizes to find a proper fit.

"Mr. Kowalski, do you have a response?" asked the judge.

Kowalski rose to his feet, pushing himself out of the chair. He began to stammer, "This is contemptible, really disgraceful, a mere ploy, an argument cobbled together from pop psychology to hoodwink this court and delay the inevitable. Any fool can see that Corporal Belmonte is mentally and emotionally fit."

"Well, I hope you are not calling me a fool, Mr. Kowalski, because I cannot judge Corporal Belmonte's psychological state merely by observing him in court. From what little I know of PTSD, its symptoms may be severe but subtle. I do not want to delay this case, but I am going to appoint a psychologist to examine Corporal Belmonte." Judge Tibbs looked down at Slidell. "My warning to you still stands, Captain. Court dismissed." This time Judge Tibbs did bang the gavel on the sounding block.

After the judge had left the bench and Belmonte had been escorted from the courtroom, Slidell walked over to the table where Sutton sat glaring at him.

"Where's Anderson?" he asked.

"What?" Sutton spat out the word.

"Where is Anderson?" Slidell repeated his question slowly as if Sutton had not understood him.

"How should I know? He didn't make partner at the firm so he packed up and left. Happens all the time," Sutton responded, and turned his back to Slidell as he grabbed papers off the table and stuffed them in his briefcase.

Chapter 58

SPECIAL AGENT KEN ABBOTT bowed his head over the steering wheel of his car and said a prayer of thanks to Jesus before he entered Kinkos on his way back from Camp Pendleton to the San Diego FBI office. The pages of the Bible he and his wife had read together before he left the house that morning spoke directly to him and were guiding his life. He repeated the lines of Leviticus to himself, "If ye walk in my statutes, and keep my commandments, and do them; then I will give you rain in due season, and the land shall yield her increase, and the trees of the field shall yield their fruit." His life was bearing fruit, and he had the proof of it in the manila envelope on the seat beside him.

Abbott took his cell phone out of the pocket of his sports coat and dialed a number at the FBI headquarters in DC. When it was answered, he spoke quickly, unable to cover his excitement.

"It's Ken, sir. I have something that you should see right away."

"What is it?" The voice was low and had a slight southern accent. Abbott could sense an undercurrent of boredom. This was not the first time he had called his father-in-law during duty hours.

"It's a letter, sir. A colonel at Camp Pendleton just gave it to me. Sir, the letter is from a lawyer for two of the Marines on trial here for the murder of civilians in Iraq, and it mentions a very important person in our government. He's dead, sir. The lawyer, I mean. I think you should read it, sir."

"Who is the person it mentions?" The boredom was still there.

"Congressman Blakely, sir."

"Has anyone else in the San Diego office seen it?" The voice now revealed a hint of interest.

"No, sir. I thought you should see it first," said Abbott.

"Good. When can you send it to me?"

"Now, sir. I stopped at a Kinkos. I will fax it to you."

"Excellent. Do you have the private number for my office fax?

"I do, sir."

"Good. I'll be waiting. And Ken."

"Yes, sir.

"Don't do anything with the letter until I've read it and given you instructions. Is that clear?"

"Yes, sir."

Abbott opened the door of the car and stepped out onto the pavement of the strip mall parking lot. He stood by the car and let the heat of the sun slowly replace the chill of the air conditioning. As his body warmed, he thought how very different things were for him now. He had been a sinner. Drunkenness and debauchery ruled his life. Satan was his master—until he met his future wife. She was a student at Biola University in La Mirada, California, an evangelical Christian college. He had crashed at a friend's house on a cross-country road trip. She was also staying at the house over spring break with his friend's sister, her roommate at Biola. Slowly and surely she had led him to Jesus, and He had saved him.

They were married when he finished college; and her father, who was a senior official with the FBI, paid his way through law school and then encouraged him to apply for training as an agent. When he graduated, his father-in-law maneuvered him into the office in San Diego, bypassing a long line of other applicants. His father-in-law made clear to him why. He was to be his eyes and ears in San Diego. A rogue office politically, the entrenched FBI personnel in it had lost their way and needed to be watched. As he walked into Kinkos, Ken Abbot was about to perform his first mission for God and family as an FBI agent.

*   *   *

Andrew Benedict had come a long way since his first days as a new agent with the FBI. He was blessed. As the current Criminal, International Operations, and Services Executive Assistant Director (EAD), he oversaw the Criminal Investigation and International Operations Divisions, and the Office of Law Enforcement Coordination of the FBI. In that capacity, very few issues at the agency escaped his attention. He managed matters affecting the national security of the United States that became known to the FBI's international and domestic law enforcement partners. The information contained in the letter that his son-in-law had just faxed him fell squarely within his jurisdiction.

As each page of the letter rolled from the fax machine, he grabbed it before it fell into the tray, reading it before the next page had finished printing. He was stunned and stood by the credenza in his office and read the copy of the letter a second time. He considered it a sign. Benedict did not believe that his life consisted of random, unconnected events strung together from a universe in chaos. His life had meaning, and he was part of a larger plan. The letter had not come to him by accident, and he was humbled that he had been chosen to be an instrument in the execution of that plan.

Once more Blakely had come into his life. The first time, Arndt had persuaded him to quash the investigation of the trafficking of children for sex in the US, and Blakely had escaped the net the FBI had cast. Blakely was a sinner and abhorrent to Benedict. But he had to protect him. God sometimes chose sinners to fulfill His design for the world. Benedict reminded himself that the Bible was full of such people. Was not even King David an adulterer and a murderer?

As all devout Christians, Benedict awaited the Rapture, a time when the Bible prophesized that Jesus would come again, descending from the sky to slay the enemies of Israel, and carry up to heaven the true believers in Him, both the dead and the living. But for the prophesy to be fulfilled, Israel must survive. The rabid dogs of the Middle East lusted for the blood of Israel, and the US could not falter. The war in Iraq must be won, and for that to happen, war financing must continue. Blakely had to be allowed to accomplish that.

Benedict bent down and put the pages into the slot of the shredder beside the credenza. The appliance hummed like a satisfied cat as the paper was pulled into it. He then picked up the phone to call his son-in-law. All evidence of the letter would be obliterated and those with the knowledge of what the letter contained dealt with.

Chapter 59

SEPTEMBER RAIN. UNEXPECTED. Out of season. As much an impediment to the smooth operation of life in Southern California as an autumn blizzard in Maine. Slidell watched out his office window as low, gun-metal grey clouds scudded over Pendleton releasing their moisture and turning the dry earth to mud. He turned away in disgust and searched his office for an umbrella that he was certain wasn't there, opening and slamming drawers and looking behind filing cabinets. Without the umbrella, he would get soaked dashing to his car in the parking lot nearly a block from his office. And waiting for the torrent to abate was out of the question. The rain might continue for hours, and he was already late. It was Anna's birthday, and he had made reservations for her, Candice, and him at their favorite restaurant in San Diego. But her birthday wasn't all they had to celebrate. The DUI case against him had been dismissed, and the psychologist's report that Judge Tibbs had ordered, declared that Belmonte was suffering from PTSD and was not presently capable of making decisions in his own interests. The trial would have to be put on hold while Belmonte underwent therapy. Tonight, Slidell thought, would be like celebrating a home run hit with bases loaded. But he had to leave now, even if it meant getting drenched. Traffic would be backed up on the freeway into San Diego. It always was when it rained in Southern California.

"Try this, sir." Fallon was holding a black plastic trash bag in front of her. She had cut out holes for arms and head. "You'll look ridiculous. But it will keep you dry. Sort of."

"This didn't come from one of our garbage cans did it?" asked Slidell, taking the bag and inspecting it.

"Of course not, sir. We have extra. And take this too." Fallon handed him an empty file folder. "It's to hold over your head," she said when Slidell eyed it suspiciously.

Slidell took the folder, held it above his head, and looked up at it. "It's big enough. I think it might work. You're a genius at field expediency, Fallon."

"Have to be around here, sir. Enjoy your evening."

The ground could not absorb the downpour fast enough, and Slidell splashed through the two inches of water awash over Pendleton as he ran to his car. When he got behind the wheel and slammed the door shut, his shoes, socks, and trousers below his knees were soaked. At least the garbage bag and file folder had worked. He was dry from his waist up. As he left the main gate of the Camp, the inside of his windshield began to fog over from the moisture he had brought with him into the car. By the time he reached the entrance ramp to I-5, his vision was totally obscured by the condensation on the window.

Slidell turned on the air conditioner to lower the humidity and wiped the windshield with his bare hand, smearing the wetness and leaving filthy streaks that obscured his vision even more. He reached over to the glove compartment, opened it, and fumbled through the clutter searching for a napkin or something absorbent as he tried to keep his eyes on the road. The car behind him began to honk, short beeps and then a sustained blast. Slidell, blind now, sensed the car drift to the right and pressed his foot on the brake pedal to slow down. Almost simultaneously a huge vehicle hurtled by on the left, rocking the car and sending a thick spray of water thudding against the windshield.

Slidell fumbled for the button on the door and lowered the passenger side window. Through the rain, he saw that he was almost completely off the road and brought the car to a stop on the shoulder. The contents of the glove compartment had spilled onto the passenger seat and the floor. Among the litter, Slidell spied a small packet of tissue and grabbed it. He tore the clear plastic wrapper off with his teeth and swiped the windshield with the entire content balled up in his hand. Finally, he could see.

As Slidell passed Exit 34, a dark blue SUV sped pass him coming the other way. The vehicle was going too fast for conditions, and he followed it in his rearview mirror. The headlights of the car behind him flashed, and Slidell wondered if the driver might be warning the SUV that it was driving dangerously or signaling him that he was going too slowly. If it was the latter, then too damn bad. He didn't like driving this stretch of I-5 at night. For the next two miles, to the Exit 36, there was nothing but sand flats and marsh on either side of the freeway—total darkness. He wasn't going to speed up.

The rain was unrelenting, and Slidell had to keep the wipers at the fastest setting to get a clear view of the freeway ahead. The rhythmic slapping of the wiper blades and the steady drum of the rain on the car put him into a semi-trance, so that he was only subliminally aware of the dark blue Explorer that drifted in front of him and slowed to his speed, keeping two car lengths ahead. He was thinking of Candice and Anna and what the evening would bring when the red taillights of the Explorer brightened, and it slowed so quickly that it appeared to be driving backward. Slidell slammed on his breaks; and his car skidded, fishtailing into the SUV.

"What the hell?" Slidell shouted. The Explorer sped forward and then slowed, again keeping a distance of two car lengths between them. Slidell peered through the rain to see if he had done any damage. The rear of the vehicle ahead was dented, and he suspected that the grill of his car might also be banged up. He drove behind the Explorer waiting for the driver to pull off the road. Instead, it continued on as if nothing had happened. Disgusted and beginning to get angry, Slidell pulled into the passing lane to drive up even with the Explorer and signal the driver. But as he did, it swerved into the passing lane, keeping in front of him. Slidell jerked his car back into the right hand lane and gunned the engine, but the Explorer cut back in front of him.

"Fuck this," Slidell said out loud and took his cell phone out of his pocket to call the police to report the road rage. A slam to the rear of his car whipped his head back and knocked the phone out of his hand and onto the floor by his feet. Dazed, Slidell fought to clear his head. As he instinctively reached for the steering wheel, he was slammed back into his seat again. He felt the car shoot forward and looked up in time to see that he was being shoved into the rear of the Explorer. Slidell jammed both feet against the brake pedal, applying his full weight. The car shuttered as it slid into the rear of the huge SUV. The Explorer accelerated, and Slidell heard clanging as one or both of the front hub caps bounced behind him on the road. His steering wheel began to wobble violently as he struggled to keep control of the car. He looked into the rearview mirror and saw the car behind him, a dull grey Dodge Charger with a Baja bumper, fall back and then come toward him, gaining speed. He looked to his front and saw the brake lights of the SUV flash.

Shit, he said to himself, and wrenched the wheel to the left at the same time he pulled up hard on the parking break. The car spun into the left lane doing one complete revolution on the wet surface of the highway before winding up facing forward again. Slidell heard the screech of brakes in front of him. He stomped on the accelerator and the engine screamed as the wheels caught the road. As he gained speed, the wobble of the steering wheel changed to a steady shiver, and the car attained equilibrium.

In seconds he was approaching the Charger and could see the Explorer in front of it, moving into the passing lane. The lights of the Del Mar Heights Shopping Center just off Exit 36 were visible ahead. The drivers of the two vehicles were forming a barrier in front of him, blocking him from the exit. Slidell glanced into his rearview mirror and searched the freeway for other cars behind him. There were none, only the dim headlights of two automobiles far in the distance. So, he thought, there must be two other drivers working in concert to slow traffic down and keep it far back, giving the SUV and Charger the opportunity and isolation to engineer a wreck. Slidell knew then that the wreck was to be fatal. In an instant, his brain shifted from a mind that reasoned to an organ of nerves that only sensed. Gone were any questions of who or why. There was nothing now but each second of the present: intense, solitary, belonging only in that moment of its existence. And Slidell experienced everything that the moment brought to his senses. He could feel the intent of the drivers who would kill him. It was as if their thoughts were announced in the movements of the vehicles they drove. He slammed his foot down on the accelerator and sped toward them.

Slidell maneuvered to the center of the road. He would wait until the last second before deciding on which side to pass. The Explorer dropped back and fell behind the Charger, both now in the right lane. He was so close that spray from the rear wheels of the Explorer splattered his windshield. Slidell edged even closer then slid the car into the left lane, pushing the accelerator to the floor. But the instant his car shot forward, Slidell jerked back into the right lane, the front of his car missing the rear of the Explorer by millimeters as it swerved into the left lane to run him off the road. He gunned his engine and came up behind the Charger and parallel to the Explorer. He was on its right now, only feet away. He slowed down, holding this position, keeping behind the Charger. The Charger would brake or the Explorer would attempt to crash into him from the left. He gripped the steering wheel, holding his left foot lightly on the brake pedal and pressing his right foot on the gas as he and the other two drivers sped through the rain toward Exit 36 like military jets in tight formation. Slidell sensed them daring him to commit himself.

He waited, straining to keep the Explorer framed in his peripheral vision while fixating on the rear bumper of the Charger. A flicker on his left caused him to turn. The passenger window of the Explorer slid down and Slidell saw the barrel of a rifle leveled at him. He spun the steering wheel, sending his car hurtling into side of the SUV. Slidell's airbags exploded with the impact, smashing into his face and chest and filling the car with a thick cloud of white dust. Half conscious and unable to see, he braked and twisted the steering wheel to the right. The car skidded to a stop on the shoulder. Coughing and swatting away the dust, he searched for the Explorer. Through his shattered window he saw it against the cement freeway divider; stationary, side stove in, a front wheel flat. Slidell checked the road ahead of him. The Charger was gone. He pulled back onto the freeway and nursed his battered car toward the lights ahead.

Chapter 60

"**A**RE YOU SURE you are okay? Tell me again you are all right."
The rain slid from the roof covering the walkway in front of
Vons Grocery Store and smacked the pavement in front of him so
hard that Slidell could barely hear Candice's voice over the phone.

"Yes, yes. I'm fine. The police will be here any minute so I haven't
much time. I need you to come and get me. The car is a total wreck.
I'll fill you in on all the details when you get here. Do you know
where the Del Mar Heights Shopping Center is?"

"I think so," said Candice.

"It's off Exit 36 of the freeway. I'm in front of Vons Grocery."

"I'm leaving now."

"Can you bring me a change of clothes? I'm soaked."

Slidell had coaxed the car as far as the shopping center parking
lot before it died in a thick cloud of steam. He found his phone
under the driver's seat and dialed 911. He identified himself,
reported where he was calling from, and told the emergency
dispatcher that someone had tried to kill him on the freeway. Then
he ran to the nearest shelter to escape the rain that poured into the

car through its glassless windows. His next call was to Candice. He did not tell her someone had tried to run him off the road or worse, only that he had been in an accident and was all right.

"I love you."

"I love you too. See you soon."

He heard the sirens first, distant and piercing; and then saw the lights, bursts of red and blue that collided over the approaching police cars in halos magnified by the rain. He waved and the two vehicles weaved through the parking lot toward him, jerking to a halt in a vee formation by the curb. As their doors opened, Slidell noticed that each car was from a different town.

The first officer to reach him was young, female, and intense.

"You Captain Slidell?" she asked.

"Yes," he answered.

"We drove by the site coming up here where you said the disabled vehicle was. Didn't see a thing. About a third of a mile north from this exit in the south bound lanes, right?" She checked the pages of the note pad in her hand.

"Yes," said Slidell. "That's correct. It had a flat tire."

The second officer was male and considerably older than the first. He spoke slowly as if to a child and did not look at Slidell but at Slidell's car still steaming under a broad cone of light which shone down from one of the tall poles that dotted the parking lot.

"The state police are looking up and down the freeway, but haven't notified us that they have found the SUV or the other car. A Charger with a tube bumper was it?" he asked.

"Yes," answered Slidell.

"Looks like they were serious." the older officer observed.

When Slidell didn't offer a response, the younger officer said, "The dispatcher said there was a rifle." She then asked, "You sure about that?"

"I know what a rifle looks like, especially one that is pointing straight at me. I'm in the military," said Slidell.

The older officer smiled and then reached into his poncho and took out a battered notebook and pen. He clicked the ball point with ceremony and said, "Well, let's get down to business, shall we?"

For the next twenty minutes, the two officers alternately interrogated him, several times repeating not only some of their own questions but each others. When they were finished, the older officer offered to drive him anywhere he needed to go. Slidell thanked him and told him that his girlfriend would be by soon to pick him up. The younger officer said they would be in touch with him as soon as they heard anything, and then they left.

As Slidell waited for Candice, he couldn't shake from his mind the last question from the older officer. It was clear that both officers had concluded that he was a victim of road rage, and the older one seemed embarrassed and almost apologetic about making the inquiry. Was there anyone Slidell knew who might want him seriously harmed or dead? he had asked.

Chapter 61

B LAKELY INSTINCTIVELY GRABBED the handkerchief from the rear pocket of his suit trousers and wiped his upper lip. He cupped his hand, hiding the pure white linen. Almost immediately beads of sweat began to form again. The nervous tick was a curse, a signal flag raised high announcing to the world an otherwise hidden fear. He sat alone in his private office beneath the Old Executive Office Building. He would not leave until his fear was under control, until the sweating stopped.

The call from Benedict had been terse. He wanted to meet and meet now, no excuses or delays. Their meeting had been short and without congenialities. Benedict showed him the copy of Anderson's letter to Slidell. When he had finished reading it, Benedict explained how it had come into his possession and told him that it would be taken care of, that nothing would ever come of it. However, something must be done first. Then he took three dominoes out of his pocket and stood them in a line on the table between them. Benedict gently pushed the first, which toppled and fell into the second, which toppled and fell into the third, knocking it over. He shook his head slowly and set the three of them up again, but this time he took back the first domino and dropped it into his pocket, leaving just two dominoes standing. He stared at Blakely for a long moment. Then, without saying a word, he walked out of the office.

Blakely knew the meaning of the pantomime. The first domino was Sutton, the second domino was he, and the third domino was the President. For two to remain standing, the first must be eliminated, and he must be the one to eliminate it. Blakely also understood the ultimate implication of Benedict's demonstration. The third domino would never be allowed to fall.

Sutton had to be erased from the picture. Alive, Sutton could confirm the existence of a conspiracy between Blakely and him to manipulate the outcome of legal proceedings against members of the American Armed Forces. Dead, and any risk that the conspiracy might become known would die with Sutton. Blakely could simply deny that he was the second person on the disk and Sutton would not be alive to prove it. Blakely, of course, would tell Sutton about the letter and intimate that the situation was under control. Sutton was bound to learn of it anyway. But Sutton was no fool and, in spite of such assurances, would act to protect himself. He might even panic and do something foolish. Blakely knew he could not take that chance.

He sat paralyzed by the irony of his predicament. He was considered one of the most powerful men in America; yet, he had no idea of how to go about having someone killed. He had destroyed careers, irreparably damaged reputations, and shattered the finances of others. Yet, anonymously arranging a murder was beyond his ken. And he didn't think he could personally stomach it. But the meaning behind Benedict's cold silence and cutting stare was unequivocal. His own life might ultimately depend on it. He brought the linen to his upper lip and held it there.

Blakely silently cursed Sutton, and then he cursed himself. The disk was meant to keep Sutton in check, a not so subtle hint that if, for any reason, Sutton thought it in his best interest to turn on him; Blakely had the means to destroy him. But obviously things had gone wrong. Somehow he was on the disk with Sutton, and the disk had gotten into the wrong hands. For now, things were under control; and Blakely wanted them to stay that way. He decided that he should immediately inform Sutton of the existence of Anderson's letter to Slidell and convince him that it was not a threat to either of them. He did not want Sutton to learn about the letter from someone other than himself, panic, and then maybe do something very stupid. He also wanted to meet with Sutton so he could personally assess the situation with him.

Blakely balled up the handkerchief and stuffed it in his pocket. He took out his cell phone and dialed Sutton's number. Sutton answered on the third ring.

"It's me, Blakely."

"Well, hello," said Sutton, "to what do I owe this honor?"

"Robert Anderson wrote a letter to the Marine captain representing Corporal Belmonte. He saw the disk I gave you. You and I were both on it. He told the captain what he saw and heard."

"Shit," said Sutton. "How do you know this?"

"The FBI has a copy," said Blakely.

Sutton said nothing. Silence.

"It's being handled," said Blakely. "There will be no investigation. Neither of us need worry."

"Does the FBI have the disk?" asked Sutton.

"No one has the disk according to the FBI. There is just the letter," replied Blakely.

Again silence from Sutton.

"I want to meet. I'm having my staff accept a speaking engagement for me in LA next week. We can meet then. I'll call you with the details." Blakely hung up without waiting for Sutton to reply.

Chapter 62

THE CALL FROM Judge Tibbs had been a surprise. Belmonte wanted to see him, she had said, as soon as possible. She did not say why. Although it was after visiting hours, Slidell had contacted the brig officer as soon as he had hung up from Judge Tibbs and had informed him that he wanted a conference visit with Corporal Belmonte within the hour. It had been granted. He now sat in the small, claustrophobic conference room in the brig waiting for Belmonte to be escorted there from his cell. Slidell was nervous. It was absurd, but he felt like some school kid standing outside the principal's office waiting his turn to be summoned, an odd mixture of dread and perverse curiosity. It had been almost two months since the day in court that Judge Tibbs had granted his motion to have Belmonte examined by a court appointed psychologist. The psychologist's initial report to the court had confirmed a diagnosis of PTSD and had recommended therapy for Belmonte before the trial continued. Belmonte had immediately entered therapy, and now he wanted to meet with Slidell.

The door opened, and Belmonte half stepped, half stumbled into the room. He was not wearing shackles or handcuffs, but the Marine escorting him held him by the upper arm, lifting the right side of his body so that he was slightly off balance. Belmonte jerked his arm out of the escort's grasp, and the Marine backed away and shut the door.

Belmonte had gained weight and looked healthier than Slidell had ever seen him. The extra weight made him appear younger. If he were out of uniform, he could almost pass for a high school junior. Slidell couldn't help himself but calculated the effect his youthful appearance would have on the trial panel. Then he remembered that Belmonte did not want him to be his lawyer.

Slidell had been standing when Belmonte entered the room. He sat down now; and, as he did, he motioned for Belmonte to sit opposite him at the small table. Belmonte slid the chair out from the table and sat, back straight, legs bent perpendicular at the knees, and both feet flat on the floor. His hands gripped the seat of the chair. He stared straight ahead. Slidell watched Belmonte and waited for him to speak.

"My head's on straight now, sir," he said.

"What do you mean?" asked Slidell.

"I am thinking clearly now. Before I wasn't," said Belmonte.

"I still don't know what you mean," said Slidell.

"I got it all wrong. I should have trusted you, but I didn't," Belmonte stammered. "You were right about Kowalski. He just wants me to plead guilty, to go along with Alvarez and Conroy. You never pressured me, sir. Not like him. You left the choice to me. He said I didn't have a choice, that I was a dead man if I didn't plead guilty, that I could never win at trial. He put pressure on my parents too. He frightened them. My mother calls me every day now crying, begging me to take the deal they're offering me to say I murdered those civilians. I can't do it, sir. I want to go to trial."

Belmonte stopped talking and looked directly at Slidell. Slidell stared back at him but remained silent.

Remarkably, Belmonte sat up even straighter in the chair. "Sir, I want you to be my lawyer, please," he said.

"And what does the psychologist say? Are you capable of making rational decisions?" Slidell asked.

"Like I said, sir, I'm thinking straight now. He says I'm ready," said Belmonte.

Slidell permitted himself a slight smile then nodded his head, just once.

Chapter 63

FALLON LAY IN bed in her room of the women's barracks, trying to read again the same page of the novel she had been reading for the past half hour. She struggled to decipher the words, to pull the meaning from them. It was late, and she was exhausted; but she would not put the book down and sleep. She had not slept more than a couple hours a night for the past two weeks, ever since she had seen the prostrate body of Robert Anderson in the Nebraska morgue. When she slept, she dreamed of him; and, in her dreams, he was alive and they were together again. She experienced the excitement that would sweep over her when she was with him. It was all so real. Upon awakening, she could still smell him, feel the softness of his skin, and hear his voice. And then came the sudden awareness that he was dead. Each time was as if she were learning of his death for the first time. The shock tore her gut, and terror overwhelmed her. If she didn't sleep, if she didn't dream, then she might hold the terror at bay. So she embraced exhaustion and fought against sleep.

For her, their relationship had been too good to be true. She knew that it was only a matter of time before he would become bored and leave her, and then the pain would be more than she could bear. So she had drawn a line beyond which she would not let her feelings for him go. The self-discipline she had learned in the Marines had served her well, and she had not crossed that line. But now that he was gone, and gone from her forever, she found herself falling hopelessly in love with him. It was insane, but she couldn't help herself; and the pain was more than she had ever imagined.

She blamed herself. He might be alive if she had stayed and listened to him at the zoo. He had reached out to her for help. But she did not see that then. When she had walked away from him that day, she felt smug and righteous. How dare he think that he could persuade her to divulge information about a client's case? He might have fancy degrees and an actor's looks, but she was not a smitten hick. She had been certain of his motives and certain of her duty to client and Corps. Now nothing seemed certain, nothing except her belief that Robert Anderson had not killed himself.

She closed the book and, without looking, reached out and placed it on the nightstand beside her bed. Then she rolled on her side and faced the wall. In the quiet of her room, the familiar night-sounds of the barracks began to nudge at the edges of her consciousness; and almost without realizing it, she began to relax. Slowly, she closed her eyes; and, as if in prayer, she whispered her lover's name.

Chapter 64

STUBBLEFIELD LEANED HIS massive frame across the table and reached for one of the dozen bulging file folders. "So what the hell are we going to do about this?" he asked, pulling out Anderson's letter and tossing it over to Slidell. He had just finished telling Slidell about his call to Agent Abbott inquiring about the status of the FBI's investigation into the letter. Stubblefield had been told that because of the persons named in the letter, the investigation was a matter of national security, and its status could not be revealed. Further, Abbott had cautioned him not to discuss the fact that the FBI was in possession of the letter.

"This is bullshit. They've wrapped their so-called investigation inside a cloak of national security. They are not going to do a damn thing. In my mind, this proves that Anderson knew what he was talking about. Blakely is being protected. Maybe Sutton too, but god only knows why they would want to protect an insignificant slime bag like him."

"Where does that leave us?" asked Slidell.

"Up the proverbial fucking creek without a paddle," said Stubblefield. "On our own, we can't prove a single thing Anderson says in his letter. The deaths of Patterson and his girlfriend were ruled a one-car accident—losing control while driving at excessive speed. No one has a copy of the disk, and its contents are inadmissible hearsay. Anderson is not alive to testify that it once existed and that he had seen and heard what was on it. His death has been ruled a suicide by a Nebraska coroner, not a homicide. Now the FBI has deep-sixed the investigation. There's nothing we can do with it that we haven't done all ready. Face it. The damn thing is useless to us."

"Unless," said Slidell, picking up Anderson's letter.

"Unless what?" asked Stubblefield.

"Unless we do what Anderson maybe should have done to begin with," said Slidell.

"And what might that be beyond notifying the police, which essentially is what we did by bringing in the Fucking Bastards of Incompetence?" responded Stubblefield.

"We give it to a reporter, confidentially. See what he does with it," said Slidell.

"You think Anderson's wild imaginings should be made public?" asked Stubblefield.

"You don't really believe that is what his letter is, do you?" responded Slidell.

"It doesn't matter what I believe. Anderson's death was declared a suicide. He actually may have been insane and delusional. Or he may have been clinically depressed because he didn't make partner at his firm and was trying to get even with those who derailed his career. We didn't know the guy, and Fallon was smitten with him. We can't trust her judgment of him. Without any proof whatsoever of what he said in the letter, wild imaginings are all we've got," answered Stubblefield.

"But a reporter may find proof," said Slidell.

"You gotta be damn careful of reporters. You turn the wrong dog loose in the field, and he'll scatter all the birds so none get shot," said Stubblefield.

"Your meaning?" asked Slidell.

"If you're going to hunt, you better have the right dog."

Chapter 65

SLIDELL STOOD IN front of Fallon's desk and waited for her to stop typing and look up at him. He normally would have called out to her from his office in mock military gravity for whatever it was he needed; but ever since Anderson's death, the playfulness had gone out of her, and he could no longer predict her reaction to him.

"Sir?" She acknowledged his presence with the one word and kept typing.

"A while back when word got out that we were representing Belmonte, a bunch of reporters called. I spoke to one of them, but I don't remember his name. I think he was East Indian and worked for one of the national news magazines. Can you please check the duplicate telephone message pads and see if you can find his number or what might be his number?" Slidell winced. In spite of himself, he had spoken to Fallon in the soft rhythms of someone trying to sooth a nervous pet or a crying child. He wanted to be caring, not condescending. He hoped Fallon hadn't noticed.

"His name is Amarphal Singh, and he works for *Time*. I'll look for his number," Fallon answered immediately, still typing.

Looking down at Fallon, Slidell had the sudden image of a blind hatchling hunched on the ground in the grass. When a boy, he'd found it lying there in his back yard. As if sensing his presence, it struggled to lift its head and uttered a single, barely audible peep before it was still again. Slidell started to reach out and touch Fallon. For her sake and for his, he felt the need to make some kind of physical connection, to simply place his hand on her head or to stroke her hair; to tell her she'd be OK. But he stopped himself and backed away from her desk. "Thanks," was all he could say to her.

*   *   *

"Sure I remember you. You are the Marine lawyer representing Corporal Belmonte in that trial at Camp Pendleton," said Amarphal Singh.

Slidell wondered if everyone had superior memories or if he just had a rotten one.

"Your area code is 312. Where is that?" asked Slidell.

"It's a Chicago area code. *Time* has an office here to cover the goings-on in the Midwest," answered Singh.

"You are half way across the country then," said Slidell. "I was hoping we could meet in person. I would prefer that. There's something I want to show you, something that may have a great impact on the case but that reaches far beyond this case. But first we need to come to terms about certain conditions," said Slidell.

"What sort of conditions?" ask Singh.

"Anonymity," answered Slidell.

"I'll be there tomorrow. I'll call you when I arrive," said Singh, and hung up.

Slidell checked his growing feeling of satisfaction. He had held out a bone to Singh and he was running for it, but would he be the right dog, he wondered.

Chapter 66

SINGH WAS TALL, at least six four by Slidell's reckoning, had bronze skin, thick black hair cut short, and a face that radiated a permanently bemused expression, which made him seem imminently approachable. And he was young.

"I thought you'd be taller," said Slidell, shaking his hand.

Singh's faint smile spread into a broad grin that revealed the whitest, most perfect teeth Slidell had ever seen on a human being. He wondered if either or both of Singh's parents were dentists.

"Me too," said Singh, and his smile got even bigger.

"Is there anything I can get you before we start? Coffee or a soda?" asked Slidell.

"No, nothing. I grabbed some coffee at the airport in San Diego on the way to pick up the rental car. I'm good, thanks," said Singh.

"Fine. Then follow me," said Slidell turning and heading for his office.

"So, how do we begin?" asked Slidell after Singh was seated and had unslung the backpack he carried over his left shoulder and placed it beside his chair.

Singh reached into a side pouch of his backpack and took out a small notebook and pen. Then he looked directly at Slidell.

"We begin by being suspicious of each other," he said.

The directness and brevity of Singh's answer surprised Slidell. He was unsure of what kind of answer he expected, but it wasn't this. Before he could respond, Singh continued.

"You are suspicious of me because of my age and what you believe to be my inexperience. You are trying to decide if I have the knowhow and balls to safeguard your identity. I am suspicious of you or more correctly of your motives in giving me whatever information you think requires that I protect its source—namely you. I have a right to be. Protecting you may require giving up my freedom. I could be held in contempt of court and jailed if a crime has been committed, your information is relevant to the prosecution or defense of that crime, and I refuse to obey a court order to reveal the source of that information. In short, I do not want to be used for a purpose or purposes I can't condone."

The smile affixed to Singh's face now made his expression look more sardonic than bemused to Slidell. But Slidell was impressed. So far so good, he thought.

"How do we overcome our mutual suspicion?" he said.

"First, you show me whatever it is you want me to see. This will all be off the record. If either of us decides not to go ahead with this, I will not use in any way anything I learn from you while we are off the record. It will be as if we never met. Do you understand?"

"I understand as long as I can trust you," said Slidell. "How do I know I can do that?"

"All I can offer you in that regard is the known integrity of the magazine I work for and my own history as a journalist and demonstrated adherence to the ethics of the profession. A list of my writing and the prizes I have won are on the Internet. If you Google me, you will also find that I have been held in contempt of court for refusing to reveal a source." Singh held out his hands and shrugged his shoulders, acknowledging that it was not much.

Slidell stared at Singh for a long moment and then slid the manila envelope that was on his desk across to him. "Take a look at this," he said.

Chapter 67

SUTTON HADN'T SMOKED for over thirty years, but he unconsciously reached into his shirt pocket for the pack of cigarettes that wasn't there. The call had unnerved him. The reporter said he was from *Time* and doing background research on a story about the Marines on trial for murder. His questions had been innocuous at first, centering on how the citizens group called Defend Our Defenders or DOD had chosen him to represent two of the Marines. He was the best attorney they could afford, he answered. The reporter had laughed. Then the reporter asked what his relationship with Congressman Blakely was. Sutton was surprised but not thrown by the question. He answered without hesitation that they had known each other in law school and had maintained a casual friendship over the years. He had always assumed that their acquaintance was a matter of public record. It was the next question that had unnerved him.

The reporter inquired about Blakely's association with DOD. Sutton did hesitate this time, and then had angrily demanded what the reporter's questions were really about. When the reporter repeated, "background," Sutton barked an obscenity at him and hung up. Big, big mistake. The reporter would now know that he had hit a nerve with Sutton and might be on to something regarding Blakely. His questions, few as they were, were enough for Sutton to put two and two together. If *Time* was inquiring into his relationship with Blakely and into Blakely's relationship to DOD, then it knew about the disk. Anderson's missing letter had found its way to the press.

Sutton quickly assessed his situation. The FBI had a copy of the letter. Blakely said not to worry; everything was being taken care of. But *Time* had a copy of the letter. Blakely had said nothing about that so he probably didn't know yet. But he would soon enough. Then what? Anderson was dead. Now there were only two people in the world who could prove the contents of Anderson's letter, Sutton himself and Blakely. This put Blakely at risk. But the risk to Blakely would disappear with Sutton out of the picture. Then no one would be left who could implicate Blakely. Sutton knew Blakely would soon do the arithmetic. He resolved that a minus sign would not be in his future.

Chapter 68

B LAKELY YANKED THE ticket from the metal box and drove into the parking garage. He wound around the corkscrew ramp up to the fourth level where he found a parking place at the far end away from the elevator and stairway door. There were only two other cars. It was late, just 1:45 a.m., but he was fifteen minutes early for his meeting with Sutton. Sutton had chosen the parking garage on the outer center of LA when Blakely had suggested that their get-together be late, nonpublic, and out of view.

Blakely turned off the engine and reclined his seat. The steady hum of the radiator cooling fan calmed him. Through the spaces of the cement pillars that separated the floors of the garage, he could see, over the speckled hills of Silver Lake, the eerie phosphorus glow of the Scientology building and, off to the right, the ribbon of lights draping the observatory atop Griffith Park. Blakely was coming down from an adrenaline high after his speech and working the crowd. True, he had spent some time in a plush private bar with a few select campaign contributors. But that had not been relaxing. He was on stage still, performing his legerdemain by conjuring the charming, erudite, powerful yet humble man he portrayed to the public. It had sapped his energy. The stillness felt good, and the silence allowed him to think.

He had come to the right decision about Sutton. Killing him was out of the question. He simply could not do it. Instead he would assure his silence and loyalty by giving him an offer he could not refuse. He knew Sutton didn't want or need money. He had enough. Even prestige would not be a sufficient carrot for Sutton. For all of Sutton's strutting, for all his money, for all of his trappings of success, he viewed himself as despised, brilliant and talented to be sure, but still despised. What he wanted, what he craved, was respect. If he had it, and if it was real and lasting, albeit grudging, Sutton would never risk losing it. Blakely had decided that he would arrange for Sutton to become a federal judge. Sutton would be king; his realm, the court. People might still despise him, but he would have an office with genuine power and influence, and people would respect the office he held if nothing else. Long live the king, he thought and smiled to himself.

Blakely heard footsteps and then a tap on the trunk of his car. He opened the door and got out to greet Sutton. That's when he saw the gun pointing at his chest.

There was no pain. He felt as if he had been gently shoved, and he even heard himself utter a faint "ugh" as he fell back onto the front seat. It was when he tried to get up that his life dissolved into oblivion.

Chapter 69

SUTTON WAS LATE. He'd gotten to Los Angeles early enough, but had dallied too long over a five course meal at his favorite LA restaurant before slacking his thirst for the better part of two hours at a posh late-night watering hole he'd heard about and just had to visit. Now he was in a hurry. He bounced his car over a speed bump and onto the fourth level of the parking garage where Blakely had said his burgundy Cadillac rent-a-car would be. He spotted it at the far end. Sutton approached the car from its passenger side and pulled into the space beside it. He looked over expecting to see Blakely, but the car appeared empty. He scanned the rear seat, saw nothing, and looked in the front again. It was then that he noticed that the driver's door was open. Odd he thought, but perhaps Blakely got out to stretch, and he hadn't seen him when he was parking.

Sutton lowered his window and called hello. He waited several seconds for an answer, but all he heard was the popping of his engine as it cooled in the late night air. Rather than sit and wait for Blakely to return, Sutton decided to get out of his car. He opened the door, swung his legs out and onto the cement floor, and then heaved himself up. The exertion was enough to make him stand for a moment clutching the door so he could catch his breath. He called hello again and then shuffled around to the driver's side of Blakely's car. That's when he saw the two legs hanging out over the side edge of the front seat. His first thought was that Blakely was napping. After all, it was late. He held on to that thought as he stepped closer. He reached out to shake Blakely's leg and wake him. But he stopped himself. There was something odd about Blakely's legs, the angle of their bend and their stillness.

Frightened, Sutton backed away and hurried around to his car. He stood between the two vehicles for a moment to compose himself, and then he tried to peer through the passenger window of Blakely's car. The glaring neon lights on the low ceiling of the garage reflected off the glass and it took a second for Sutton's eyes to adjust. Blakely stared up at him with an odd twist to his mouth. Blood covered his chest.

"Fuck," Sutton screamed and threw himself into his car. He fumbled for his key and nearly dropped it trying to get it in the ignition. As he raced down toward the exit of the garage, he knew with absolute certainty that whoever killed Blakely was also after him.

Chapter 70

A RNDT HUNG UP from the President and looked again at the headline of the *Washington Post* spread out on his desk. The death of Blakely was practically the only news being reported in DC and across the country. Few facts were known about his death other than he had been shot, his wallet taken, and his car rifled through. The cautious speculation was robbery. Rampant speculation had him in a rented car in a parking garage late at night in LA for a sexual assignation. Political pundits were already predicting a total collapse of the President's war efforts with Blakely's death; no Blakely, no passage of the war funding bill. This last bit of public conjecture worried Arndt and prompted his call to the President. They both decided something had to be done about it quickly.

Arndt got up from his desk and walked to the window of his office. Outside, down on the streets and in the parks of DC, all appeared normal. The leaves were just beginning to show tinges of color, pedestrians wore light jackets or sweaters, and the traffic in the streets was still heavy with cabs and the cars of tourists. But unseen Washington reeled under Blakely's death. Nature abhors a vacuum, and political power abhors it even more. Even as Arndt stood at his window, he knew that forces were at work to use Blakely's death to wrench power away from the President and derail the war effort.

Hard experience had taught him that when chaos reigns, when fear and uncertainty are widespread, anything can and will be believed. And he understood well how the bold dissemination of disinformation had changed the course of campaigns, political fortunes, and party agendas. Arndt formed the theory in his mind. Blakely had been murdered elsewhere. His body taken in his rental car to the parking garage and the scene made to look like a robbery or worse, a sexual encounter gone terribly wrong. Why? Because some deranged zealot seeking capitulation with the enemy had put two bullets through his chest. Blakely was a casualty of the war every bit as much as a fallen soldier on the battlefield, a hero who had given his life defending his country, for the brave American men and women who were dying in Iraq.

Arndt grabbed a pen from the drawer of his desk and began writing the talking points he would disseminate to his party's media whores; and as he wrote, he began to imagine the public backlash in favor of the war and how Congress, hearing the rising clamor of constituents, would ultimately release the money to finance the war. He would get the funding bill passed. By god, he would.

Chapter 71

SUTTON HAD PARKED his car at the end of his block and sat low in the front seat watching. His condo was gated and manned around the clock by a doorman, a concierge, and a security guard. He was confident no one would be let in who had no business there. Yet, he continually scanned the street, searching for anyone who might be watching or waiting for him. He had arrived from LA early that morning. It was almost noon when he called the doorman to send someone outside to park his car when he pulled up in front of the entrance. He didn't start the engine until he saw a uniformed condo employee walk to the curb and wait. When he entered his unit, he immediately went from room to room closing all the curtains. He then poured himself a large glass of vodka, straight, and collapsed on his couch in the darkened living room. His hand shook as he raised the glass to his lips.

He had to get control of himself, he thought. He had to stay alert and keep focused. He could not allow fear to imprison him in his own home. And he had to admit that he was afraid. But he resolved not to fight his fear but to embrace it. His fear would keep him sharp, vigilant. And it would keep him alive. He thought of the gun in the drawer of his bedside table, a pocket pistol but a Ruger LCP .038 Auto. Concealable and accurate, it would now be his constant companion.

Sutton lifted his glass to take another gulp of vodka, but it was empty. He was surprised. The four fingers of Belvedere had had no effect on him. He got up and walked to the bar. He poured himself another glass and took a long drink. He stood for a moment feeling the 80 proof alcohol warm his throat. Then he picked up the bottle and returned to the couch.

He took a second swallow of vodka and began to consider his options. It was not his nature to go through his days waiting for whoever had killed Blakely to try and kill him. He would act to make that scenario too risky, too dangerous for the person or persons. But what action must he take? The killing of Blakely, a well known, respected, and powerful congressman, was an enormous risk, and someone had taken it, confident that their identity would never be discovered. What would make killing him, an unknown, local lawyer, too hazardous for them? Sutton could think of only one source whose power trumped Blakely's. That left out going to the federal authorities for protection in return for revealing the conspiracy Blakely had engineered and his own part in it. The federal authorities already had knowledge of the conspiracy. Blakely had said that the FBI was handling any fallout from Anderson's letter, and now he was dead. It was not inconceivable that someone in the Bureau had arranged Blakely's murder to cover up proof of the conspiracy. The final step in handling Anderson's letter logically and unquestionably would be his own murder, Sutton thought. There was, of course, the possibility that Blakely was the victim of a random, violent robbery; but Sutton would not stake his life on it.

As the vodka eased the tension in his shoulders and spread its magic down through the muscles of his back, Sutton realized how tired he was. He was tempted to lie down and let the plush cushions of his couch enfold his whole body. But he could not permit himself the luxury of sleep, not yet, not before he decided what he must do. He rose from the couch and carried his drink into the dining room. Sitting in one of the straight-backed Malacca wood chairs at the glass-top table would keep him thinking.

He next considered going to the press but almost instantly rejected the idea. The press could offer him no protection. And he remembered the call from the *Time* reporter. He was certain that the reporter either had Anderson's letter or knew of its existence. He looked down at his feet through the cut crystal of the table top. He was taken aback to see that his shoes were badly scuffed and that there was a rip through the cuff of his left pant leg. He wondered when and how that had happened. It must have been when he was running to his car after finding Blakely dead.

Then it hit him. Anderson had run, thinking he would be safe; but as Sutton himself had proven, you could never run fast enough or far enough to escape those intent on catching you. Sutton resolved not to make that mistake. He knew now what he must do. He would stay put and bargain for his life with those who wanted what he had and could keep him alive to get it.

Chapter 72

THE HUGE, FLAT-SCREEN TV flashed sporadically, filling the den in Stubblefield's home with bursts of light as the studio cameras alternately bounced from one talking head to the next. Stubblefield could not believe what he was hearing. Blakely's body was not yet cold, and already the bombasts of the news networks were lending credence to conspiracy theories by overworking their sagacious voices and mock judicious expressions.

"Far be it from me to be a fear monger, Andrew. You know me better than that, but just look at the facts. One of the most powerful men in America is shot under suspicious circumstances. The facts as we know them—sketchy as they are—suggest that his body was moved. The double shot to his chest screams of a professional execution. And he had enemies, viciously vociferous enemies in the peace, or should I say surrender, movement."

The speaker vanished and another head filled the TV screen, looking to the right and nodding vigorously.

"True, Ted, all true." The head turned, facing the camera. "But I'm just saying that we can't discount an assault and robbery. The LA police haven't completed their investigation yet, and it may be just a bit premature to…"

The first head returned, eyes drilling into the camera lens.

"Oh come off it, Andrew. That's the problem. People are afraid to tell it like it is. This is not the time for the faint of heart, not when things like this happen. Congressman Blakely was not afraid to speak the truth no matter who disliked hearing it. That's probably why he's dead now."

The camera panned back showing both heads now attached to bodies seated behind an oval studio desk.

"Are you saying…"

Stubblefield pointed the remote at the TV as if it were a gun and clicked. The room went dark, and he and Bella sat on the couch in silence.

Bella reached over and touched Stubblefield's hand.

"This is bullshit, Bel. What the hell is happening?"

"Blakely's death was a shock to everyone, darlin', they're just trying out loud to come to terms with it. Everyone's just venting," said Bella.

"It's more than that. The same crap is being spewed on almost every news network. They're trying to make the bastard a five star hero. Hell, babe, you read Anderson's letter. Blakely was a scumbag who wanted my Marines found guilty and was working to make it happen," said Stubblefield.

"You only have Anderson's word for that darlin', no other proof. You might be jumping to conclusions." She waited for the explosion.

"Don't be so goddamn naive. This isn't the time for it," he bellowed.

"Yes, Ted," she said sweetly.

Stubblefield raised his arms in mock surrender. Bella's sarcasm had not gone unnoticed.

Chapter 73

FALLON STOOD BEFORE the full length mirror in her bedroom and adjusted the wig so that no trace of her own hair showed. The wig was black, cut short; and it altered her looks completely. With the new makeup she had purchased, she could barely recognize herself. She had practiced countless times applying the makeup, fitting the wig, and changing into slacks and a blouse that tastefully complemented her new hair color and makeover. Her metamorphosis could be accomplished in just under three minutes. Perfect, she thought. She was noticeable but not memorable. And she mirrored the look of a thousand other women in San Diego.

Even the sidearm had not been a problem. She was amazed at the number of unaccounted-for and untraceable weapons scattered over the base. They had been purchased or acquired as trophies and smuggled in country by Marines returning from duty in Iraq, Afghanistan, Africa, or South America. She discovered that such arms were a common currency in camp, and she had bartered for one as easily as a school boy swopping for baseball cards.

She picked up her purse and slung it over her shoulder. She felt the weight of the weapon inside. She was ready. All she needed now was the opportunity.

Chapter 74

"I T'S SUTTON." THE two words were spoken as one, a quick chop—Izzuttin.

"I know who it is," said Slidell. "What do you want?"

"I need your help." These words were spoken slowly, one after the other, like cards being placed on a table.

Slidell held the phone to his ear, saying nothing.

"Don't hang up," said Sutton. "Nothing's free in this world. I know that. I can offer you something in return."

"There's nothing you can offer me that I could possibly want from you. Except for you to take yourself straight to hell," said Slidell.

"I can help you win your case."

"Like I said, go to hell." Slidell started to hang up the phone.

"Lose the attitude, Slidell. You owe it to your client as his attorney to hear me out," blurted Sutton.

Slidell hesitated and then said, "Maybe you're right, but I don't owe you squat."

"Like I said, lose the attitude. I know about Anderson's letter. I can only guess what he told you, but I'm certain of one thing: you need me to prove whatever he suspected might have been happening."

"I promise nothing in return," said Slidell.

"I'll take that chance. But what I have to say must be said in person, not over the phone. When can we meet?"

"If I do meet with you, I will have someone with me to witness and record your every utterance, understood?"

"If you bring Stubblefield, I won't agree," said Sutton.

"I'll bring whomever I damn well please," said Slidell.

Chapter 75

STUBBLEFIELD TRIED TO push the front passenger seat of Slidell's car farther back.

"For fuck sake, why didn't you buy a car with some goddamn legroom?"

"Why didn't your mamma have shorter kids, sir?" quipped Slidell.

"She did. My sister's six-three, and she drives a Lincoln Town Car. Now there's a vehicle with some damn room for a body's legs," said Stubblefield.

"So you think Sutton is going to admit to the allegations of Anderson's letter?" asked Slidell.

"Not all of them and certainly not to murdering Patterson. But he might tell what he believes will help us without hurting himself too much," said Stubblefield.

"Why, and why now?" asked Slidell.

"I've been wondering about that," answered Stubblefield. "I'm not sure, and I wouldn't bet the farm on it; but my guess is Blakely's death has Sutton scared, and he wants to come in from the cold. He knew Blakely and probably trusted him. He's alone now with no one to protect him. He may not trust whoever is behind Blakely. They could leave him twisting in the wind if the scheme to hang Belmonte and the other Marines comes unraveled, which it might because of Anderson's letter. He's decided to come clean about the conspiracy in return for some guarantee he won't go to prison for life."

Slidell shook his head. "So why is he looking to us to make that deal? Shouldn't he be talking to the US Attorney's office? If you're right, he is going to admit to a federal crime."

"I haven't figured that part out yet, but I'm sure he'll enlighten us as to where we fit into his warped plot to save his ass," said Stubblefield. "Now tell me once more where we are meeting the motherfucker," he added.

"Zia's Bistro. It's on India Street in Little Italy.

"Bistro? What the hell is a bistro?" bellowed Stubblefield.

"Don't worry. They have steaks on the menu."

"They damned well better," said Stubblefield as he tried to coax his seat further from the dashboard. "And we ain't paying. He is."

*   *   *

The tall rectangular windows of Zia's Bistro opened onto the streets of Fir and India, and Sutton searched the passing pedestrian traffic from his table along the far wall looking for Slidell and whoever might be with him. He had arrived late to avoid being alone at the table, waiting. He was now on his second martini, and still Slidell had not arrived. He had just resolved to leave in ten minutes when he saw Slidell and the giant Stubblefield crossing Fir. As they entered the restaurant, he waved; and a waitress brought them to his table.

"Gentlemen, thank you for coming. Sit down, please." Sutton did not get up from his chair to greet them or shake their hands.

Slidell and Stubblefield sat down, and the waitress asked if they wanted anything to drink.

"Just water for me," said Slidell.

"Coffee for me," said Stubblefield. "No pollutants. Black, please."

"One more when you get a chance, just like this one," said Sutton, raising his martini glass with one hand and pointing to it with the other.

"I hear the almond crusted salmon is delicious here," said Sutton.

"I'm a Marine. Why would I eat a fish?" said Stubblefield.

Sutton attempted a smile but couldn't tell if Stubblefield was trying to be humorous or was mocking him.

"I'm ordering steak, the biggest one they got. And you're paying, right?" continued Stubblefield.

"Certainly," said Sutton. "Order anything you like, my treat, of course."

"Look, let's dispense with the pleasantries. You said you had something to tell us that could help Belmonte. What is it?" said Slidell.

"Hold on a minute, Kemosabe. First things first," said Sutton.

"You hold on a minute, you fat fuck," said Stubblefield, leaning across the table toward Sutton until he was just inches from his face. You're insulting my Native American grandmother." The patrons at the table next to them looked over in alarm.

Sutton leaned back until his head touched the wall. "Okay. Okay. I mean, take it easy. It's just an expression." Sutton held up his hands in a gesture of defense and conciliation. "Maybe you're right. Maybe it is better to get right to the point." He waited until Stubblefield settled back into his chair before he leaned forward again.

"I know about Anderson's letter to you. I also know that without my testimony the letter is worth less than crap to you in this case. I am the only one alive who can verify the truth of what Anderson wrote."

"So you admit killing Patterson and his girlfriend and Anderson too," said Slidell.

"Anderson's speculation that Patterson's death was not an accident is just that, speculation, or more accurately the wild imaginings of a troubled mind. And Anderson's death was a suicide. But he may have gotten something right; and if he did, it would guarantee that the case against your client will end in a mistrial or dismissal of the charges against him. But you need me to verify it; in court, under oath."

The waitress arrived with their drinks and asked if they were ready to order.

"Give us another minute, Honey, we haven't looked at the menu yet," said Sutton.

When the waitress left, Slidell spoke first. "So you're saying that you entered into a conspiracy with a United States congressman to arrange the guilt of innocent Marines in a case against them? Because that's what Anderson wrote in his letter."

"I'm saying nothing yet," replied Sutton.

"What actions did you take in furtherance of the conspiracy?" asked Stubblefield.

"Make a guess as long as we're playing that game," said Sutton.

"Alvarez's and Conroy's accusations against Belmonte are bull-shit. They are an exchange for guilty pleas that you scared them into taking, and their false testimony could hang Belmonte. Bingo, three Marines guilty," said Slidell.

"You make it sound so easy," said Sutton.

"For that to be admissible evidence at trial you'd have to testify against your own clients. And if you did, you would be admitting that both you and they are guilty of suborning perjury in a military trial; not to mention your violation of almost every ethical duty to a client, including attorney-client privilege," said Slidell.

"The privilege doesn't hold if your client is committing a crime, especially if someone's life is on the line. As for me, I would be coming clean before my clients had an opportunity to lie under oath at trial; before any harm was done. My testimony would prevent a crime from taking place," Sutton countered.

"Assuming your clients didn't hold to their story and accuse you of lying," said Slidell.

"Why would I lie about something like this?" asked Sutton, genuinely taken aback.

"What do you want from us?" asked Stubblefield before Slidell could respond.

"I want to be treated in the case as a material witness whose life is in danger. I want to be housed on base at Camp Pendleton, under guard, until I testify and my testimony becomes public, very public. Then the cat's out of the bag, so to speak, and my death would only serve to confirm my testimony." Sutton saw Stubblefield and Slidell glance quickly at each other.

"What makes you think your life is in danger?" asked Slidell.

"Blakely told me to make sure the Marines were found guilty; that it was imperative they be found guilty. I know he wasn't acting on his own. He was being used. Then the FBI got Anderson's letter connecting Blakely to me and me to the Marines, and now Blakely's dead. Anderson's also dead; so right now, I am the only one who can link Blakely with the Marines. Ergo, those who want the truth of what I know put forever out of reach can only do that by killing me, just as they killed Blakely," said Sutton.

"You're insane," hissed Stubblefield who started to lean again across the table toward Sutton.

Slidell put his hand on Stubblefield's shoulder to restrain him and Stubblefield settled back into his chair. "Why is it so important that the Marines be found guilty?" he asked Sutton.

"Blakely wouldn't tell me, and he paid me enough that I didn't care," answered Sutton.

"And who wants to kill you?" asked Slidell.

"I can't answer that," said Sutton.

Stubblefield stood up and took out his wallet. "I've had enough of this," he said, and threw a twenty dollar bill down on the table. "That's for the waitress. Suddenly I'm not hungry anymore. Let's go," he said to Slidell.

"Wait," said Sutton. "What's your answer?"

"Don't call us. We'll call you," answered Stubblefield, as he and Slidell walked out of the restaurant.

"You have two days. That should be enough time. Then, no deal, and I move on to other options," Sutton called after them.

Chapter 76

NEITHER SLIDELL NOR Stubblefield spoke until Slidell merged into the traffic on I-5 off the ramp at Hawthorn Street, and they were headed north out of the city.

"That shit wants to use us to help save his miserable, fucking life," said Stubblefield.

"He may also help us save Belmonte's life," said Slidell.

"A life for a life then, but it's not even close to a tradeoff. Belmonte's a hero. Sutton deserves to be strapped to a gurney in a prison chamber with injections of lethal drugs coursing through his veins," said Stubblefield.

"Divine retribution, do you believe in it?" asked Slidell.

"What the hell are you talking about?" asked Stubblefield.

"You know. The atonement for sins. 'Vengeance is Mine,' sayeth the Lord. In the end, maybe he'll get what he deserves," answered Slidell.

"Bullshit. There can be no god when there are creatures like Sutton squirming over the planet," said Stubblefield.

Chapter 77

FALLON, OF COURSE, knew when and where Sutton would be meeting with Slidell and Stubblefield. As soon as they had left the office for their appointment, Fallon had quickly dressed in civilian clothes and taken the Greyhound bus from Oceanside into San Diego. The shoulder bag she took with her contained her disguise and the gun she planned to use twice. She had purchased only a one-way ticket. She would not be returning. The ride had taken less than an hour, giving her plenty of time to change into her disguise in the station restroom and walk the twenty minutes from Broadway to India Street. When she sat down on a bench at the courtyard fountain just outside of Zia's, she could see through the windows of the north wall the table where Slidell, Stubblefield, and Sutton sat talking. She watched and waited, slowly, methodically turning the pages of a book she held in her lap. She thought of Robert, their last moments together, his cry for help which she had ignored. She believed she was doing what was right, and he had died. Now there was no right or wrong for her, only a resolve to reassemble the world as it should be. Her reasoning was pure, her mode was simple: Sutton had murdered Robert and unbalanced the world; she would kill Sutton and return the world to equilibrium.

When Stubblefield and then Slidell stood, she closed the book and put the strap of her bag over her shoulder. As they left the restaurant and strode passed the fountain, she got up from the bench and began walking toward the entrance where two valet parking attendants stood by the door. Sutton was between them. As she approached them, Sutton handed a ticket to one of the attendants who grabbed it and hurried up the sidewalk past her toward Fir Street. Fallon hesitated. She held the gun in her hand inside her shoulder bag pointed at Sutton, but there were people behind him nudging him aside to get out of the restaurant. She decided to walk on and then double back for a clear shot. Innocent blood would not be on her hands when she turned the gun on herself after shooting Sutton.

Fallon turned around just as a cream-colored Lexus pulled up to the curb in front of Zia's and a parking attendant jumped out and held the door open. She saw Sutton dart from the entrance and push his heavy body past the attendant, grabbing the keys as he put one foot into the car. She heard herself shout "No," and she began sprinting toward Sutton. Sutton looked up at her just as she pulled the gun from her bag. He dropped his keys and plunged his hand inside his sports coat. What happened next was like a dream, vivid but unreal. Fallon heard two sharps cracks and the squeal of tires. Sutton spun and crumpled to the street. Then all was still, engulfed in a heavy silence splintered moments later by the terrified cries of people rushing in all directions for shelter. Fallon stood transfixed within the confusion. She had not fired her gun. Someone else, she realized, had shot Sutton.

Chapter 78

ARNDT HAD EXPECTED the call from al-Asadi. The chill wind that had blown down from the Hill and through the White House was now a warm, inviting spring breeze. Blakely's death had changed everything. No longer was there a clamor for cutting off funding for the war by killing the war appropriations bill. Now congressmen could not board the funding train fast enough in light of their constituents' ferocious backlash against antiwar extremists who they believed were responsible for Blakely's death. Arndt did not need al-Asadi anymore to assure passage of the bill.

"How are you, my friend?" said Arndt.

"My health is good. And you?" asked al-Asadi.

"I've been better, but I can't complain," answered Arndt.

"We must never complain. Allah provides for us even in ways we cannot understand. Is it not true?" said al-Assadi.

"The God of Abraham shelters each and every one of us," responded Arndt.

"Yes," stated al-Asadi, almost in a whisper.

Arndt waited for al-Asadi to continue speaking, but there was only silence.

"You have much on your mind," said Arndt, breaking the silence.

"Yes," said al-Asadi, again almost in a whisper.

Silence.

"Are you there my friend?" asked Arndt, honestly thinking their connection might have been broken.

"What I want to say is difficult to say," said al-Asadi finally, "to a friend."

"I'm listening," said Arndt.

"When I was very young, my mother would tell me a story. It was my favorite. I never tired of hearing it. There once was an oil merchant in ancient Baghdad who would sell oil from two large leather jars strapped to the sides of his donkey. He would walk the streets, calling for customers, and ladle oil from the jars into the bowls or casks they carried to him. He was careful to give them an exact measure for their money and to remember the number of ladles full of oil he had poured. That way, at the end of each day, he knew how much oil he had taken from the jars and how much was left for the following day. One day he ran out of oil before noon, which was impossible from his calculations. He checked the jars for leaks but found none. He refilled the jars, but again he ran out of oil much too soon. Day after day this happened. He took to staying up night after night to watch that oil was not being stolen from the jars, but no thieves came. He could not understand how he was losing oil. Eventually his business failed, and he had to take to the streets as a beggar. It was not till years later; after poverty had made him sick and old before his time, did he discover what had happened."

Al-Asadi paused and in spite of himself, Arndt asked, "What did happen?"

"It was sad, really," continued al-Asadi. "The merchant's brother-in-law, jealous of his success in business, had taken the ladle one night and replaced it, by the next morning, with one which looked exactly the same but was slightly larger. Therefore, every time the merchant served a customer, he was pouring more oil than the customer paid for. He never noticed nor suspected his brother-in-law of trickery." Al-Asadi paused again, but this time Arndt did not speak.

"The story is simple but has much to say about life, does it not, my friend?" said al-Asadi.

"I believe it may," said Arndt.

Their conversation ended a few minutes later after Arndt had pressed al-Asadi on his view of the progress of the training the US provided the Iraqi army, and al-Asadi had urged Arndt to provide him with more intelligence on the number of insurgents and their infiltration routes into Iraq. Neither had overtly mentioned the Marines on trial, yet Arndt knew that the story al-Asadi had told him was a cautionary tale meant to warn him that their deal must not be broken. Even a politically crippled al-Asadi had the power, time, and patience to frustrate or even stymie American objectives in Iraq.

*   *   *

Arndt felt exhausted. Somehow the conversation with al-Asadi had drained him of energy. He realized he was tired more often now. He kept himself in shape. He jogged every day, worked out at his gym every other day, drank very little, and ate mostly vegetables with an occasional serving of fish or chicken. But this wasn't enough to stave off the fatigue that increasingly overwhelmed him. The constant vigilance, the ceaseless skirmishing, and the eternal plotting extracted a toll. Like an aging boxer, it was taking him longer to recover from each bout in the ring. His monk-like devotion to party and office had ultimately left him isolated and bereft of true friends, a partner, or family he felt close to. He had preferred it that way, no encumbrances and no emotional ties to cloud his judgment. The Lone Ranger, but now just alone.

He also sensed his control over things slipping away. His choice of Blakely to handle the matter with the Marines had been a mistake. Things had started to go wrong, very wrong; and Blakely had not been able to handle the situation. Benedict had understood that before he had, and now he was in control. Arndt wondered just how far Benedict would go to clean up the mess and to complete what he had begun.

Chapter 79

KILLING SUTTON HAD been easy. The team had worked well. All professionals. His driver's timing was perfect, and the two team members on the street had panicked the crowd with screams and shouts of misdirection immediately after the first shot was fired. No one would be able to remember the van or anything about the driver and passenger in the confusion they had generated. There had been no collateral damage; not even the valet standing almost beside Sutton had been hit. However, something strange had occurred that concerned him. A team member had seen a woman run towards Sutton just before the drive by. It was almost as if she had known what was about to happen and was trying to warn him. But that was impossible.

They had taken the van into the hills to a remote spot and had set it on fire. The heat generated by the accelerants they had used rendered it beyond identification. No one would discover the hulk for years, if ever. The team had dispersed thereafter, going back to their jobs and lives, to resume being ordinary citizens, indistinguishable from any other of the millions of working stiffs in

America. But they were special, members of a domestic sleeper cell, anonymous, highly trained, and unknown but to a select few. Assembled only in cases where the national security was threatened, they never questioned their orders.

Benedict was relieved but far from satisfied. Things had gone badly, very badly, with that Marine captain. Two members of the team had been injured in the car chase on I-5, and they were barely able to get their vehicle off the freeway and hidden before the police were cruising the area in force. The mission to kill Sutton had not made up for that failure.

Chapter 80

SINGH HAD BEGUN to equate his role as an investigative journalist with that of the one cynical member of an otherwise enthralled audience at a magic show. All magic, he knew, was misdirection and manipulation. It was the artistry of performance masking the obvious; the illusion of impossibility. While all eyes followed the magician's left hand as it rose with fingers fluttering, he kept his affixed to the magician's right as it palmed the gold coin. Where everyone else detected nothing but the bare inside walls of an upright box, he deduced the presence of mirrors simulating depth and shielding the assistant inside. Singh's purpose was to uncover the concealed and to detect the hidden.

But the Belmonte trial had turned his view of both investigative journalism and prestidigitation inside out. Where the Belmonte case was concerned, the trick and the secret of its performance were already known. It was the magician who was being concealed. Anderson's letter had revealed that the ploy was to create the illusion that the murder conviction of three combat Marine's was the end result of a duly convened and properly conducted general court-martial. Sutton's confession to Slidell just before he was killed disclosed how this deception was to be accomplished. Identifying who wanted the Marines found guilty and why were the puzzles Singh had to solve.

Singh was convinced that the deaths of Patterson, Anderson, Blakely, and, now, Sutton were meant to hide the identity of the master manipulator. He figured the magician must be someone with the power to control Blakely and to kill him if that control was lost. He also guessed that it was someone who exercised power anonymously and who possessed the means to protect that anonymity. Such people were often surrogates with little power of their own but who wielded the power of another. They were drawn to power and, like a parasite without a host, could not survive for long away from it. So, Singh had come to the center of power to look for the magician.

Washington, D.C. welcomed him with its monuments, memorials, and secrets.

Chapter 81

T HE RAIN HAD stopped. The skies of Southern California were again an infinite blue. The trial was scheduled to begin in two days; and all things seemed possible, even the successful defense of three Marines accused of murder. The word had come from Boswell, Noonan, and Clark within a few days after Sutton's death that Privates Alvarez and Conroy were not going to enter a plea and were demanding a trial. The even better word was that they wanted nothing more to do with Boswell, Noonan, and Clark, were firing the firm, and would ask the court for leave to have Slidell represent them. Slidell had agreed. Representing all three of the Marines would not change his trial strategy, would require no further preparation of a defense, and, in fact, would eliminate the anticipated bullshit accusations against Belmonte by Alvarez and Conroy. Slidell would not need a continuance to be ready for trial.

"So what do you think?" Slidell sat across from Stubblefield at the table in the small conference room of the offices of The Regional Defense Counsel and waited for his response to the draft of his opening statement.

"Too long," said Stubblefield.

"Really?" Slidell was astonished. The few typewritten pages were all that was left after days of ruthless editing.

"The closer the bone, the sweeter the meat," said Stubblefield. "You gotta slice it down to the bone, and you haven't done that yet. Hell, twice I had to banish from my debauched mind lascivious thoughts of the tight, moist thighs of a Jamaican stripper so I could pay attention. Shit, that's what you're competing with when you deliver one of these damn things to a panel in a military trial. Make it too long and everybody's mind starts to wander. You gotta pull them into your story and keep them there."

"Where the hell do I begin to slice? There's not much left," said Slidell, letting the pages fall to the table from his hands.

"Get rid of the part about the investigations. Save that for the closing argument. Bring it up in the beginning and you make that issue too important. We want to minimize it," said Stubblefield standing up.

"But trial counsel will use their opening statement to hammer home the results of the NCID investigation. We've got to respond," said Slidell.

"We'll fire back at them on that issue, but not in our opening. Save it for closing. They won't stress it that much anyway. They've too much else to cover. Ignore it, and it will lose its fizzle and go flat. Don't forget the first rule of an opening statement; spend the time telling your own story, not responding to the other guy's. If you do nothing but answer the trial counsel's opening, you just make their version of events seem more creditable, even by denying them. If our story is good, and it better be damn good, it will make the panel forget most of what the trial counsel said."

Slidell knew Stubblefield was right. Judge Tibbs had given them a lucky break concerning the Naval Criminal Investigation Division report on the deaths of the civilians. The investigators from the NCID had taken and then inexplicably lost all records of the investigation by General Maxwell. Slidell had argued before Judge Tibbs that since an arm of the prosecution had lost or maybe even destroyed evidence valuable to the defense, a mistrial should be declared or, at the very least, the results of the NCID investigation should be excluded from the trial. Judge Tibbs had rejected both arguments, but had ruled that the panel could be informed only that both investigations had been conducted, how they had been conducted, and the conclusion reached by each investigation. That meant that the panel would never hear or see the forensic evidence gathered by the NCID. Slidell now had the opportunity to argue that General Maxwell's investigation clearing the Marines was based on the most reliable evidence because it was conducted well before the NCID investigation. How strong an argument Judge Tibbs would allow him make remained to be seen, just as it wasn't yet clear how far Judge Tibbs would let trial counsel argue that the later investigation was more thorough, more objective, and thus more reliable.

"OK, I'll nix the part about the investigations, but nothing else," said Slidell, "visions of Jamaican whores be damned."

Chapter 82

"IS TRIAL COUNSEL READY?"

"Yes, Your Honor."

"Then you may begin."

Cheryl Schmidt stood, nodded to Judge Tibbs, and then turned to the panel of military personnel sitting in judgment of Corporal Samuel Belmonte and Privates Victor Alvarez and William Conroy.

"Murder in time of war is a crime. When young men and women must resort to killing to defend a way of life or life itself, then it is imperative that the killing be justified and only in furtherance of life. When the killing becomes wanton, random, or vengeful, then there can be no justification for it; and the perpetrators must be punished to preserve the way of life we cherish and, as soldiers, are sworn to protect."

Reynolds sat to the right of Schmidt and nodded in silent agreement. *The son-of-a-bitch is trying subtly to influence the panel* thought Slidell, and almost rose to object when he thought better of it. He would only draw attention to the ploy, look petty, and maybe annoy the panel with the interruption. He remained seated.

"That way of life does not condone murder. You will hear and be shown in this trial how three Marines ignored what they were fighting for. We will present you with evidence of how insurgents, by remotely exploding an IED, killed all but three members of Corporal Belmonte's squad, how the insurgents escaped the attempts of the three surviving members to kill them. You will see how for reasons personal to themselves—for vengeance—the three survivors cowardly chose innocent, defenseless civilians, beat them, and then shot them again and again until they were dead, how they took the lives of a woman, her father, and her two children—a beautiful teenage girl and a young boy.

Schmidt then began ticking off the evidence that she would present to the panel and highlighting its import to the guilt of the defendants. She eventually came to the NCID investigation.

"You will hear how a team of highly skilled experts in forensics and crime thoroughly investigated the killings and concluded that murder had been committed. This team was more experienced, trained, and thorough than were the few officers from the same unit as the Marines on trial before you today who looked into the killings prior to the NCID investigation, an investigation which was ordered soon thereafter."

Nice touch thought Slidell, Schmidt's use of the phrase 'looked into' when speaking of the officers of Belmonte's unit compared to her use of the much stronger and more credible word 'investigation' when speaking of the NCID. It would be difficult for him not to respond in his opening statement.

"Gentlemen, at the conclusion of this trial we will ask you for a verdict of guilty. Thank you," she concluded.

Schmidt sat down with an air of exhaustion. Reynolds placed his hand on her back, leaned toward her, and whispered something.

Schmidt hung her head as if in prayer. Slidell was sure the tableau was rehearsed and meant to send the message to the members of the panel of the long work in preparing the case and of the faith placed in the panel to come to a correct verdict, a verdict of guilty.

Judge Tibbs broke the silence in the court room.

"Captain Slidell, do you wish to give an opening statement?"

"Yes, Judge, I do."

"Then you may proceed."

Slidell rose from his chair and then walked around the table and stood in front of it. He preferred a more intimate atmosphere when speaking to a panel. He wanted no barriers between it and him. He would speak without notes so he would not break the connection he desired to establish with each member. He took one step forward, but only one, careful not to get too close and invade the panel's space.

"Trial counsel has told you that a woman, her father, and her two children were killed in Iraq. That is true. She has also told you that these were innocent civilians. That too is true. And she has said that those innocent civilians were killed by these three Marines sitting before you today, Corporal Samuel Belmonte, Private Victor Alvarez, and Private William Conroy." Slidell slowly gestured toward his clients. "Unfortunately that is also a sad truth." Then Slidell raised his voice and said, "But what is not true is that those deaths were murder."

Slidell made sure to make eye contact with every member of the panel. Each member now appeared to listen intently to what he was saying. By narrowing the issues in the case, by his admissions and then sudden shift in focus, he hoped he had succeeded in breaking the thrall established by Schmidt. He thought he had won the panel's attention.

"In every war, the highest casualties are borne by civilians, but especially in this war," he continued. "The evidence will show that the insurgents were using the mother and her children as human shields as they fled the burning building in which they had hidden. Corporal Belmonte and Privates Alvarez and Conroy would not have fired their weapons at the insurgents if the insurgents had not been shooting and killing Marines as they ran. Private Jorge Mendez was shot and killed by the escaping snipers as Corporal Belmonte was trying to save his life. To stop their wounded and defenseless comrades from dying at the hands of the enemy, they shot back. They shot back even though noncombatants were placed between them and their targets. The horrible irony of battle is that you sometimes have to kill to save. The impossible choice thrust upon Corporal Belmonte and Privates Alvarez and Conroy was to let their comrades meet certain death or risk killing innocents to save them. Whatever their decision, people would die."

"The Marines in their platoon had a mantra, a refrain that reflected the hard truth of war, 'You gotta kill who you gotta kill to save who you gotta save.' You have to kill to save." Slidell walked back to the defense table and stood beside his clients.

"The evidence will show that Corporal Belmonte and Privates Alvarez and Conroy attempted to avoid hitting the civilians, as they were trained to do, but that there was no hope of saving their fellow Marines unless they tried to kill the snipers who were shielding themselves with the civilians, as they were also trained to do. You will hear that the use of human shields was almost universal among the insurgents in Iraq at the time. That in order to protect our soldiers in the field, the rules of engagement sanctioned engaging the enemy in spite of its use of this appalling battle tactic.

Further, the evidence will show that the father died in the burning house during the firefight in the home and that Belmonte, Alvarez, and Conroy did not know of his existence until the Navy brought the charges they now face."

Slidell paused. Then he continued. "At the end of this trial, after you have heard and considered all the evidence, I am confident that you will enter a verdict of Not Guilty in favor of Corporal Samuel Belmonte and Privates Victor Alvarez and William Conroy. Thank you."

*   *   *

Slidell placed his cell phone next to him on the cushion, leaned back, and put his feet up on the coffee table. He spread his arms out and rested them along the back edge of the couch. He smiled. The first day of trial had gone well, better than he and Stubblefield had expected. He felt confident. Today had proved that he still had talent as a litigator and that his instincts had not deserted him.

Candice had wanted to know all about the day, and her excited questioning of him had kept their phone conversation going for almost an hour. Now he could feel himself beginning to decompress from the high-wire act of the trial.

As his body and mind calmed, exhaustion traded places with elation. A drink, he thought, just one to push back the fatigue and toast the day. He remembered where he had hidden the bottle. It was under the sink, invisible behind the green cylinder of the disposal. He imagined the weight of the glass in his hand, the sharp rattle of the ice, the breath of the whiskey filling his nose. He was strong now, tired but strong enough to stop at one. As Slidell got up from the couch, his phone rang. He bent down to pick it up and then stopped. He stood and then began walking toward the kitchen. The phone was still ringing when his hand found the neck of the bottle.

Chapter 83

STUBBLEFIELD SAT AT the defense table with Belmonte, Alvarez, and Conroy and tried a third time to call Slidell. For the third time, Slidell's cell phone immediately answered with the voicemail message. Damn, he thought to himself, where the hell is he? Judge Tibbs had ordered that the trial start promptly at 9 a.m. It was now almost 9:45 a.m. and still no Slidell. He knew he could not placate Judge Tibbs with any more excuses or pleas for patience. It was clear he either would shortly have to beg for a day's recess or, more likely, be forced by Judge Tibbs to handle the trial in Slidell's stead. Neither option appealed to him.

The door to Judge Tibbs' chambers swung open, and Stubblefield watched as Judge Tibbs strode to the bench and glared down at him. There was shuffling and the muffled scrape of clothing on moving bodies as everyone in the courtroom stood up.

"That's it," said Judge Tibbs before Stubblefield could speak. "I'm not waiting a second longer. Colonel Stubblefield, you're representing Corporal Belmonte and Privates Alvarez and Conroy at trial today. Ms. Schmidt, call your first witness."

"Judge, I'm sorry." Everyone turned as Slidell entered the courtroom. "I had a flat tire; and when I tried to notify the court that I would be late, I discovered that my cell phone was out of juice. A damnable combination of events. Never happened before. My apologies to the court." Slidell set his briefcase on the table and stood next to Stubblefield.

Judge Tibbs sat down and then slowly shook her head. Stubblefield could sense her relief in the slight drop of her shoulders. "Very well, let's proceed," she said.

As the crowd in the court seated itself, Slidell whispered to Stubblefield, "It's not what you think. I really did have a flat tire, and the battery is dead on my phone."

Stubblefield examined Slidell's face. It was clean-shaven, and his eyes were clear. Then he scanned his hands. He could see smears of grease and dirt. Last, he checked out his uniform: cleaned and pressed.

"I told you, it's not what you think. I was tempted, very tempted; but I didn't touch a drop," whispered Slidell, looking straight ahead, unsmiling, as Schmidt's first witness approached the witness stand.

"State your name and rank, please," began Schmidt.

"Lieutenant Jason Greene, ma'am." The Marine officer sat on the edge of his chair, leaning slightly forward. He was young—Stubblefield placed his age at about 25 or 26—with ginger hair and a serious face.

"You were the platoon leader of the first platoon of Bravo Company, Third Battalion of the 8th Marines in Fallujah, Iraq, on the 14th of May last year?"

"Yes, ma'am," answered Greene.

Schmidt was leading the witness and cutting corners to get quickly to the heart of Greene's testimony. Stubblefield liked that and was glad that Slidell was not objecting.

"And Corporal Samuel Belmonte and Privates Victor Alvarez and William Conroy were members of the second squad?" stated Schmidt, continuing to lead her witness.

"Yes, ma'am."

"Now, I want to direct your attention to that day, May 14, when your second squad encountered the IED."

Beautiful, thought Stubblefield. 'Encountered the IED' was like saying that a house reduced to nothing by a tornado had met with inclement weather. That should go over big with the members of the panel who were combat veterans.

"Did you receive a situation report from the squad?" continued Schmidt.

"I received several sit reps from the squad," answered Greene.

"Did you receive one after it encountered the IED?"

Great, there it is again, Stubblefield cheered to himself.

"Yes, ma'am."

"Please tell the judge and the panel about that report."

"Well, Corporal Belmonte called it in. He said that they had wounded and dead and needed medical help immediately, that an IED had blown the squad apart. I asked him how many Marines were down, and he said the entire squad except for him, Alvarez, and Conroy were either wounded or dead. He gave me the squad's coordinates and described where it was in the city. He gave me street names and intersections."

"Did he tell you that civilians had been killed?"

"Objection. Leading." Slidell stood and almost shouted the objection.

"Sustained," said Judge Tibbs. "Don't lead."

"Yes, Judge," said Schmidt.

"Did he say anything else?" asked Schmidt.

"No. That was about it," answered Greene.

"Did you go to the scene?"

"I'm sorry?" said Greene, confused.

"Did you send aid to your squad?" Schmidt tried to clarify her line of questioning.

"Yes, of course," responded Greene.

"When?"

"Immediately."

"Did you go yourself?" pressed Schmidt.

"Of course," said Greene, who seemed both surprised and annoyed by the string of questions. "I was the first one there."

"Please tell us what you saw when you got there," Schmidt pressed.

"The best way to put it is carnage. There were bodies and body parts all over the courtyard and in the area in front of the house where the first team had found the snipers. The house was burning, in full flame. You could feel the heat from the street."

"Did you see Corporal Belmonte and Privates Alvarez and Conroy?"

"Not at first. There was thick, black smoke blowing over the courtyard from the house, and they must have been covered by the smoke. I saw the three of them come out of the smoke a few moments after I exited the humvee and ran into the courtyard."

"They were not attending to the wounded?" Schmidt asked with feigned surprise.

"Objection," said Slidell.

"Sustained," said Judge Tibbs.

"Did you learn what they were doing when you got to the squad's position and could not see them?" continued Schmidt.

"You mean before they came out of the smoke, ma'am?" asked Greene.

"Yes," answered Schmidt.

"No. Things got real busy real fast, what with trying to find out who was still alive and what help we could give."

"At any time, did Belmonte, Conroy, or Alvarez tell you there had been civilian casualties?"

Slidell was on his feet immediately. "Objection, Judge."

"Counsel, I caution you again not to lead. I want that stopped. Understood?"

"Yes, Judge. I'm sorry," said Schmidt. "Lieutenant, did you learn at some time that there had been civilian casualties?"

"Yes, ma'am." Answered Greene.

"When and how did you learn of the casualties?"

"A medic from the platoon told me that he found an Iraqi woman and two kids dead in the courtyard near the house. I asked him where they were, and he took me to them."

"What did you see?" asked Schmidt.

"It was difficult to see anything where they were, the smoke was so thick. I confirmed that they were dead and then got back to helping with the evacuation of the wounded and taking care of the bodies of our dead."

"Could you tell how they died?"

"Yes, all three had been shot multiple times," answered Greene.

"Just a few more questions, Lieutenant; and then I'm finished," said Schmidt. "When you first saw Belmonte, Conroy, and Alvarez, what did you notice about them?"

"How do you mean, ma'am?" asked Greene.

"What was their demeanor, how were they acting?"

"Well, I guess you could say they were agitated. Conroy was especially jumpy. I noticed that both he and Alvarez kept looking at Belmonte whenever I asked them a question. They both seemed real nervous"

"What did you say to them?" Schmidt moved closer to the witness stand.

"I asked them if there were any hostiles in the area, who was still alive, and where the wounded were on the ground."

"How did they respond?" Schmidt looked at the panel as she waited for Greene's answer.

"Like I said, only Belmonte answered my questions. He told me the snipers had escaped and that most of the squad was dead. He also seemed very agitated," added Greene.

"Did he say anything else to you?"

"No ma'am."

"Thank you Lieutenant. No further questions." Schmidt returned to the trial counsel's table and sat down.

Lieutenant Greene stood up and started to step away from the witness stand.

"Not so fast Lieutenant," said Judge Tibbs. "Captain Slidell, do you wish to cross examine?"

"Yes Judge, I do," said Slidell. He walked around the defense table and stood just in front of it, back from the witness stand. Lieutenant Greene sat back down.

"Lieutenant, how long had you had command of the first platoon prior to May 14?"

"Three days, sir," answered Greene.

"And how long had you been in Iraq prior to that time?"

"Three days, sir."

"Before Iraq where were you stationed?"

"Quantico, sir."

"And you were completing your training at the infantry officer's course there, is that correct?"

"Objection, leading, Judge." Schmidt was on her feet.

"This is cross-examination, your honor. I'm entitled to lead the witness," Slidell responded.

"It's argumentative then, Judge." This was clearly a bullshit objection and Stubblefield wondered if Schmidt was just trying to break the rhythm of Slidell's questioning.

"Rephrase your question Captain Slidell," Judge Tibbs ordered.

"Why were you at Quantico?" Slidell asked with a shrug.

"I was completing my training as an infantry officer," answered Greene.

Stubblefield noticed two members of the panel smile. One even shook his head.

"Was the first platoon, Bravo Company, Third Battalion your first assignment?" continued Slidell.

"Yes, sir."

"You had not seen or experienced combat prior to that assignment had you Lieutenant?"

"No, sir." Greene's answer was barely audible.

'I'm sorry. I didn't hear your answer. What did you say?" said Slidell.

'No, sir," repeated Greene, much louder this time.

"Now, you have told us you were the first to reach your squad, is that correct?"

"Yes, sir."

"And you have described the scene as a carnage?"

"Yes, sir."

"Had you ever before seen men dead or wounded in battle?" asked Slidell.

"No, sir, not before this."

"What was your reaction when you first got to the scene of the battle?"

"I was stunned, sir. It took me a few seconds to understand what I was seeing, and then I began running to the bodies on the ground to see if I could help anyone."

"As you ran to the bodies, could you see their wounds?"

"Yes, sir. Some were pretty awful."

"At that time, could you tell if any of the wounded had been attended to?"

"I don't understand, sir?"

"Well, did you notice any fresh medical dressings on any of the wounds, tourniquets, or other evidence of medical attention?"

"Actually, I did, sir. A few of the wounded I saw had been bandaged and one had a tourniquet, as I recall."

"Before you saw Corporal Belmonte and Privates Alvarez and Conroy come out of the smoke, did you see any other Marines on their feet or giving aid to wounded Marines?"

"No, sir. Everyone I saw but Belmonte, Conroy, and Alvarez was either down wounded or dead."

"Then isn't it fair to assume, Lieutenant, that it was Corporal Belmonte and Privates Conroy and Alvarez who gave them that aid?"

Before Greene could answer, Schmidt was on her feet. "Objection, your honor, argumentative."

"Sustained. Careful Captain," said Judge Tibbs.

Slidell did not respond to Schmidt's objection or acknowledge Judge Tibbs' warning, but continued immediately with his next question. "Lieutenant Greene, you testified in answer to Lieutenant Schmidt's questions that the bodies of the civilians were in the smoke when you saw them, is that correct?"

"Yes, sir," answered Greene.

"That you were led into the smoke by a medic to find the bodies of the civilians?"

"Yes, sir."

"Were there also the bodies of either dead or wounded Marines in the area covered by the smoke?" asked Slidell.

Greene hesitated before he answered, thinking. "I'm not certain, sir, but I believe I did see other bodies."

Damn. Good work, thought Stubblefield. Slidell had skillfully planted doubt in the minds of the panel members. Perhaps Belmonte, Conroy, and Alvarez could not have been on a rampage killing civilians if they were attending to their wounded comrades. The sustained objection didn't count for squat. You can't unring a bell. But Greene had testified on direct that he had not found out about the dead civilians from Belmonte, Alvarez, or Conroy. It was evidence that they were hiding something; circumstantial but powerful nonetheless. Stubblefield wondered how Slidell would handle that testimony.

"Lieutenant, when you saw Belmonte, Conroy, and Alvarez coming out of the smoke, they were running into the courtyard weren't they?"

"Well, yes sir, they were."

"They were running toward where the dead and wounded Marines lay."

"They were running in that direction, yes, sir."

"And you stopped them."

Greene hesitated for a second. "I guess so, sir."

"Well, didn't you?"

"Yes, sir."

"And you questioned them?"

"Yes, sir. I had to know if there were any hostiles and, if so, where they were. I also wanted to know about the wounded."

"How long did you question them?"

"Hard to say, sir."

"Was it more than a minute?"

'Yes, sir."

"Three minutes?"

"Maybe, but not more than three minutes."

"Corporal Belmonte answered all your questions, didn't he?"

"Yes, sir."

"You didn't ask about civilian casualties, did you?"

"No, sir. I didn't think to. I was more concerned with the Marines who were injured."

"Exactly, Lieutenant, and, in fact, when you finished questioning Corporal Belmonte, he and Privates Alvarez and Conroy immediately ran to the medics and began directing them to the wounded didn't they?"

"They were helping the medics, yes, sir."

"Thinking back on it Lieutenant, wouldn't you now describe the demeanor of Belmonte, Conroy, and Alvarez during your questioning as anxious, anxious to help save their fellow Marines, rather than agitated?"

"Objection." Schmidt was back on her feet. "He's invading the province of the Panel, it and it alone must decide whether..."

"That's enough counsel," interrupted Judge Tibbs. "You are the one who opened this line of questioning on direct. Captain Slidell now has a right to explore it. You may answer the question, Lieutenant."

"I'm sorry, ma'am. What was the question?"

Slidell repeated it.

Greene lowered his head for a moment and then raised it. He turned to the panel. "No, sir," he said. "They were agitated, definitely agitated."

"Thank you, Lieutenant. No further questions, Judge," said Slidell.

Beautiful. Stubblefield was elated. Slidell had deftly given the panel an alternate, more convincing scenario for Belmonte's, Alvarez's, and Conroy's actions and had made the observations of a young, inexperienced lieutenant appear misguided. He hoped that the rest of the day would go as well.

Chapter 84

IT WASN'T EVEN noon yet, and Candice was deliciously exhausted. She had spent the last three hours in Anna's tow, zigzagging, backtracking, and leapfrogging from one apparel store to the next shopping for the all-important ensemble. Anna had insisted they go to the Fashion Valley Mall because it had all the cool stores—a Zara's had just opened there—and they could go to Numero Uno Pizza for lunch and then to the movies. It had become a tradition every year to devote a day to shopping together. However, now that Anna was older, these special days were becoming more expensive—a lot more expensive—and lasting much longer. Still Candice cherished them. Anna's excitement and enthusiasm and her inexhaustible energy made the cost and the effort worth it. Besides, Candice thought, she could catch her breath at lunch and the movies.

"What do you think, Mom? Really, tell me the truth." Anna held up the lime and rust striped top with the neck that draped over one shoulder. They were back in Nordstrom's for the third time, and Anna was modeling the top for the second.

"Honey, like I said when you showed it to me earlier this morning, you're a bit too young for that style."

"Yeah, but I'm older now than I was then, so how does it look?"

They both laughed.

"Let's try Bloomingdale's next just for fun," said Anna, still smiling as she hung the top back on the rack.

As they walked down the midway between the facing stores at the mall, Candice spotted in a window a pair of shoes exactly the style and color she needed.

"Anna, let's stop here a minute. I want to take a look at those shoes."

"Mom, those shoes are horrible. There's nothing there I could possibly wear."

"They are not for you, honey, they're for me, and they're not horrible," said Candice.

"Mom, please. I know what happens to you in a shoe store. You take hours. Can't you come back here on your own?" Anna pleaded.

"I promise I'll be quick. I'll just try on the one pair," said Candice.

"Okay, but can I go in that store while you're looking?" said Anna, pointing across the midway.

"No. I don't want us separated. I'll just be a minute."

"Mom, you can see me through the window. The clothes I want to look at are right there. See?"

Candice debated with herself about letting Anna go. She did not want to be one of those over-protective mother hens, always clucking at the chicks in her brood. She knew she had to give Anna more and more space and not smother her, but how much and when?

"Okay, but stay in sight. I mean it," she said.

"Sure thing, Mom," said Anna, and darted into the store.

Candice realized almost immediately on entering the shoe store that Anna was right about two things: She could see her, and it was going to take longer than a minute to try on the shoes and a few other pairs she spied. Twice she looked out the window to check on Anna, and both times Anna saw her and waved. The third time Anna clutched the sides of her jeans, wiggled as if pulling them on, and then held up a pile of clothes.

Candice shook her head and mouthed no, but Anna had already left for the changing room. All right, that's it, she said to herself. She had made clear that Anna was to stay in sight. Anna had disobeyed her, and now they were going home. She didn't care how much Anna protested or if the day was spoiled. She had set a reasonable limit and Anna had deliberately gone beyond it.

"Where's the fitting room?" Candice asked the first clerk she saw as she entered the clothing store.

"Over there, ma'am," said a young woman, pointing to the sign on the far wall.

At the changing-room entrance, another female employee asked Candice how many items she had.

"None," said Candice, "I'm looking for my daughter. Did you see a young girl—eleven, blond—come in just a moment ago?"

"No, I didn't," said the woman. "No one's come in for a while."

"Are you sure?" asked Candice.

"Pretty sure," responded the woman.

"Do you mind if I look?" said Candice.

"Be my guest."

Candice entered the changing room and called out Anna's name. When she got no answer, she began pushing open the doors to each stall, one after the other, until she had checked them all. Every single one was empty.

Candice fumbled in her purse until she found her phone. She dialed Anna's cell and heard Anna's ring tone coming from outside the changing room. Candice ran toward the sound, expectant and relieved but still angry. Then she stopped. Beneath a carrousel of brightly colored designer shorts, Anna's phone lay open on the floor.

"Oh my god," she said.

Chapter 85

THE CALL CAME as Slidell was leaving court.

"We have the girl." The voice reverberated as if it were bouncing off tin, sounding distant and mechanical.

"What? Who is this?" said Slidell, not sure if he had heard the voice correctly.

"Shut up and listen. I'm only going to say this once," said the voice. "We have the girl, and if you want her back you will follow my instruction to the letter."

"Who is this?" Slidell demanded.

"Last warning. Say another word and I will hang up, and the little bitch will disappear forever. There are men in certain parts of the world who believe fucking a virgin will cure them of AIDS. Girls like her can be easily swallowed in the market for blond, adolescent cunt. Are you getting my drift, Captain?"

Slidell froze, and his hands began to tremble. He tried to hold the phone to his ear without shaking.

"The Marines will plead guilty to all the charges against them, they will do it in open court, and they will do it in the next twenty-four hours, starting from this moment. You will not contact the authorities or tell anyone about this call. If you adhere to these simple directions, the girl will be released unharmed. If you don't, you will be responsible for what happens to her. Can you live with that, Captain?"

The question was rhetorical; the connection was dead.

Slidell checked his phone for the number of the caller. It had been blocked.

Slidell held the phone in front of him, staring at the screen. The sudden jangling of the ringtone startled him, and the phone almost fell from his hand. Slidell jammed the talk button and screamed, "Listen you son-of-a-bitch…"

"What? Chuck is that you?" The voice this time was Candice's, and she sounded terrified.

"Candice, I'm sorry. I thought you were someone else," Slidell stammered.

"Chuck, please. Help me, please. Anna is missing. She's gone. I lost her at the mall. No one will help. Mall security couldn't find her and has stopped looking. The police aren't doing anything. It's too soon they say. I need you, Chuck. Help me. I know something's happened to her. Please, I need you."

Chapter 86

THE TWO CALLS together had the cumulative effect of an eviscer-
ation. Slidell literally felt as if his vital organs had been ripped
from his body. He had tried to reassure Candice that Anna was OK
and would be found soon; to say the things she needed to hear
immediately to hold herself together. But he couldn't make his
words convincing and had hung up hurriedly mumbling that he was
leaving the camp and would be with her soon. He walked to his car
like the old victims of syphilis he'd seen on the streets of New
Orleans as a boy, stiff-legged, jerky, barely able to keep his balance.
He stumbled the last few steps to the car, opened the door, and
collapsed into the driver's seat. He gripped the steering wheel, took
in deep gulps of air, and squeezed his eyes shut in an effort to stop
his rising panic and to clear his head so that he could think. His
panic only increased.

Slidell sat up and opened his eyes and then squinted into the late
afternoon sun burning through his windshield. He lowered the
visor against the glare and saw, on the back of it, Candice and Anna,
cheek to cheek, smiling identical smiles at him in the photo he had

put there weeks ago. He stared at it for a moment and then flipped the visor up with a quick slap. He couldn't bear to look at it.

As Slidell sat, he became aware, casually at first and then with an intensity that surprised him, of the energy that surrounded him. It was palpable, almost electric. The rhythmic thwap of Cobra attack helicopters beat against the roof of the car as they swooped low across his vision on their way to Munn Field. Shifting clusters of uniformed men and women surged over the dry grasses. The dust in the wind brought the faint smell of diesel fumes and mess halls, metaphors, he thought, of the two universal constants of all armies: soldiers had to be moved and fed, moved and fed.

He had once embraced the Marines without reserve—*Semper Fidelis*, always faithful. He had believed in the creed. But faithfulness to duty and to the Corps had cost him Mary; and, with her death, he swore that he would never again pay such a price. Plunging Anna, a child, into a life of unimaginable abuse and consigning Candice to a living hell of never knowing what became of Anna were unthinkable, acts that would make living with himself impossible. Nothing was more important to him than the two of them. He could not exist without them. Yet, if he turned his back on his duty now, it would exact another kind of toll, one that was also far too high. Saving Anna and Candice would mean sacrificing Belmonte, Alvarez, and Conroy, relegating innocent men, boys really, to a purgatory of hard labor and isolation that, he knew, would forever rob them of their youth and promise—a living death for them, an everlasting stain upon his soul. With growing clarity, Slidell realized that he had only two options, that he must choose between them, and that either choice would destroy the lives of others and his own. *You gotta kill who you gotta kill to save who you gotta save.* The words of the mantra came to him in all their terrible irony.

Slidell started the car and backed out of the parking space just as a convoy of camouflaged MTVRs rumbled past the lot. He felt the quake caused by their bounce on the road pass through his body. He would go to Candice first and try to comfort her as he acted out a charade to hide his knowledge of Anna's plight and his involvement in her fate. Then he would do what he had to do.

Slidell's cell phone rang and hummed against his thigh as it vibrated. He stretched out his leg and arched his back lifting himself slightly off the seat to free his pocket so he could reach for it, holding the steering wheel with one hand.

"Hello," he said, fearful that it might be Candice again.

"Chuck. I wanted to tell you something before we left court today, but didn't so I'm calling to tell you now." It was Stubblefield. "I don't say this kind of thing often. Hell, I never say it. But here goes. You did well in court today, very well; and I was proud to be at your side. There, it's said."

Slidell continued to hold the phone to his ear, but there was only silence. Stubblefield had hung up.

"Shit," he said out loud.

Semper Fidelis. Stubblefield lived by the creed. And so did Belmonte, he thought. Slidell silently cursed them both.

Chapter 87

BAAN AL JARRAH SAT shoulder to shoulder with seven other reporters on the wooden bench reserved for the press in the small courtroom at Camp Pendleton where Corporal Samuel Belmonte and Privates Victor Alvarez and William Conroy were on trial for their life. The other reporters were all male, all middle-aged, all overweight, and all pale. Thin, young, and dark-complected, he stood out like a single raisin on a plate of plump, white grapes. And as far as he could tell, he was the only foreign correspondent in the courtroom. NINA or the National Iraqi News Agency had sent him to the States to cover the trial. Although young, he had two superior qualifications for the assignment: he had graduated from Al-Nahrain University College of Law in Baghdad, and he had been interrogated by CIA agents while detained in Abu Ghraib prison. Thus, he was familiar with legal systems and the effectiveness of interrogations in small rooms. So far, he had performed his job well. The trial of the Marines was big news in Iraq, and his dispatches from the courtroom were read all over the country. He had been granted a byline, and that meant that his reputation as a journalist was spreading both in the profession and throughout Iraq. He was pleased, so much so that he barely noticed the discomfort of the bench.

The door to the judge's chambers opened, and the bailiff came to attention. Everyone in the courtroom stood up as Judge Tibbs entered, climbed the stairs to the bench, and then stood behind her chair; her hands gripping the sides as if she was suspending a shield in front of her.

Al Jarrah waited for her to sit, but she did not. Instead she motioned for everyone to be seated as she remained standing. Odd, he thought. She usually takes her seat while everyone else is standing. There was something else odd, too, something not quite right; but al Jarra felt he might be imagining it and put it out of his mind as Judge Tibbs began to speak.

"Counsel, I understand you have a matter to bring to my attention?" she said, looking at Slidell.

Slidell stood. "Yes Judge. My clients wish to enter a plea of guilty. Trial counsel and I have discussed a plea agreement, and we have come to an understanding."

There was a communal gasp of surprise in the courtroom.

"Is that correct?" Judge Tibbs was now staring at Schmidt.

Schmidt rose from her chair and glanced over at Slidell. "Yes, Judge," she said.

Al Jarrah could not believe what he was hearing. The trial had been going well, very well, for the defense. He had weighed every piece of evidence submitted, analyzed the effect of the defense's cross-examination of the trial counsel's witnesses, minutely observed the panel's reaction to the testimony of the witnesses. The defense had effectively eroded the trial counsel's case and created serious doubt about the guilt of the Marines—at least in his mind—

in its own case. Al Jarrah leaned forward, intent on hearing every word.

"That's correct," answered Schmidt.

"And what is the plea, counsel?" Judge Tibbs was still looking at Schmidt and still standing.

"In exchange for a plea of guilty by each defendant, trial counsel will recommend that the court enter a sentence of fifteen years hard labor."

"And your clients agree to this, Captain Slidell?"

"They do, your honor."

"Have the defendants approach the bench, Captain."

Slidell turned and signaled the Marines to come forward. Judge Tibbs waited until they stood in a line facing her. Then she spoke.

I have been informed that trial and defense counsel have come to an agreement concerning this case. I want to make certain that each of you have been fully informed of that agreement and that you fully understand it and its consequences, so I am going to ask each of you a series of questions. Before you answer any of my questions make sure you understand the question. If you do not, you are to speak up and say so. Do you understand?"

All three Marines said, "Yes, ma'am," in unison.

"Fine. I will begin with Corporal Belmonte," continued Judge Tibbs.

Al Jarrah noticed Belmonte glance quickly at the other two Marines.

"Has your attorney explained the agreement to you?"

"Yes, ma'am," answered Belmonte.

"Part of that agreement requires you to plead guilty before me today. Do you understand?"

"Yes, ma'am."

"Has the effect of your plea of guilty before me been explained to you?"

"Yes, ma'am."

"Do you understand that the Uniform Code of Military Justice gives you the right to a trial before a military panel and that by pleading guilty you are giving up that right?"

"Yes, ma'am.

"Further, do you understand that by pleading guilty, you are agreeing to a sentence of fifteen years hard labor?"

"Yes, ma'am."

"Do you have any questions of me?"

"No, ma'am."

Belmonte had stood at attention with his head held high and answered each question in a steady voice. He gave al Jarrah the impression that he understood perfectly well what he was doing and that he was even proud of it. Good, thought al Jarrah, he would work that observation into his dispatch under the theme of, *American Soldiers Proud of Killing Innocent Iraqi Civilians.*

Al Jarrah listened impatiently as Judge Tibbs repeated her litany of questions for the other two Marines. Each parroted Belmonte's answers.

When her last question was answered, Judge Tibbs said, "I accept the agreement of counsel and the pleas of the defendants." She then stepped down from the bench and went into her chambers.

Al Jarrah waited for the bailiff's declaration of, "Court dismissed," but it never came. Instead the bailiff just stood at his post by the side of the judge's bench after Judge Tibbs had abruptly vanished.

Everyone in the courtroom remained seated for a few seconds, silent and uncertain of what to do, before the first of the reporters bolted for the door. Al Jarrah was the second person out of the courtroom.

It was only after al Jarrah had filed his dispatch that it finally occurred to him what was odd about the proceedings he had just witnessed: Upon Judge Tibbs' entry into the courtroom, the bailiff had not intoned the now familiar, "All persons please rise. A general court-martial convened by Lieutenant General Jonathan Wiederman, commander First Marine Expeditionary Force, Camp Pendleton, is now in session, Military Judge Gladys Tibbs, Colonel, U.S. Marine Corps, presiding." The bailiff had begun the court session as he had ended it—in silence.

Chapter 88

ANNA SENSED HER body from outside herself. Heavy, slow, unresponsive to her demands, it sank deeper into the darkness. She observed it, at first, with detachment and curiosity as a shadow within a shadow, without definition. As the shadow receded into the greater darkness, she groped for it, tried to pull it back; but her arms were so heavy she could not lift them. She could only watch, helpless, as the blackness began to swallow her. Something was wrong. She wanted her mother and called out to her, but no sound came. Then she tried to scream, but the only sound she heard was the faraway cry of a wounded animal.

Chapter 89

"EAST MAIN, EL Cajon." Four words spoken in not more than a second; then nothing. The mechanical voice still buzzed in Slidell's ear as he turned to Stubblefield.

"She's somewhere on Main Street in El Cajon," he said.

"That's not far, twenty minutes at most," said Stubblefield.

"Twenty minutes and a world away," said Bella.

"What do you mean, babe?" asked Stubblefield.

"Darlin', it's the weekend of the annual Mother Goose Parade. There'll be a million people there. Don't you remember we use to take the kids there when they were young?"

"Yeah, I remember it. Those fuckers have dumped her in the middle of the biggest event of the year in San Diego County. Hell, that sorry excuse for mayhem draws the largest crowd for Thanksgiving west of the Mississippi. It'll be like looking for a needle in a hay stack," said Stubblefield.

"Anna will try to get to a phone or beg someone to call Candice for her," said Slidell. "She'll tell us where we can find her."

"She will if she is in any condition to," said Stubblefield.

"You're not saying they have harmed her are you?" said Bella.

"Babe, we don't know what they may have done to her. We don't even know if she is still alive. This may be a ruse. They've never given any proof that she was alive since she disappeared." Stubblefield turned to Slidell.

"Call Candice. If Anna hasn't contacted her, then we get our asses over to that parade and start searching for her, now."

Slidell reached for his phone on the coffee table and tapped the speed dial for Candice's number.

"Yes?" she answered. The one word seemed to carry all her fatigue and worry, and the weight of it pushed down on Slidell She had not heard from Anna.

"Candice. Anna is somewhere in El Cajon. We're coming to get you."

Chapter 90

THE DRIVE INTO El Cajon was like entering a ghost town: empty streets and sidewalks. And silence. In the distance they could see the tops of huge balloons, the rubber heads of animated movie, TV, and storybook characters swaying from side to side as they were pulled forward on long, sloping lines. Stubblefield drove toward the balloons, headed toward Magnolia and Main. As they got closer, parked cars began to line the streets, sporadic at first and then jammed solid along the curbs, some even double parked or nosed up on the parkways. Siren blasts from fire engines mixed with the thrum and blare of marching bands, tapped and then pounded against the windows of the SUV. People swelled into the thousands, milling in streams that lined both sides of Main Street. And the crowd was teaming with children.

Stubblefield stopped the SUV in the middle of Magnolia Street. He turned off the ignition and yanked the handle of the parking brake. Up ahead, a half block short of the intersection with Main, was the assembly area for the parade. Flowered floats, convertibles with celebrity occupants sitting high on the top of the back seats, equestrians on nervous horses, marching bands in bright uniforms, and manic clowns in queues, waited their turn to enter Main and join the flow to Second Street.

"We start looking here," Slidell said. "She may be in the parade somehow and not in the crowd."

They had decided earlier on searching in pairs, all except for Slidell who would be alone. Stubblefield would work with Bella on the south side of Main, and Candice and Fallon would work the north side. Slidell had made sure everyone had fully charged cell phones, that they all had each other's numbers. They would be in the street with the parade, so he, Stubblefield, and Fallon wore their uniforms in case they were stopped by the police or parade security. They would look official and could act with authority, especially since they discovered that the Marine Band was marching in the parade. Slidell had exacted a promise from Stubblefield, Bella, and Fallon before they had picked up Candice. For her benefit they would act on two premises: that Anna was alive and that she was imbedded in the crowd. Slidell prayed that both were true, but he couldn't help playing out in his mind the different scenarios of how he would react with Candice if they were not. The scenes were not pleasant. They had heard nothing from Anna.

Stubblefield, Bella, Fallon, and Candice clambered out of the vehicle—no one even bothered to shut the doors—rushed to their positions on either side of the route, and began their search, half jogging, half running along the edges of the parade. Slidell hung back. He would search more slowly, probing not only the surface of the crowd but penetrating its depth, isolating groups and delineating their individual members, visually pulling Anna from the blur of humanity that surrounded him—if he could, if she were there.

Slidell stepped between a high school marching band made up almost entirely of drum lines and a float carrying a beauty queen ensconced atop a waterfall of exotic flowers. As the parade rolled on to Main Street, he immediately felt daunted. The spectators were families packed shoulder to shoulder, five and six deep, and seemed to be made up of innumerable young, blond girls, with painted faces or wearing masks of their favorite movie heroines. They would never find Anna.

The sound of the band was deafening, and Slidell decided to move to the front of the float. As he did, a man perched on impossibly high stilts and dressed as Uncle Sam almost collided with him. The man pretended to topple and lose his balance. The crowd gasped. Then the man lifted one long leg and swung it over Slidell's head. The kids in the crowd clapped their hand and roared with laughter. Uncle Sam pretended to topple again—another gasp—and then wobbled to a stop, upright. The kids jumped up and down and applauded as the man raised his top hat to Slidell, smiled, and then moved on down the street with long, punctuated strides.

The incident had somehow unnerved Slidell, and it took him a while to regain his focus. The crowd was in constant motion, people turning around to those behind them, reaching for those in front of them, sitting down, standing up, some darting into the street for the celebrity autographs, toddlers being lifted on or lowered from shoulders, babies raised high above heads; the combined energy of more than a hundred-thousand souls translated into contained chaos. Slidell tried mentally and visually to stop the movement or at least slow it down so that he could see, but the struggle exhausted him and made observing even more difficult. The crowd became a miasma of colliding shapes and colors without definition or nature.

Then an epiphany. All he had observed was the movement, the motion, the commotion. He had not been looking for the stillness. Yet, he had glimpsed it; sensed it for just a second: a hush engulfed by the din, a single leaf untouched by the breeze, a lone child not laughing, clapping, gasping, or jumping with delight. He ran back to where he had encountered the man on the stilts; and there he saw her, a thin, young figure in a Cinderella mask standing perfectly still amid the flurry around her. He walked up to the figure and raised the masked. It was Anna, staring into his face.

Chapter 91

"ALL PERSONS PLEASE rise. A general court-martial convened by Lieutenant General Jonathan Wiederman, commander First Marine Expeditionary Force, Camp Pendleton, is now in session, Military Judge Gladys Tibbs, Colonel, U.S. Marine Corps, presiding."

Judge Tibbs entered the court room and seated herself at the bench before the bailiff had finished uttering the words that officially opened the court.

"Everyone please be seated," she said when the bailiff had finished.

The day before, Judge Tibbs had issued a press release stating that a special session of the court would be held the next day at 0900 hours. All parties to the case were present. Slidell, Stubblefield, and the three accused Marines crowed the defense table. Schmidt and Reynolds occupied the trial attorneys' table. But behind the bar, in the spectator section of the court room, Judge Tibbs saw only three persons, all in the section reserved for the media. One, a rotund, balding man, she recognized as a local reporter; another was the dark skinned young man who came to court every day wearing jeans and a long sleeved, blue dress shirt—she had pegged him as a foreign correspondent; the last was an enlisted Marine in uniform whom she knew to be with the *Scout*, the Camp Pendleton military newspaper. She had hoped for more media attendance, but these three would do.

"I wish to make an announcement from the bench concerning what took place three weeks ago in this courtroom, ostensibly as an official session of the general court-martial of Corporal Belmonte and Privates Alvarez and Conroy. It was not an official session of their court-martial; it was a fabrication, a staged occurrence sanctioned by me for one purpose—to save a life. Captain Slidell supplied me with creditable evidence—very creditable evidence— that this court was under attack, attack by forces that wished to subvert the outcome of this trial and undermine the military justice system itself. In order to accomplish that end, the life of a young girl was held as ransom. To save her life and to defend against the assault on the integrity of our system of justice, all parties to this case agreed to participate in the staging that took place here. The pleas of the defendants and the pronouncements of this court at that time have no effect and do not stand. All parties to this case understand that."

Judge Tibbs paused and looked at the three reporters. She saw the jaw of the bald newsman literally drop and his eyes widen to the size of pie pans. She probably had given him the scoop of his lifetime. The young Marine, obviously confused, fidgeted with the garrison cap and note book he held in his lap. The foreign correspondent, head down, was furiously texting in spite of the bailiff's standing prohibition against the use of electronic devices in court. They hadn't heard anything yet, she said to herself.

"What I say now is official and part of this court martial. I firmly believe that unlawful command influence at the very highest levels has been asserted in this case. I am ordering that the influence be vigorously investigated and that until that investigation is concluded, this court martial will recess. I am further ordering that Corporal Belmonte and Privates Conroy and Alvarez be released from custody and returned to their units until such time as the investigation results in a finding, at which time I will issue further orders regarding their custody and the disposition of this court martial."

Judge Tibbs knew it wouldn't take long for the reporters, two of them at least, to put two and two together. The highest levels of command went beyond military commanders to civilian authority. She had publically implicated someone in the United States government in kidnapping, extortion, and treason.

Chapter 92

ARNDT SHUT THE door to his office and locked it. He stood for a moment and then turned and walked to the window. Five stories below, the streets of DC spread out into the fading light like the spokes of a wheel, the traffic sparse, the city emptied hours ago of its bureaucrats and scrambling tourists. It would be a while before a sea of young, self-important GS-somethings flooded the avenues and boulevards gladly heading toward the pricey bistros and bars to spend the tax dollars paid to them for services rendered to their country. Arndt wanted to remember the city like this: quiet, still, poised on the edge of a transition that would infuse it with new life. He wanted this to be his last memory.

He picked up the gun from his desk. What was it Benedict had said to him? He had been a good soldier; he had served his country well. Yes, he thought, his whole life had been in service to his country, and in the end to its president. No family, wife or children, no life of his own, only a life devoted to others who could greater serve the greater good. Now his death would be of service, perhaps his greatest service to his country, to his president. The media frenzy generated by the trial of the Marines had taken on a life of its own since the judge's announcement. The investigation initiated by the judge could not now be controlled. It would eventually reach to him. But it must go no farther; it must never reach the President. Benedict told him what he must do and had given him the gun. He had understood and agreed.

He put the muzzle of the gun in his mouth and closed his eyes. The white monuments of the city he loved glowed crimson in the setting sun; all was still, resting, waiting. He pulled the trigger.

Chapter 93

THE FIVE-CAR CONVOY of black Mercedes sedans sped through the streets of Baghdad rocking into turns and backtracking as it snaked along a convoluted route from the prime minister's resident to Parliament. Hakim had configured the route just moments before the convoy left the residence and had waited before the prime minister was ready to leave to pick the car in which al-Asadi would ride. He had chosen the fifth. The windows of each Mercedes were made of bullet-proof glass, and the undercarriage and sides were reinforced with steel. Riding in each car were three heavily armed men, the security guards of al-Asadi, all hand-picked by Hakim. Al-Asadi himself wore an armored vest while traveling in the convoy and carried an automatic pistol on the seat beside him.

Al-Asadi rested in the back seat of the car and reviewed the agenda for the emergency meeting of Parliament that he had convened. The joint Iraqi and American assault on Ogedi's forces had been a success. The news of the American Marines' guilt in the killings of Ogedi's family had been broadcast throughout Iraq on television and in the press and had silenced opposition to the attack on his army as al-Asadi had hoped it would. Al-Asadi had brilliantly used the announced guilt of the Marines to prove to doubters that Ogedi's accusations against the sons of Naseri for the murders were only an excuse to war against Naseri and remove him as competition for power in Parliament. However, without his army, it was now Ogedi's power in Parliament that had diminished to virtually nothing. The demise of Ogedi's influence had resulted in the rise of Naseri, a supporter of al-Asadi in Parliament. Al-Asadi had shrewdly worked to consolidate his strength with Naseri's to form a new and stronger alliance, one that would assure al-Asadi's continuation as prime minister. The plan had worked, but now things had begun to unravel. The guilt of the Marines had been revealed as a ruse to the shock of the people of Iraq. Ogedi had publically branded al-Asadi as a fool and a puppet for being used by America to bend Iraq to its will. He also called him a despot for turning the Iraqi army on its own people to preserve his power and position. More and more people were listening to Ogedi and believing his words. If al-Asadi did not quell the rising outcry in Parliament against him and his party, he would soon be thrown from power or worse. He began rereading to himself the speech he would give to Parliament. It was a good speech, he thought.

*   *   *

From the third floor window, a man watched the dust of speeding cars rise over the low, brick buildings bordering the street that paralleled his own. He waited, knowing that the cars would turn and pass below him. Soon he could hear their tires grinding the dirt of his street, and he saw the first black Mercedes pass beneath him. He counted. At the fourth car, he pressed a button on the cell phone he held in his hand. The explosion of the two five-hundred pound

bombs buried in the center of the road ripped through the fifth
Mercedes, blazing a hole through the floor and the roof, incinerat-
ing the occupants, and hurling the three-ton automobile four stories
into the air.

Chapter 94

T HEY WERE ALL in the Stubblefields' back yard in spite of a rare November frost that had settled over Southern California that morning. Stubblefield had insisted. Smoke billowed from the grill as he worked over its red hot grate like some giant medieval blacksmith bent over his forge.

"Won't the neighbors complain?" asked Slidell coughing and tying to wave the thick smoke out of his way as he came toward Stubblefield.

"Hell, no. The bastards should be so lucky. Just inhaling this elixir from three-inch steaks covered in the best homemade rub you can imagine and grilled to perfection by yours truly is a better culinary experience than dining at Donovan's of Downtown. Probably the whole neighborhood is out there competing for lungs full of it," said Stubblefield. "Anna seems to be doin' just fine," he added, as he tenderly pressed down on a steak with a mammoth hand and then turned it over with a grilling fork. He nodded to where Anna, Candice, and Bella were huddled together upwind and talking animatedly.

"Yes, she does. We're very relieved," said Slidell.

Candice and he had been worried that the trauma of the kidnapping had done terrible psychological damage to Anna, but the doctors and psychologists who examined and tested her had all agreed that she had not been physically harmed and that she had been so heavily drugged that she had no memory of the experience, unconscious or otherwise. Time would tell, but for now she was her normal self. And so, thank god, was Candice. She had not blamed him for what happened to Anna. For the two of them, time would also tell, but for now they were as close as they had ever been, closer even.

"It was you who gave me the idea to stage a false plea," said Slidell. "I haven't told you that, and I want to thank you."

"I know I'm brilliant, but how in the hell did I do that?" asked Stubblefield.

"When you called me after court and said you were proud to be at my side that day. I realized that I could count on you, and…"

"Now don't go getting all sentimental on me, I can't take that shit," interrupted Stubblefield.

"Just hear me out. Before Anna's kidnapping, we could not prove what we knew was happening in the case. Sutton, Blakely, and Anderson were dead; and nothing in Anderson's letter could be verified. But when Anna was taken, they, whoever they are, exposed themselves. They committed a fatal error. They had done something that revealed their objective, and we could prove it. With that proof, I knew that in addition to you I could count on Belmonte, Alvarez, Conroy, Judge Tibbs, and even Schmidt to agree to a staged plea of guilty in open court."

"How could you be so sure?" asked Stubblefield.

"*SemperFi*," answered Slidell.

Epilogue

Along I-5

THE RAVEN SPREAD its wings and let the updraft of air sweeping in from the ocean carry it high above the freeway. As it traveled in slow ascending spirals, it never took its eyes off the shiny object that flashed from the trees below. In time, its primal curiosity overcame its caution, and it banked and slid down the current of air until it landed on the limb of the tree that held the precious item. With increasing boldness, it sidled along the limb toward the branches that clutched the silver disk. Grasping it in its beak, it leaped from the limb and again soared above the trees, but before it had risen to a safe altitude, smaller birds began to harass it. They pecked and pestered until it lost its hold on the wonderful thing it had found. The disk, sparkling in the sun, fluttered down to the cluster of houses below. The large, black bird cawed once in disappointment and then climbed higher into the sky.

THE END

Acknowledgments

To my fellow members of The Ancient and Honorable Bibliophilic Society of Oak Park: John Morris, Robert Karrow, Gary Strokosch, and Jonathan Alpert. Best friends and true who read multiple drafts without a wince or a curse.

And to Patti Cone and Michael Gorham who were there at the beginning and at every step along the way.

THANK YOU

Made in the USA
Las Vegas, NV
09 December 2024

13732006R00207